The
New
Manifesto

Or
The Slow Eroding of Time

The New Manifesto

Or
The Slow Eroding of Time

Arthur B. Johnson

Edited by Sam Ernst

Smith Ralston Excelsior

for True Love.

"If it's not worth destroying, it's not art."
- R. Smithwaite

CONTENTS

Foreword

I first encountered *The New Manifesto* on the recommendation of a friend. Unsolicited reading suggestions are always something of a quandary: as much as I enjoy connecting over literature, I've found that what captures my friends' interests often fails to align with my tastes. Thus, my usual strategy is continual evasion. Saying "I haven't gotten around to that yet" (even if I have no intention of doing so) is always easier than providing an honest assessment. Such are the travails of the liberal arts professor.

Indeed, *The New Manifesto* would have stayed on the perpetual "to read" list were it not for the earnest persistence of my friend, who, knowing my habits, forced my hand by buying me my own copy as a birthday gift. It is far harder to put off questions about something to which you have ready access. Thank goodness for her perseverance, because the novel hit me like a revelation.

For a while, I felt as if I had been inducted into some secret society with exclusive membership. Who else knew about this strange book? Why didn't more? And so, I became a *New Manifesto* evangelist, sharing and recommending it to all within earshot. I have to give credit to the saintly patience of the commuters on the Haverhill Line for enduring my daily efforts to spread the Johnsonian gospel. Some were even kind enough to say they would try the novel. Whether or not they ever did is beside the point, just building awareness of Arthur Johnson's work felt like victory enough.

Eventually, like all acolytes, my zeal for proselytization faded. My love for *The New Manifesto*, however, remained steadfast. Thus, I channeled my passion into writing essays and articles that explored the many layers of Johnson's writing. It was these articles that led the editors at Smith Ralston Excelsior to invite me to write this foreword. I accepted without hesitation: for if there is truly a soulmate for everyone in the world, then I am equally a believer that novels can be paired with individuals in the same way. At the risk of sounding cliché, *The New Manifesto* may well be my novelistic Juliet. In the paragraphs that follow, I begin with brief contextualizing comments, then explore some of the themes that have struck me as central to the novel's appeal.

When the manuscript for *The New Manifesto* was found in several twine-bound stacks on top of Arthur Johnson's writing desk after his passing, it was unclear if the various parts were intended as a single volume or stand-alone short novellas. It was even unclear whether the document was meant for publishing or merely as a diversion for friends and family. The will-triggered letters that came months later provided no firm guidance. When Smith Ralston decided to move forward with publication as a single volume, there remained the question of proper ordering. The beginning and end were clear enough, but the sections located in-between could be arranged in any number of possible configurations. Again, Johnson's letters offered no authoritative statement on how to best proceed.

Ultimately, *The New Manifesto* arrived in the form you now see thanks to the patient advocacy of Johnson's trusted editor, Sam Ernst. Were it not for his dedication to preserving the work as it was bequeathed to him, it may have taken a drastically different form (if it had been published at all). He has said that his primary contribution, excepting a handful of small copy-edits, was the addition of part numbers to each of the section headings. These, he argues, add a nice symmetry to the novel. Equally important was the editorial board at Smith Ralston. Their willingness to accept Ernst's recommendations is a true testament to the trust that is built over longstanding author-editor relationships.

The publishing context adds a layer of complexity to one of the major themes of *The New Manifesto*, authorship. Whether John G. Bailey's encyclopedia entries, Annabelle Laetner's dream journal, or the interstitial segments that speak directly to the authorial process, there is a consistent effort throughout the novel to explore the mechanistic process of writing, our sources of inspiration, and the stumbling blocks we encounter along the way. Reading a book about the challenges facing an author writing about a cast of characters with their own written output is, of course, a third-order abstraction. Perhaps Johnson created this Gordian knot to underscore just how complicated the notion of authorship can be. Our daily lives are jumbles of potential inspiration and influence such that it is difficult to ever definitively claim sole ownership over an idea.

This concept is further explored in the progression of the main sections. *The New Manifesto* begins with the memoir written by James Gordon Brecht as he reflects back on his life. This fairly straightforward conceit eventually gives way to a choose-your-own-adventure format where the narrator takes delight in mocking the reader for the choices made in "authoring" his or her tale. In fact, the most triumphant ending in this section invites the reader to add their own words to the blank page. Ultimately, the message seems to be that the tales we tell are as important in defining us as the actions we take.

Another dominant theme in *The New Manifesto* is temporality. Time is consistently presented as an obstacle (at best), or even an outright enemy. Nowhere is this more evident than in the interstitial segues. The omniscient narrator describes an anonymous author who constantly bemoans and battles time—its constrictions, the responsibilities it brings, and its overall scarcity. This is evidenced by the frequent checks of word count and writerly pace, as well as multiple references to the time of day. The character manages to find some respite in his dreams—one of the few human experiences that obliterates (or at least alters) our temporal perceptions. In fact, I argue that the novel's many dream sequences represent the paradoxes of the creative cycle. After all, being productive and waiting for inspiration are mutually exclusive, yet that is the balance all artists must strike.

As a final matter of consideration for this foreword—for surely, there is much to consider in *The New Manifesto* beyond the thoughts I've collected here—I would like to interrogate the form of the novel itself. While it's true that the order of the sections was finalized without Arthur Johnson's direct input, there exist moments of interconnection independent of their sequencing. For instance, in the penultimate paragraph of Part 4, Chapter 27, John G. Bailey mentions in passing that he is tempted to add invented characters to the history he records—heroes able to solve the problems facing the world in which he resides. This brings up the possibility that Part 2, with its encyclopedic epigraphs, was actually written by Bailey. A theory perhaps bolstered by the characters' shared initials.

Similar points of crossover exist elsewhere in the work: James Gordon Brecht's mention of an abandoned choose-your-own adventure novel; Annabelle Laetner's dreams of meteor impacts; the final protagonist's novel draft, always poised on the brink of failure; the interstitial narrator's observations that are then mirrored in the other sections at random intervals. It all creates a tightly knit, circular web of self-referentialism such that each section contributes some bit of understanding to each of the others—which leads to a classic "chicken or the egg" conundrum.

In fact, several scholars have theorized about the order in which *The New Manifesto* was constructed. Were its sections written sequentially or simultaneously? Did the points of overlap arise organically, or were they intentionally inserted in the course of revision? The interstitials ostensibly track the writing of the novel in real time, but I am of the opinion these were not written contemporaneously with the other sections.

If one takes into consideration the firsthand accounts of both author and editor, the four self-contained parts were written separately, at different points in Arthur Johnson's career. Only later, after abandoning these works because he found them too short for publication—especially given his reputation as an exhaustive biographer capable of producing thousand-page tomes—did he come back to them, struck with the idea of stitching them all together with an overarching narrative. It was this device that allowed Johnson to see *The New Manifesto* as something more than a collection of short stories. And, in my opinion, it is what makes the novel the magical journey that it is. For here, we see the author's soul laid bare. The trials, the tribulations, the self-doubt, the neurotic tendencies, and ultimately, the peace that comes with perseverance. It is this brutal, ungilded honesty which draws us in and allows us to see ourselves in Johnson's characters. Everyone imagines what it would be like if our life circumstances were different. In *The New Manifesto*, we see an author struggling against his unwieldy imagination, exploring the potential inherent in other identities. We all have internal monologues, but they are seldom presented with such wonderment as they are here. Johnson's voice becomes our own. When we turn the last page, we not only feel as if we have read an otherworldly novel, but we feel as if we have written it.

Yes, for every person, there is a novel which resonates most sublimely with their spirit. *The New Manifesto* is mine and, I believe, many others'. It is a uniting narrative showing us that despite our different paths, there is much we have in common. There is comfort in that.

Dr. James L. Vanderworthy
Bradford College
May 8, 1999

Editor's Preface

When I got out of graduate school, fresh-faced and full of optimism, I had the good fortune of finding a copy-editing position at the offices of Smith Ralston Excelsior. Though I've been here going on three decades, and have worked with many talented authors, my interactions with Artie Johnson were always a highlight. He was of the old school, devoid of the entitlement and pretension so common in the current generation of writers. His manuscripts were clean and when disagreements did arise, we were always able to settle them with a thoughtful conversation over a cup of tea. I like to think I knew him pretty well and would even go so far as to call us good friends. Yet I never heard a whisper that he was working on a fiction novel. I don't even think Doris, his wife of thirty-nine years, knew.

In the margins of the manuscript, he describes *The New Manifesto* as four failed attempts at fictional biography. The ultimate success or failure of the work is left to the individual reader, but for me, it is a marvelous, yet heart-wrenching experience. After all, the language is characteristic of his fastidiousness as a writer—only unlike his previous work, it has a lyric quality. I also suspect there is just as much autobiography as there is fiction present in these pages. I hate to imagine him closing his notebook for the last time, feeling that this—his most inspired creation—was a failure.

But I am probably too close to Artie, his words, and his history to pass any sort of public judgment. Obviously, as his friend and editor, I am a believer. And maybe, since this is the last work of his I'll ever read for the first time, my thoughts are clouded with sentimentality. So be it.

Artie, if you're reading this in the afterlife, I hope I haven't been too overbearing with my edits. There are some sections I think you left as a prank. You always did like to bury little nuggets in the prose to make sure I was paying attention. Your contagious laughter paired with my deliberative anguish—that's my enduring image of our friendship and it's the thing I'll miss most in the years that remain. Let this last collaboration be our memorial.

Goodbye, dear friend.

Publisher's Introduction

The New Manifesto is something of a mystery. When we first received word of it, we did not know what to expect. Was it a manuscript or simply a writer's journal? Normally, the details of an author's life give an indication of how to best handle posthumous publication, but here, they provide no guidance.

Arthur Blythewood Johnson was known primarily as a biographer, with several well-respected tomes to his credit including *The Life and Times of Edward Hopper* (not to be confused with the similarly titled work by Westheider and Philipp) and *Cayce and His Acolytes: The Occult in the Early 20th Century*. Aside from the biographies, his only other published volume is a small collection of poetry: *Reflections on Chincoteague Island*. Thus, the discovery of *The New Manifesto* manuscript came as quite a shock.

Given his authorial output, it is easy to at first assume that these ideas were never intended for publication. In fact, this is the assumption we operated under for many months. Smith Ralston takes great pride in preserving our authors' intents and wishes—this is one luxury of being a niche publisher. Perhaps, were our roster more broadly famous, we would be tempted to cash-in on any available work, but the nature of modern publishing means that we must be absolutely sure a title is marketable before proceeding. We cannot take up projects on a lark, no matter their apparent quality. We were content to let Arthur Johnson's final manuscript find its resting place in our archives. There are, after all, worse fates for someone's life's work. But then, we received a most curious letter.

It seems that Mr. Johnson had taken it upon himself to set up a system whereby pre-written letters would be mailed after his death. Post-mortem bureaucratic processes being what they are, it took several months for the will to be read, and its contents disseminated. This triggered the release of three letters. One for his family. One for his trusted friend and editor, Sam Ernst. And one for another person whose name he chose to keep anonymous. The contents of the letter we received at Smith Ralston made it clear that this indeed was a manuscript for a novel and that we could publish it if we so desired.* With that new perspective, we knew we had to make the document available to the reading public. It is our great honor to publish *The New Manifesto*. Never before has one of our books gained the cult following that this one has. We could never imagine when we made the first small print run that we would be one day releasing another print run, let alone one so large. For that, we owe our thanks to Arthur Johnson, the tireless editing of Sam Ernst, and you, the reader.

---

* The letter that came to Sam Ernst is included in the appendix for your reference, as is a brief biography prepared by the same.

Part 1: A Prelude

1.

He sat down to write:

> *The first point being: There is a spot in the parking lot where water drips from no apparent source. Mid-air it materializes, governed by gravity it splatters on the ground. Every day. Without fail.*
>
> *The second being: This vantage point is remarkable. Yesterday, it afforded a view of five airplanes at once. All without having to move my head.*

What a fantastic way to begin a novel. Let's begin again.

2.

"I am done for," he thought, and closed his book.

3.

He woke up knowing there was something important about Winesburg, Ohio. Or was it Gainsbourg? Or Ginsberg? What exactly the item of importance was, or its relation to the facts at hand, he couldn't remember. "No bother," he thought as he left the house to walk his usual afternoon route. Yes, there was the spot where the water dripped. There was the man with his placard. The famous aphorism came to mind: "There's something endearing about a panhandler who writes his sign in cursive." To be sure, few took the time any longer. Fewer still made the aesthetic nod to the color red.

4.

He was writing a book. A book he never finished. This is a story of failure.

5.

It was mid-February. The snow was melting, having long overstayed its welcome. Its waterlogged retreat revealed matted grass; sheaves of gray and brown interwoven like straw strewn through hail-battered cornfields. There are two weeks every year where it is impossible to determine whether it is the end of autumn or beginning of spring. He proposed the addition of a fifth season. An interloper, it would remain unfixed, open to personal assertion. This season would have no name.

6.

"Writing is easy." He smiled and drew a large exclamation point at the end of his sentence.

7.

He had heard it said that mountainous regions were incapable of producing great literature. All of the celebrated works of the past several centuries came from the plains or the coast. Something about vast, flat expanses inspired the imagination.

Living in a subalpine valley, he knew he was doomed. He considered giving up, but then realized he could simply lie about his home's location.

8.

With each step across the wet pavement, he could feel the clod of snow on the bottom of his shoe slowly dissolve. Until at last, his sole was back in contact with the earth.

A plow truck scraped across the nearly bare concrete sending up a shower of sparks. New stars extinguished as they hit the roadside snowbanks.

9.

He hadn't meant to begin writing. But then again, how many people sit down and say: "I'm going to write a novel"? The beginning had been effortless. From it had stemmed a variety of subjects, themes, plot avenues, and character formations.

(He had planned to come back to this paragraph at some later point to add more detail and description, but never did.)

10.

Here is where his ideas ran dry.

11.

He began writing two days before his twenty-sixth birthday, deciding that he would dedicate his book to true love. The love we all harbor somewhere down deep in the burial mounds of our memory. The paradox of celebration and mourning. Love unrealized.

If he wrote quickly, he could finish it tonight. That would leave time enough to read a few pages of *Doctor Zhivago* before he went to sleep. But he did not finish tonight.

12.

He hadn't intended on his novel becoming a failure either. But in keeping with the rhetorical outburst from #9, who sits down and says: "I'm going to write a failure"? He could trace the failure to nothing in particular. Perhaps it was his dedication line. He'd read so many that were far better. They usually contained words like "darling" or "my dearest friend and supporter." Some writers referenced multiple people. Some writers even thanked people. He was not one of those writers.

13.

Once, he'd read about a man named Al Herpin who'd rejected the notion of sleep entirely. Years went by and Mr. Herpin was as alert and thoughtful as ever. Finally, he died, just like everybody else.

He wished to be the new Al Herpin, but found it impossible since his mind was awash with sleepy phrases like:

"We are living in momentous times—it's not every day that you get to witness the unmaking of an empire."

or

"This is my hope: to live out my days in peace among the receding glaciers."

or

"Billionaires buying out the floodplain."

All good phrases to be sure, perfect for letters to his nieces or his true love, but certainly not fit for the sleepless. When his letters yielded no reply, the phrases found homes in his "serious writing."

14.

One night, he dreamt he was Al Herpin. Since he was sleeping, the dream proved fruitless.

15.

Maybe he would just write a book of short stories. He wasn't having much luck with anything beyond a paragraph. But the thought of ending a story in a matter of pages filled him full of hollowness. Surely, he had more to say than that.

16.

"What's your timeline?"

He pretended not to hear her. Sometimes people just go away if you pretend not to hear them.

"What's your timeline?"

However, this tactic did not work on the persistent.

"My what?"

"Your timeline."

"For what?"

"This book you're writing."

"I'm not writing a book." *(Oh my God. I've told people about my book?)*

"Oh."

The conversation came to its inevitable end. Once again, he proved that persistence never pays.

17.

He distrusted books that drew conclusions for their readers. His conclusions were his own, not to be dictated by the whims of an author.

He felt like a peanut butter sandwich, having concluded they were good.

18.

Given the book's title, he was finding it surprising how little manifesting was being done. He kept having good ideas but kept forgetting them by the time he got home. It was time for a new hobby. Or at least a new title.

"What about *The Book of Aphorisms*? I can just write pithy phrases and attribute them to invented people."

He went back and added one at the beginning of his novel, and while it fooled you, the reader, he found it difficult to come up with realistic names.

19.

Here was where the globe stole his gaze. Lost in dreams of remote islands, his sentence trailed... off.

Saints Helena and Kilda rocked him to sleep.

20.

Once, when asked his profession, Satie claimed the title of gymnopedist.

A long sigh rose slowly, escaping like a tidal bore— churning against the incoming breath. He could make no such claim.

"I am only an aphorist," he thought.

21.

He went to the spot where the water dripped. There he stood, gazing into the sky, trying to muster his best "inquisitive look." There was nothing for it. Stare as he might, the heavens would not divulge their secret. The perfect blue was tight-lipped; the horizon's fade to white was its laughter.

22.

"I will write to frustrate." At first, he forgot to define the intended target of that frustration but found one in throwing his manuscript across the room.

23.

Six months after her death, he received a letter from his grandmother. He imagined it in the cargo hold of a plane, shuttled back and forth across the Atlantic in search of him. "I hope all is well in Scotland. Try wearing a kilt and playing the bagpipes! Miss you sweetie."

Grandmothers are magical creatures. His once predicted the future: "One day, they'll play your songs on the radio." And she was right. Once, in the middle of Wyoming, the songs he loved came gushing through the radio in rapid succession, an oasis interrupting the unending, barren expanse of highway.

24.
For once, life was not accentuated with a dull throbbing. He was thirsty and drank deeply.

Yet, headache gone, he found he was now haunted by an unslakable thirst.

25.
"Perhaps I shouldn't be writing this way," he thought. "My words flow more freely with a pen in hand and a gentle breeze filling my lungs. The sun does me a world of good. I don't want a gaudy expanse of cloudless sky, only an errant ray escaping its vaporous bonds now and again."

?

Part 2: An Assemblage

DAMASCUS, Pennsylvania – A small township on the Pennsylvania/New York border. Its primary industries in the 20th century were timber, agriculture, and bluestone mining. It is notable for the fact that in the early 21st century, it became a center for natural gas production. It is also notable as the birthplace of James Gordon Brecht...

I promise every word of this is true. I open with that admonishment simply because I know the nature of the Brecht clan. We are liable to be skeptics and hyperbolists, always taking to the extremes when it comes to storytelling. With Brechts as the intended readers, I want to be clear that this is all fact. Hopefully, you will add my "memoir" to the great book of family history without feeling the need for "accuracy" edits. What follows may at times seem fanciful, impossible, or even tarnished by faulty memory, but you must believe what I say.

In 1971, when I was at the tender age of eight, my father informed me that Brechts were Eagles fans. Seeing as how I was a Brecht, my allegiance was required for Philadelphia. But I harbored impure thoughts—I dreamt of rooting for the Steelers.

In our house, there were only two laws: the laws of God the Father and the laws of my father, the god. Philly was just over 150 miles away. Pittsburgh was more than twice that. Distance dictated our loyalties. To my old man, it didn't matter that New York was closer than both. Besides, both the Giants and Jets played in New Jersey, which didn't say much for their understanding of geography, let alone football. We lived in the great state of Pennsylvania, so we had to root for the nearest Pennsylvanian team.

But as I lay in bed at night, waiting for sleep to wash over me like the Delaware, I dreamed of honorable steel men, massive crucibles, and red-hot, glowing ingots. Then I would pray my Hail Marys, ask for forgiveness and close my eyes.

Every morning, I imagined I'd woken up in a new, unfamiliar house. After I'd rummaged through the drawers that happened to be filled with clothes my size, I'd wander downstairs and introduce myself to the kindly woman who seemed to be one of my caretakers.

"Good morning ma'am. My name is James Gordon Brecht. It's a pleasure to make your acquaintance. Lovely place you've got here."

The woman would greet me with a smile, fix me a seat at the kitchen table, then offer me a plate piled high with blueberry pancakes.

"Good morning James," she would say. "I trust you slept well."

"Oh, very well, ma'am. This is one of the most peaceful places I've stayed in quite some time."

At that point, a loud, older gentleman would come blustering into the kitchen complaining about a sports score from the night before. He would swallow his curses as soon as he saw me, weaving a distinctively garbled tale of foul play, witless refs, and the nefarious people who rigged the system.

I was always too shy to formally introduce myself to the man, so full of poise and self-confidence did he seem. I always suspected that he owned the establishment. Nonetheless, he'd give a brief smile and nod while walking by and would tousle my hair as if I were a loyal Labrador retriever. As such, I'd often finish my breakfast on the floor since it was a place more suited to a dog.

When my meal was complete, I would be shooed away to get dressed for school. Since I went to St. Vincent's in Honesdale, I always knew what I would be wearing. Even if I hadn't gone to Catholic school, I probably would have adopted a daily uniform anyway. I never gave much thought to what to wear. My mind was elsewhere.

I would sit by the front window, waiting for the bus, huddled up between the radiator and the coat closet, soaking in the warmth that would power me through the day. Eventually, the bus would come and my mother would hand me my backpack as I bounded out the front door. "Have a good day James. Love you!"

I'd find my seat on the bus with well-wishes in my ears and the smell of hot metal lodged in my sinuses. The other kids sat in early morning delirium, absently staring out the windows. This was always my favorite time on the bus. My face pressed against the window in silence, its rattle connecting me to the world outside. As we wound our way through the hills, my compatriots would gradually be shaken to life. By the time we pulled into the St. Vincent's parking lot, the din of voices was more in keeping with that of youth.

School would proceed in a cascade of English, mathematics, Latin, social studies, science, and religion. We began with our morning prayers and the nuns kept us on a breakneck pace through lunchtime. Knuckles were rapped and the disobedient were punished. The best strategy was simply to keep your head down. When lunch came, we marched down to the small cafeteria, forming a long line that waited patiently by the doorway to be admitted on a class-by-class basis. Seniority ruled as the older grades would be the first to snake their way along the outside wall to the stack of fiberglass lunch trays, all faded shades of sea green, yellowed cream, and weathered red brick. The trays would then be slid along the counter, in front of a scooping squad of Polish grandmothers who ladled out our daily allotment of meat, potatoes, and vegetables presented in one of five ways, according to the day of the week.

By the time my turn came, I was always already daydreaming. I would count the tiles on the floor—first the white ones, then the black, making note of each new stain or spill that hadn't been there the previous day. At the end of each week, this slate would be wiped clean by vigorous mopping and I would begin my observations anew. If my eyes weren't on the floor, they would usually be surveying the assembled hordes, scanning slowly back and forth, looking for the most subdued table. Eventually, the hungry impatience of those in line behind me would boil over into insistent prodding.

Once we finished eating, we waited yet again, squirming under the watchful eye of the mother superior, until the recess bell rang. For a brief twenty minutes, the concerns of the school day dissolved and we were left to our own, more rambunctious, inclinations. Footballs, baseballs, and tetherballs traced arcs through the air. All found their targets, intentional or otherwise. Recess was essentially one big game of chicken—a constant cycle of tempting and then avoiding physical harm that consumed our time until the bell rang again and we lined up, breathless, to return to class.

Afternoons mirrored the mornings: more lessons in obedience. The hands of the clock would crawl as if hindered by relativistic effects. The day ended with our "evening" vespers. Once finished, I would often stay to help the teacher wipe the chalkboard clean. Thus, the bus ride home was suffused with the comforting smells of incense and chalk dust.

This was the template for my days. During the summer or on the weekends, a different cadence emerged. Daily chores, welcomely aimless free time, family dinners, and Sunday drives. I lived in tune with my Circadian rhythms and left the clocks confined to the school day. My concerns were weeklong campaigns and exploratory expeditions that crisscrossed the back yard. I knew every branch of every tree. Every lump of uneven earth. Picked countless bushels of berries from the creekside. It was my first and only stint as ruler of a fiefdom. While my people loved me, the demands of time eventually dictated that I rule in absentia. Someday, I may return to reclaim my crown.

This pattern persisted throughout my years in primary and secondary school. My daily interests and passions evolved as I aged, but not so substantially that one would be unable to recognize the second grader next to the eleventh grader. I was a model of consistency.

2.

DR. ELLEN SCHMIDT — Most famous as the medical researcher and behavioral expert who came up with the theory of the lucid coma—the notion that some patients experiencing a coma are not even aware they are incapacitated, but instead perceive themselves to be living vibrant, dream-like lives. Though there have only been a few documented cases of lucid coma, the nature of the condition has led to it being more extensively written about than other varieties of prolonged unconsciousness. Dr. Schmidt began her research at the University of Scranton...

Having given you a sense of my earliest years, I think it would also be of value—before going much further—to give you some psychological insight. People have always said that I never think in straight lines. It might be true—I have always found curves rather elegant. Growing up in a turn-of-the-century farmhouse, the graceful radius of the crown molding in the living room easily won-out over the sharp-edged ceiling in my bedroom. Which is a roundabout way of saying my thinking is often circular. Things keep coming back to me.

Take my dreams. Ever since I was young, two have re-appeared on a regular basis. In the first, I have lost the ability to move at speed. My legs still function and I suffer no pain, but I move as if mired in molasses. Everyone around me strides on as if nothing has changed. But for me, the world is suddenly out of phase. Voices become high-pitched and each step becomes frustration. Try as I may, my legs churn in vain. The resultant feeling is something akin to treading water—

momentous exertion without measurable progress being made.

It reminds me of Christmastime. And not because of the ginger molasses cookies that have always been one of my favorites. No, instead, molasses and Christmas are inextricably linked in my mind because of the stories Uncle Mike told every Christmas Eve dinner. He relished his role as family bard and found us all a willing audience as we struggled to stay awake for midnight mass with so much food in our bellies. Instead of Dickens, we got one of a stable of stories—tales of polar explorers, Sami reindeer herders, or oozing, syrupy floods that engulfed entire towns. I was always the one to vote for molasses, fascinated by the idea of destruction by baking ingredient. Apparently though, my notions of slow-motion flooding were incorrect. It has been reported that the Boston Molasses Flood of 1919 consisted of a wave forty feet high, moving at thirty-five miles an hour. Nonetheless, the image of a slow-creeping wave persists for me, coloring my dreams.

The second dream always begins with me in a familiar basement hallway. Stairs lead up to the right. Rich wood paneling adorns the walls like a West Egg mansion. Set in the wall beneath the stairs is a large rectangular vent.

At this point, I usually realize that someone is coming for me. My avenue of escape is the vent—I pull it off, climb in, and replace it carefully. Then, I climb through the ductwork, across metal grate floors, up and down ladders through the hidden underbelly of the building. Eventually, I find a duct angling upward and it leads me to a peaceful forest waterfall. There, I take my rest.

Despite what you might think, each of these dreams brings me immense comfort upon waking. I take them as evidence that my mind is still functioning as it always has—proof that the cogs are all still turning as they should be. It's a great way of keeping self-doubt at bay.

I give you all of this psychological background so as to forestall any concern you might have should you find record of my childhood visits to Doctor Schmidt. Though she was known around town as "the shrink," she was more accurately a neuroscientist. It's true that my parents were a touch concerned with some of my behaviors. Sitting too close to the television and becoming unresponsive. My habit of conducting thought experiments in a dark, closed closet was particularly perplexing, but they left me to my fortresses of solitude. I'm sure the rumors of "crazy Uncle James" will no doubt circulate, but I promise that the aforementioned dreams were about as strange as my childhood psyche could muster.

If you must know, the visits to Dr. Schmidt were part of a study for which we were compensated. You should also know that I was a willing accomplice. I can still clearly remember walking through the hospital doors and being led down the hall to a consultation room. Soon thereafter, I was secured in a chair suspended on an articulated arm above the doctor and my parents. I looked down and could see them looking up at me. Images of my internal organs were projected for all to see. The black and blue-white of x-ray slides illuminated the cavernous space. From there, I was taken into a small room where lab-coated individuals tested my manual dexterity, pattern recognition, and problem-solving skills. At the end, Dr.

Schmidt concluded that I had advanced aptitude, but no concerning behavioral traits. In other words, I was just a precocious youngster. She assured my parents that I would turn out alright. Any odd habits they noticed were likely just a phase I would grow through. We stopped by the hospital cashier on the way out. My deal-seeking, coupon-clipping father never looked so delighted as when he carefully slid the check into his shirt-pocket. He gave it a self-satisfied little pat, and off we went to the appliance store.

You see, the money from the study gave us the means to purchase a new color TV with remote control. We were the envy of every house in the area. My father was always an early-adopter. At last, he could watch his Eagles games in full color right in the comfort of our home. Bill Bradley and the club-footed Tom Dempsey never looked so good. On weekdays, there was the evening news ritual. Walter Cronkite gave us his honest assessments as I fell asleep with my head resting on my father's chest. He was still sweaty from his bike-ride home. The smell of Speed Stick coupled with the gentle rise and fall of his breath soothed me to sleep.

Later in the evenings, PBS documentarians took their cameras to wander the halls of old castles, telling ghost stories that I wholeheartedly believed. My family only encouraged this belief in the supernatural. Deadpan stories of relatives' haunted houses. Swamp-gas visions of the Virgin Mary. Maybe it's part and parcel with Catholic mysticism: when long-dead saints intercede in your daily life, it's easy to imagine other forces doing so as well. Given my news-hour naps and the high frequency of pre-bedtime public television ghost stories, my march upstairs to sleep often became a harrowing experience. Every creak of the stairs was pure malevolence.

The attic door and the pull-string light that lay behind... I can't help but shudder recalling it. When I slipped into bed, the blanket, pulled up tight over my head, was my insulating cocoon. It kept me safe then and still does to this day.

3.

EUROPA FLATS, Gibraltar — An otherwise nondescript settlement on the southernmost point of the Gibraltar peninsula, Europa Flats is significant in that it sheltered James Gordon Brecht after his journey from Gibraltar to Ceuta and back. More remarkable still are the reasons he embarked on such a venture...

Shipping runs in the family. And so, from a young age, the idea of seafaring took hold and germinated in me. Ships in bottles. Pirates. Navigational charts. Sextants. These were the objects of my fascination. The margins of my high school notebooks were filled with nautical doodles. I could recite maritime history from the Greek fire used in the battles for Constantinople, to the junks of China, to the ore ships trolling around the Great Lakes. I was invigorated by the exploits of Thor Heyerdahl and his balsa wood raft, Shackleton's sailing ship encased in ice, and the ironclads of the American Civil War.

Having no idea what to do with these interests in a land-locked town, my guidance counselor recommended I attend the Merchant Marine Academy in Kings Point, New York. I must admit, the idea had its allure. Adventure lay just on the other side of four years of schooling. But it was equally tempting to play Huck Finn and float down the Delaware to Philadelphia to see what opportunities could be had. In the end, my sense of discretion—coupled with threats of disownment—won out over my desire for immediate adventure. Before I knew it, I was a midshipman studying to become a marine engineer.

Most of my classmates gave themselves willingly to regimentation. While it was not entirely disagreeable, there were elements of the pseudo-military life that wore on my soul. I cared little for the shine of my shoes and the state of my sleeping rack. Combine that with the sinus-stinging smell of bilge water, and you'll understand why I changed careers at the first opportunity.

But I don't want to give the impression that college was all bad—no, there were parts I enjoyed a great deal. For one, there was the secret spot in the library that became my refuge. Most perused the technical collection, but I found salvation in the dust-coated half-row of history books. Biographies of philosophers and essays on the natural world became my stock in trade. Most of the books I opened had never been checked out before. A biography on the life of Martin Buber. Leopold's *A Sand County Almanac*. Gibbon's *History of the Decline and Fall of the Roman Empire*. In reading these, I sheepishly came to the realization that my childhood fascination with ships lay more with the history than the maritime. Call me a slow learner.

It turns out the collection was something of a pet project of head librarian Captain Daniel Goust. At first, when I brought my selections to the checkout desk, he assumed that I had been assigned them as some sort of penal project. But as my persistence extended far beyond the bounds of normal compulsory work, he ventured an inquiry.

"You're a glutton for punishment, my boy."

"Yes sir," I said with a smile.

Recognizing a kindred spirit, he quickly took me under his wing. Along with being head librarian, Cpt. Goust was also the curator at the on-campus American Merchant Marine

Museum. This provided the fodder for many of our early conversations. Later, as our short discussions ballooned into hour-long chats, he asked if I was interested in seeing the archives. Clearly, I was elated at the opportunity. He took me down to the basement, where, behind a locked metal door, in pristine climate control, shelf after shelf of crates and boxes waited to be catalogued. We put on white gloves and he showed me a few of the treasures he'd found.

"You know," he said, "I don't have as much time as I'd like to come down here these days."

"Yes," I replied absently, engrossed in the artifacts before us. I also wondered exactly what kinds of time demands would keep a small-school reference librarian from archival work.

"I could use a hand sorting through all of this stuff, but willing participants are hard to come by. If you have any time, you'd be welcome to do some digging."

"That sounds fantastic!"

Soon enough, I had a key of my own. That few of my classmates were even aware the school housed an archive made it all the better.

Instead of late-night carousing with the midshipmen, I preferred the quiet of Saturday morning. A walk down to the beach to see the shoreline of City Island reflected in the improbably still Long Island Sound. The smell of saltwater and decaying seaweed, gentle fog lifting on the fringes of the bay. From there, when my studies allowed, I would walk over to the archives and spend a few hours helping catalogue the Academy's vast holdings. One weekend, I came across heretofore forgotten crates of ship's china. Another, it was a stack of old gramophone records, all in pristine working order.

In them, I saw a metaphor for my life, which seemed to be caught in the grooves of my ancestors. I'd ride along peacefully for a while, only to skip unexpectedly to the next track like the needle on a faulty turntable. Extended time in an archive will get anyone thinking about family history. Here were the musty relics of the dead. What would the Brechts leave behind? And who would paw through our heirlooms? We have a proud lineage. Take my mother's father—he too was a merchant mariner. One day, his ship was anchored somewhere off Gibraltar and a nearby munitions ship exploded with such force that he was knocked backward across the deck. He got up, made mental note of the experience, and went back to work. They fished bodies (living and dead) out of the water well on into the evening. He helped salvage thirty-three crates of oranges, a few bales of rubber, and seven men who were found clinging to the debris. That night, he wrote it all down in his journal—a journal from which my mother read to us every night before we went to sleep. So there is precedent for this "memoir" I'm embroiled in. I can only pray that some descendant's mother will likewise make time to religiously read my words aloud at the close of day.

But I am getting ahead of myself. I'm a figment or a memory for those who are reading, but as the one writing this now, am still fully alive, hoping to make something of the time I've been given. Back then, to the archives. Lifting the lid on a nondescript box, I was awed to discover a collection of 18th century ships' lines drawings. As I gasped, I inhaled the stale box air. It smelled like old beef stew. The vellum was yellowed and brittle on the edges, but otherwise in good condition. Seeing the artistry evident in the lines and lettering made me somewhat self-conscious about my hackneyed attempts at coaxing a fair line from the splines. Once, I even forgot to leave room for a rudder. At that point, I knew my strengths were better suited to the engines and machinery of marine engineering than the artful ambiguities of naval architecture. And I would have readily given both up if I could have made a career at the museum.

But life winds innumerable, mysterious paths. Who knew if I'd ever get the chance to play curator? After all, my top priority at the time was filling my service obligations as a merchant mariner as quickly as possible.

Upon our December graduation, we were required to take a job in the shipping industry. Unsatisfied with the choices brokered by the school, I sought out my own, more interesting options. A friend of a friend knew a Greek shipping magnate who promised me a berth aboard one of his cargo vessels in the Mediterranean. Proximity to fine foods and sun-flecked beaches sounded good to me.

My journey to the port of Piraeus began on a frigid night in Montreal. I had been in upstate New York visiting Uncle Mike for Christmas and Mirabel International was the closest major airport. For my first time flying across the ocean, the polar jet stream had deigned to see me off in style. Snow flurries swirled gently down and I watched the engine exhaust send little white snakes skittering across the ground. As the nervous smokers in the seats around me worked their way through their first packs, I settled in, closed my eyes, and fell asleep in the enveloping cloud of nicotine.

I slept soundly and didn't wake until we had landed in Amsterdam. There, I waited for several hours until it was time to board the plane to Athens. No sooner had the takeoff acceleration pinned me back to my seat, than was I sleeping once again. It was only the characteristic squeal of the tires and roar of engine braking that caused me to open my eyes. By that point, we were on the ground and Helios was high in the sky. I felt a long way from home.

Craning to see more out the window, all that greeted my eyes was an endless expanse of tarmac. The sun glinted off a chaotic mess of airplanes and weather-beaten stair cars. After deboarding the plane, we made the long walk across the concrete to collect our bags in the lone, central building. It was appropriately spartan—more like a hangar than the terminal buildings I was accustomed to in the U.S. I had nothing to declare, so walked through customs unhindered. Everyone else did too, as there was no one manning the desk. If there are any burgeoning airport designers in the family, please remember that first impressions do make a difference.

Beyond the doorway lay a throbbing mass of humanity. Most of them were shouting, careening off one another like molecules of gas in a high-pressure vessel. For a moment, the seas parted, and I saw a taxi stand out along the curb. I threaded my way through the crowd, found an amenable driver and was off toward the docks of Piraeus. Actually, if you want to get technical, the ship was anchored in Perama, but the two cities are largely indistinguishable, separated only by a container shipping facility. All I knew was that the entirety of the two ports was inhospitable.

The taxi ride was nothing short of terrifying—and I had ridden through the middle of Manhattan with a driver who thought the sidewalks were fair game. We reached speeds on city streets I had never previously achieved on the interstate. We swerved into oncoming traffic, only to swerve back through narrow gaps at the last possible moment. In situations where I have no control, I've learned it's best just to place your trust in fate. Either life meets an abrupt, fiery end, or you make it through alive. Somehow, I was able to sit back and relax after a few minutes. The path was circuitous. At several points, a burning high-rise came into view. Either Athenian office blocks were all dangerously combustible, or we were doubling back on ourselves. We came to a stop under a bridge where I was instructed to hand over my passport to a man sitting in a corrugated metal hut. Despite the walls being rusted through in places, he maintained his illusion of security by sitting behind a barred window. The taxi driver gestured that it was now time to leave. Though I had not previously traveled internationally, I was pretty sure I wasn't supposed to leave my passport with strangers. What's a young man to do? A harrowing hour later, my faith in my driver was rewarded as we pulled up, safe-and-sound, beside the docked ship.

The scene that greeted my arrival was one of confusion. I was accustomed to the orderly, clean trappings of the U.S. merchant marine fleet. The ship before me was rusted and battered, its deck crawling with a motley crew. The din of voices and machinery was deafening even from inside the car. Dockside wasn't much better. Burnt-out husks of concrete buildings were everywhere. I detected motion in the shadows of one nearby structure. Stumbling out over the rubble came a grizzled man waving a broken ouzo bottle in my direction. No sooner had my seabags and I been deposited on the slip, than did my taxi speed away. I was beginning to second-guess my Greek odyssey.

With nowhere to go but aboard, I quickly heaved my bags up to the main deck and looked around for someone in charge. Everyone seemed to be swinging a sledgehammer. All were dressed in grimy boiler suits more suited for deck swabs than ships' officers. Apparently, my bewilderment showed. A swarthy boatswain walked toward me, flailing his arms wildly. His Greek commands only earned my raised eyebrow. He about-faced in disgust and, soon, a gentler-looking younger fellow approached, cigarette dangling from his lips.

"You must be the new third mate."

I nodded my head and he stuck out his hand.

"The name's Tinu. Captain Michalis told me to keep an eye out for you."

I thanked him and told him my name as he shouldered one of my bags to lead me to my quarters.

"We don't get many Americans coming through."

"I've got a friend in the company who helped set this up."

When I said that, I thought I could hear him try to repress a laugh.

"I'm just looking forward to getting underway," I said, ducking through a hatch that led toward the officers' block. We reached a door that read "3RD MATE" in all caps. In homage to the pirate life, someone had etched-in a tasteful "y" at the end. Tinu set my bag down and turned to me as he fished in his pocket for his ring of keys.

"You know this ship will never sail, right?"

I feigned ignorance—an act that was helped by my actual lack of knowledge.

"They bought this ship to scrap. We're just here to knock the rust off and polish her up before the salvage crew comes in to run her aground for the Indian shipbreakers."

I couldn't manage a response more intelligent than an awkward "hmmm…" This was not what I had expected. The position had been described to me as "a great learning opportunity." While I was sure to learn some lessons, I now had a feeling they would be different from those I'd initially anticipated.

Tinu finally found the key but hesitated as he reached for the lock. He looked me in the eyes and said, "I'm sorry for the state of the room. The last third mate left in a hurry and we haven't had a chance to tidy it up. We're glad to have you aboard." It looked as if he was on the verge of saying more but thought better of it. He unlocked the hatch, pushed it open and walked quickly down the hallway and around the corner.

I was left staring into the dark abyss. There was an unavoidable foulness in the air, but a pale glimmer of sunlight through the curtains on the far wall gave me some hope. It took a little while for my eyes to adjust, but soon I was able to make out some basic details. I slid my hand along the inside wall, groping to find a light switch. When I did, I wished I hadn't.

Filth and squalor don't begin to describe the accommodations. Though the room was spacious by naval standards, much of it was taken up by stacked bags of rotting trash. Open cups of yogurt on the desk grew mold inches thick. The sheets were full of cigarette burns through which various insects wriggled in and out. The en suite head and shower were out of order.

I gathered up the worst of the trash and carried it down to the main deck to set atop a garbage pile I'd noticed earlier. This is common practice on most ships—once you are far enough off shore, you just push the garbage overboard. This particular pile was probably started by some hopeful soul who thought the ship might actually sail one day. Just as I was setting the trash down, I heard a loud voice behind me:

"Ey boy!"

I turned around and could only assume that the bearded man with the wooden leg, eye-patch, and shoulder-mounted parrot was Captain Michalis. Let me take a moment to clarify that this description is no exaggeration. Most would think the stereotypical picture of a pirate is just a product of our collective imagination—an outlandish image perpetrated upon our consciousness by Hollywood—and my inclusion of it, evidence of whimsical artistic license. I would have been inclined to agree until I saw the man standing in front of me. I had stepped through the looking glass, it seemed.

"You are tired, so I will not make you work today. Tomorrow we begin at sunrise. You should sleep now."

I stopped by the officers' mess on the way back to my room. Though it was past standard feeding hour, the Filipino cook happily fixed me a plate of spaghetti and boiled hot dogs tossed in a generous helping of vegetable oil. He stood there smiling as I scarfed it down—it was my first "proper" meal in thirty hours. Once I finished, I went back to my room and collapsed into slumber on the vinyl couch opposite the bed.

I hadn't bothered to set an alarm, trusting in the decorum of the ship's horn to blast me awake. When it did, I rifled through my luggage, but couldn't find my cadet's uniform. (This is a common occurrence when I travel—I once forgot to bring underwear.) Improvising, I opened the cabinets in my room and found a boilersuit from the former ship's medic, complete with red cross and rod of Asclepius embroidered on the breast pocket. I slipped it on, zipped it up, and went downstairs to get my breakfast—one egg over-easy and a fried fish head. Seeing the offering, my appetite quickly waned, so I went outside to receive my instructions for the day.

We all lined up at midships and were handed twenty-pound sledgehammers. Then, Captain Michalis proceeded to give us an exhaustive demonstration of how to bang rust off pipes. After each hammer swing, he'd turn to us and say "See...? Like this." Though the instruction period stretched for a full twenty minutes, the actual task was, as he kept saying, self-evident. The sledge-heaving lasted a few days. When we finished, we were given brooms and plastic bags to gather the mess we'd made. We threw the detritus over the side, splashing into Perama harbor below (apparently, the normal rules of waste disposal didn't apply here). I'll spare you the tedious details about the remainder of my time aboard the M/V *Visigoth*, but after a few weeks of optimistically sweeping garbage and cleaning up oil spills, I decided to seek alternative employment since I did not seem to be moving up in the world. Captain Michalis begrudged my departure but assured me it would be no problem to transfer my passport between shipping companies. By that point, I had forgotten that my passport even existed. Maybe things were not as dire as they had seemed.

Regardless, when the ship's horn sounded, I walked down the gangplank with my bags and didn't look back. I proceeded straight across the shipyard to another, nicer looking vessel. It was captained by Sezer Stakis, a gentle Cypriot of some repute. Once I explained my situation, he welcomed me aboard, offered me a position as deck cadet, and assigned me to the pilot's quarters. It was there I had my first shower since coming to Greece. The water ran black with the toils of weeks past and I felt renewed.

Unlike the *Visigoth*, my new berthing, the refrigerated cargo vessel M/V *Orion* was still in working order. We sailed from Perama to Gibraltar and anchored there to await our cargo instructions. Cavendish bananas were experiencing a resurgence in popularity on European tables, so maybe we'd go to Central America. If I was lucky, we would sail through the Panama Canal—one of the world's great engineering marvels that I had long wanted to see.

Knowing my grandfather's explosive history at the Gibraltar anchorage, I winced every time I heard a ship's engines crank to life. Alas, the laws of generational stoichiometry meant that his excitement would have to be balanced with my tedium. I stood on the bridge with the Ukrainian First Mate, learning to read navigational charts, listening to the radio chatter, and gazing at the rock looming out of the sea. For being the lifeblood of the modern economy, the merchant marine corps is not as organized or efficient as you might think. We sat there anchored for weeks, waiting for cargo instructions that never came.

To pass the time, I devoured the ship's meager library. I read E.W. Pickett's *History of the Rock: Gibraltar Then and Now*, Winston Moorehouse's *Memoir of a Life Spent in Surgery*, and Susan K. Hellman's *Hope Beyond Hope*. I have never since been able to find copies of these books, so I sometimes wonder if I just made them up; but at the time, they proved a welcome respite from the doldrums of bridge duty.

When cargo instructions failed to come through after the fourth week (and it didn't look like they'd be coming any time soon), I decided it was time to move on. The rest of the crew thought I was crazy—how often does one get paid to sit in anchorage for months? But I wanted more than a paycheck. The cost-conscious Captain Stakis welcomed my decision. At breakfast, he handed me my passport (a minor miracle), hailed a passing tugboat to take me ashore, and I was off. As far as I was concerned, my obligations to the shipping industry were fulfilled. The job-placement staff at King's Point might have disagreed, but I wasn't so sure that any record of my time in the Greek fleet would be communicated back to them anyway. At the very least, they couldn't fault me for not trying. Maybe the sailor's life wasn't for me. Nonetheless, I soon learned that the sea wasn't done with me yet.

As HMS *Tug Mumbles* came alongside in choppy seas, the first mate tossed a rope ladder over the side. There, it dangled, swinging like a pendulum five feet above the tugboat's gunwale. He took my bags and tossed them one-by-one toward the tug. Miraculously, only one missed the mark, but the *Mumbles* crew were able to quickly fish it out of the water with a long hook. I clambered down the ladder and eyed the ever-narrowing-and-expanding gap. If I timed it wrong, I would be pinned between the ships. When I made the jump, time stopped and I enjoyed the momentary sensation of flight. My subsequent landing on the tug was undignified, but all birds look awkward on the ground. Soon, we pulled away and charted a course toward the harbor that clung to the west side of the rock.

While underway, I inspected my bags. Thankfully, the one that hit the water was filled with my clothes, not my books. The dry boilersuit I brought along from the *Visigoth* would have to suffice for the time being.

Just as we rounded the peninsula and the port came into view, a regal-looking pigeon alighted on the rail. I immediately noticed a small band around its left leg, emblazoned with the Moroccan flag. It appeared as if the band held a small tube. I was under the impression that messenger pigeons had fallen out of favor decades ago, but my eyes told a different story. I inched my way toward the bird as it cooed softly, but it took off before I could make a closer inspection. I watched it glide toward land with a sense of purpose.

Before it could reach its final destination, however, I saw the telltale flash of talons as a kestrel came swooping-in to spear it out of the sky. Locked in a mortal struggle, the two birds tumbled toward the ground with the grace of a lumpy, feather-covered bowling ball. About fifteen feet from the ground, the attacker disengaged and flew off to find less resistant prey. The pigeon struggled to regain buoyancy by flapping its broken wings, but failed, crashing to the ground in a discernible puff of feathers.

While this drama unfolded, we had pulled alongside the dock. I grabbed my bags, thanked the *Mumbles* crew and followed my curiosity in the direction of the downed bird. My navigator's intuition did not fail me and soon, I was looking down at that poor, lifeless creature. Though the bird was clearly dead, the mysterious message tube remained, so I bent down and delicately removed it from its holster. I looked around nervously, to see if its master (or intended recipient) had come to collect the remains, but the surrounding alleys were empty. And so, I unscrewed the top, retrieved the tiny scroll of paper inside, unrolled, and read the message. The contents were indecipherable to my eyes—some manner of code which I hadn't the patience to crack. The sender's name was clear, however—Prince Mehdi al-Ayouch—and the tube had an address along its edge, which read, "Belyounech, Morocco."

Having studied the local navigational charts in exhaustive detail during our anchorage, I knew the town was just across the strait. Figuring the message and messenger were important to its sender, I made a snap decision to inform the prince of the bird's demise and failed delivery. I found a ferry schedule and learned that another cross-strait ferry wouldn't depart until the following evening. With a message like this, time could be of the essence. Were I another man (or a marathon swimmer), I might have decided to try my luck with the ocean, but discretion won out. But being that I was on the waterfront, I spied another option. A number of sea-going rowboats were tied up at a tourist shop. Since the shop was closed and the boats wouldn't be needed until the following weekend, I figured that it wouldn't hurt to borrow one. So I walked down to the shore, stashed my bags in a quiet corner as karmic collateral, untied a boat, grabbed some oars, and set off.

When I was several hundred yards out, I began to grasp the enormity of the task I had undertaken. Over my shoulder, Africa sat huddled low on the horizon, paradoxically looking as if it were both standing guard and seeking refuge. Each stroke seemed to move me no closer to my goal. Thankfully, the breeze coming off the cool water was invigorating after weeks in the stale heat of the ship and it powered me onward. Despite the visual cues indicating a lack of progress, I knew there was but one way forward. My arms reaching for the European shore, then pulling back, inching me closer to Africa one beat at a time.

I became absorbed in the monotony. For a while, my mind was limber enough to think on other topics. But 'round the halfway mark, I had to devote renewed focus to the task at hand. Reach, pull, lean. Catch, drive, extract. I could feel the current tugging the boat as the Mediterranean and Atlantic battled to empty themselves into one another. Eventually, my perseverance led me through and I beached my rowboat on the African continent. It had taken me four hours to row across.

When I stepped ashore, my arms felt like jelly and despite the multi-hour exertion, I was chilled to the core. Nearby, some fishermen were sitting around a bonfire on the beach. As I staggered up to them, they gave me the wary but sympathetic look one gives to a mumbling beggar. My docile condition must have won them over because they soon offered me a warm cloak and a space by the fire. I sat there silent for an hour, warming myself as they looked me up and down. They fed me fish stew and dried bread, and soon, I was revived—at least as revived as one can be after a four-hour row.

Remembering my mission, I enquired as to who might have sent the pigeon across. The fishermen knew right away and led me (still in my cloak) toward a fortress perched atop the cliffs overlooking the beach. We came to the wrought-iron gates and a guard asked our purpose. I related my tale and was immediately shown into the central palace. It was a wonder of Moorish design, all archways, marble floors, and intricate mosaics. In the great hall, I was instructed to wait while the guard went to fetch his master. Soon, Prince al-Ay-ouch greeted me kindly. Though he was only a lesser prince in that country—the title was not officially recognized but was more of a local honorific—the surroundings were no less lavish.

"So," he said, after we had exchanged introductory pleasantries, "you have found one of my birds."

"Yes, I'm afraid I have some bad news..." I explained the kestrel attack, how I'd come to discover the message on the bird's foot, and how rowing across the strait to deliver the message back to its sender seemed the only logical course of action at the time.

"Amazing. Fate is smiling on me today. But I would argue that yours was an act of faith, not logic." The prince took the small message tube from me and rolled it between his tobacco-stained fingers with the ease of a lifelong smoker. Without a second thought, he raised it over his shoulder and a servant scuttled out of an unseen corner to fetch it. Somehow, the tube had been replaced by a lit cigarette. Taking a deep drag, the prince exhaled a bluish puff of smoke before continuing.

"The note you intercepted was intended for a high-ranking Gibraltarian friend of mine. We've been working—in secret—to design a hydropower bridge that will span the strait. Not wanting to let the details of our calculations fall into our competitors' hands, we have—until now—been exchanging encoded messages via homing pigeon."

Another puff of smoke. "What you found was our final pigeon—the one carrying the last and most critical part of the work. My friend needed the information by day's end to meet the filing deadline for our patent application."

I wondered what the prince would have done had I not come along. Fortune favors the lucky, as they say.

"If we fail to submit the full calculations by midnight, our provisional patent will expire, and our plans will be made public, much to the delight of the naysayers. They write-off our ideas as delusional fantasy, saying we're just like the German Atlantropists who wanted to dam the strait decades ago. But unlike them, our design is feasible."

The prince spoke, absorbed in his reverie, drawing punctuation in the thickening smoke. At some point while he was talking, a fresh cigarette materialized in his hand. To this day, I have no idea how it got there.

"What is certain is that our opponents would rather not see our two continents connected. Once our patent is secured, however, there is nothing they can do to object. My friend and I have acquired the necessary right-of-ways."

Reestablishing eye contact, the prince paused for an awkwardly long moment before continuing again.

"You have proven your trustworthiness. If I tell you where to go, can you relay the calculations to my friend across the strait? You will be handsomely rewarded."

I knew there was not another ferry departing in time and didn't think I had another multi-hour row in me.

"Do you have a motorboat you could spare?"

"I would, but my competitors know my yacht well and would waylay any effort to cross in that fashion. Moreover, their informants within the Gibraltar Port Authority would raise the alert even if we tried to take you partway. As you proved, however, smaller boats can still slip through undetected. What I can do is loan you some rowing assistance."

Prince al-Ayouch turned and gestured toward the dark hallway behind him, and there appeared the broad-chested bulk of a man born for rowing. At that moment, I half-wondered if the prince was some sort of conjurer able to summon life from thin air.

"This is Hamza, my faithful, trusted servant. He will help you row back to Gibraltar."

Hamza responded with a silent nod. With only nine hours left until the patent deadline, there was little time to dawdle. I bade the prince a fond farewell and took a waterproof tube containing the calculations. Hamza and I walked wordlessly down to the beach where I had pulled the boat ashore. As anyone in the family can attest, when I'm forced into unexpected collaboration, it is my custom to strike up a conversation. In this case, I ventured several inquiries, but, each time, was rewarded with silence. I could take the hint that Hamza was not a talker.

Despite the advantage of having a fresh set of arms doing the rowing, the way back was slower and more difficult—the tide was stronger and a thick fog had descended. But Hamza was steadfast. About a half-mile from Gibraltar, we could finally see the city lights glowing through the murk. No sooner had the lights come into view than a shape loomed suddenly off the starboard bow. We were directly in the path of an oncoming freighter. I had always thought that doom's approach would be heralded with fanfare and commotion. All we heard was the steady rumble of a bow wave and all we saw was the impossible angle of the prow blotting out the fog-filtered moonglow overhead.

Hamza put all of his strength into several big pulls. It was enough to propel us to the Gibraltar-side of the ship, but we overturned in the wake and tumbled headfirst into the cold water. I came to the surface clutching the tube containing the calculations and was able to grab hold of the inverted rowboat but saw no sign of Hamza.

Minutes passed and so did the freighter. My chattering teeth and gasping breath kept me focused on the task of survival. Struggling shapes in the swirling eddies stole my attention every so often, but my compatriot did not surface. I was hoping that Hamza's talent for holding his words meant that he was equally adept at holding his breath, but each elapsed minute further strained credulity. It wasn't until the ship had passed and the wake died down, that I saw Hamza bobbing in the water on the opposite side. I think we were both relieved to see the other. He gave me a big wave and came swimming in my direction. With us both clutching the side of the rowboat for flotation, we kicked our way into shore. To power me, I started counting out the Fibonacci sequence in metronomic fashion. When the numbers started getting too big to handle, I spiraled back to the beginning of the sequence and started anew. Together, we eventually reached the European mainland. We had made the return trip in eight hours. One hour left.

The destination was not far. My ocean-numbed body stumbled through the neighborhood to a house on a nearby side street. Somewhere along the way, Hamza sublimated back into the darkness from which he first materialized. Left alone at an unassuming doorway, I knocked a pattern of prime numbers and collapsed inward as it opened.

"My good man, why are you all wet?"

I responded with an outstretched arm and the tube containing the calculations. My host ran through his small home and brought me a glass of water, a loaf of bread, and a blanket.

"I am sorry to leave you in this state, but I must be off to the patent office!"

With that, he closed the door and left me alone on the floor. I gulped down the water, inhaled the bread, and passed out there on the concrete, drool pooling beneath my cheek. Before losing consciousness, I remember coming to the peculiar conclusion that the taste of the floor was reminiscent of the smell of the Honesdale post office back home.

When I came to the next morning, I was somehow wrapped in a blanket on a couch near the fire. There was fresh fruit, dried fish, and more water on a small table beside me. On another table was my neatly folded boiler suit, which looked to have been cleaned and dried. I attacked the provisions ravenously and must have made some noise in doing so, because soon, the man from the night before shuffled into the room.

"Ah, so you're awake I see. You'll be pleased to know that we got our patent. You have helped lay the groundwork for a new peace between the continents. For that, we are in your debt. I spoke with Prince al-Ayouch this morning and he has wired your promised reward to the following Swiss bank account."

The man produced an envelope containing an account number and corresponding access instructions. I tried to thank him for his hospitality, but he would have none of it and left me to rest. Other than soreness and exhaustion, I felt remarkably well. I enjoyed the fire's warmth and passed out once again. When I awoke, the table had been cleared and I found a small note stating: "I had to go out. Yours, Antonio."

At that point, I was feeling well enough for a stroll to loosen my joints. I stepped into my boiler suit from the *Visigoth* and wandered down to the spot where my journey had begun. There, in the place I had initially found it, stood the rowboat, looking good as new. Satisfied that Hamza must have taken care of the loose ends, I grabbed my still damp bags (the karmic collateral had apparently been sufficient) and walked back to the house. Antonio hadn't returned. I've always been uncomfortable imposing on the goodwill of others, so I gathered my things and went on my way. The nearest airport, and the taxis to take me there, were just a short walk across the Spanish border. My Gibraltar experiences may not have been as explosive as my grandfather's, but they made a lasting impression on me nevertheless.

4.

RADAC, Pejë District, The Autonomous Socialist Republic of Kosovo — This tiny Kosovar hamlet lies on the border with Montenegro. Its rugged beauty and bucolic charm make it a popular waypoint on journeys between the two countries. Otherwise, it does not see much traffic from those outside of the area. Nonetheless, it did serve as the location for what became known as "the miracle of Radac" ...

As I walked across the border from Gibraltar into Spain, I was immediately approached by what looked like a customs official. He looked me in the eye and solemnly made the sign of the cross over his heart. Neither fluent in Spanish nor the local Catholic customs, I simply nodded, traced a cross over my breast pocket, smiled, and got into the taxi he had so courteously arranged for me. I've always found that Catholics can identify one another in a crowd—I assumed he must have seen me and wanted to do a good deed for a fellow initiate. We wound northward along the Costa del Sol until we reached Malaga. There, I was met by another uniformed official who motioned me into a large building, gave me a stack of papers, shook my hand, and hurried me down a long corridor toward a tarmac. Before I could really tell what was happening, I was loaded on a plane headed east. Since the taxi ride had been so pleasant, I wasn't overly concerned with my destination. Below me, I watched Majorca, Corsica, and Elba glide by. Over the Adriatic, we began our descent into the Balkans.

Let me pause here. If you're from the doubting Thomas side of the family, I'm sure you will question the veracity of this series of events. "How could he so easily take this all in stride?" you might ask. For one, I've always had a knack for attracting strange happenings, and in this case, I was more than a little bewildered. After weeks at sea and my adventures with the prince, the waiting taxi and subsequent plane ride didn't seem so odd. I'll also say that incredulity will only get you so far in this life. If you want to spend your time drawing lines between what you believe and what you don't, that's your business—it won't change what happened or the words on this page.

Nonetheless, I know my family—you require context in order to believe, so here is an additional aside. After the death of General Franco, some Spaniards were put off by the rapid growth of personal liberty, preferring the watchful eye of government in everyday affairs. In hopes of rekindling the flames of Spanish autocracy, these groups established a variety of exchange programs with like-minded autocrats in the Eastern Bloc: tradespeople and service workers were loaned for the agitator philosophers necessary to incite revolution. Thus, Spanish civil engineers labored building the infrastructure in places like Belarus and Czechoslovakia, while early-career politburists came to Spain espousing controlled economies and encouraging the proletariat to rise up. Thanks to my heavy-handed foreshadowing, you have now realized what was happening before my younger self did.

We landed in a jewel of a city nestled in a mountain valley. When I stepped off the plane, I could sense a special kind of fervor in the air. As in Spain, a taxi and a bespectacled bureaucrat were waiting for me. We grinned, had a vigorous handshake, and were off into the winter night. Without a word, I was deposited in the lobby of a grand hotel. The bell-hop took my bag and showed me to my room. Out the window, I could see snowflakes drifting lazily down through yellow cones of light. All this spy film was missing was a man in a trenchcoat and fedora. But the city square was largely deserted—its only occupants the breeze-rustled banners hanging from streetlamps and balustrades. One depicted a bobsled team, another an ice skater. It was January 1984—just a month before the Winter Olympics would be held in Sarajevo. Happy to at least know where I was, I pulled back the sheets on the bed, stripped down to my undergarments, and slept soundly until dawn found its way through the hotel curtains.

Almost as soon as I had cinched my belt in the morning, ready to face the day, I heard a polite knock on the door. It opened to reveal the bureaucrat from the night before, still grinning. I wondered aloud where the day might lead us, but his shy nod told me we did not share the same language. Too groggy to attempt the hard work of translation, I grabbed my seabag and followed my handler to yet another car. I got in and he started driving. Trying to explain my state of mind at that moment will be futile, but it was something like exhilarating exhaustion. The silence only heightened the feeling. We wove through pristine valleys and over rugged mountain passes until we entered the Socialist Autonomous Province of Kosovo.

I hadn't eaten for a day and a half (airplane food doesn't count), so I was famished. I touched thumb to forefingers and brought them to my open mouth to pantomime eating. There was a spark of understanding in my companion's eyes. We pulled up near the first cafe we encountered, got out and proceeded to eat great quantities of lamb and eggplant casserole. The meal was accompanied by the best coffee I have ever consumed. To this day, I can still taste its luxurious flavor—thick, sweet, and darkly creamy. Mr. Grins never stopped smiling the entire time we ate. Now, with some food to fuel my thoughts, I began to ponder my current predicament. Surely, whoever brought me here didn't intercept me in Gibraltar and send me to Yugoslavia for a delightful cafe luncheon. There must be some quid pro quo expected.

Soon enough, the quid and quo came to light. After lunch, we proceeded across the town square to a small, whitewashed building. My companion opened the door with a great flourish, smiled even more broadly than before, and presented me to the young people assembled inside. The room erupted with cheers and applause. Not knowing what to do, I smiled awkwardly and bowed my head slightly. I was handed a flimsy textbook and left alone with the Kosovar youth staring at me expectantly.

Knowing no other course but forward, I looked in sheepish silence from my new students to the book in my hands. What I initially mistook for Albanian was in actuality English gobbledygook presented in fancy script. The title did not inspire much confidence: *Sample Metal-Psychics for Ewes and Meats*. If I said it quickly aloud, it made a modicum of sense. Poor translations are one thing, but the book appeared to have been put together by some homophonic savant—the translator knew roughly what the words should sound like but had no idea of their meaning.

Though I have always fancied myself to be well-read, metaphysics has never been a strong suit. Couple that with my lack of Balkan language skills and you can imagine my initial dismay. But since the textbook was written in seeming English, I held on to a glimmer of hope. I flipped through the first dozen pages and found more of the same intractable language. Some of the gems I remember reading aloud:

"Nay sure is alter hound us. Weeds donut eggs is inane vacuum. Why?"

"Air is throttled is the feather of tuff yield."

"Hew masked a bough treasons import ants."

My audience sat in rapt attention, nodding along to my every word. Luckily, once I got past page fifteen, the book became dominated by vivid illustrations. I had previously imagined it impossible to convey metaphysics via picture-book format, but I was wrong. As I held up the first picture, slowly panning from right to left so the students could see, I saw an epiphanic wave break across their faces. A lanky, unkempt young man in the back shot his hand up. I acknowledged him and he spoke. Everyone shook their head in agreement. After only a few more pictures, a bell started ringing and the class dismissed itself. The students got up, gathered their belongings and filed outside respectfully.

Just as I was wondering what to do next, my handler appeared in the doorway and led me across town to my accommodations. The room was a small, unadorned space on the fifth floor of a brutalist concrete building. Still, what furnishings it had were comfortable. Out my window, I could see the streets alive with activity. A high apartment row, a squat building full of market stalls, and a minaret. This was a land without architectural coherence.

From my perspective, I was caught up in what I took to be an elaborate boondoggle. It seemed I would be teaching a course in government-approved metaphysics and provided with room and board in exchange. While I had never anticipated such a turn of events, it was a new place and the work seemed like it could be a rewarding challenge. The reality of the situation was even stranger than I had imagined. Metaphysics was just an activity to pass the time. But I will explain that later. For the moment, pedagogy held my interest and occupied my time.

In my class were twelve young men I came to call "the Apostles": Mathias, Markus, Lucas, and Jeton were the ringleaders. They traveled en masse, quietly conversing, dutifully reading their books, and writing in their journals. There was also a Tomor. Though he himself was as full of faith as anyone I had yet met, I was doubtful that he would amount to much. The group even had a Marigona who followed them around. Clearly, I had spent too much time in Catholic school. Nonetheless, the mnemonic has stuck with me to this day.

Over the next few weeks, I settled into a comfortable pattern of teaching, reading, and exploring the countryside on foot. I seemed to be reaching my students bit by bit and greatly appreciated their patient studiousness. They were quickly learning snippets of English, whereas I struggled with even the most basic Albanian phrases. Honestly, I made a better English instructor than a metaphysician. But it didn't particularly seem to matter how I structured my lessons. The students were appreciative, so I was happy.

I was living through that time in youth when one can't help but feel productive, hale, hardy, and full of boundless energy. The surrounding landscape was one of the most beautiful places I had seen. I traversed the depths of Rugova Canyon, explored the snowy Sar Mountains, and walked through the frigid spray of the towering waterfall on the White Drin. Class would end for the day and the students would go back home to help tend their farms. I, on the other hand, wandered free over relatively untrammeled nature.

This general bliss continued uninterrupted for about a month. One morning, my grinning friend reappeared. Since he had deposited me in my one-room flat, I had not seen him a single time. I had almost forgotten how I had come to reside in the town of Peja. But the flesh and blood reminder was standing in front of me. He beckoned me to follow him once more, and so I did.

Out to the car we went. On the passenger seat, a surgeon's smock and pants lay neatly folded. On top of them was a rusting, well-used stethoscope and old-fashioned headlamp. His gestures seemed to indicate that these were for me.

"What a strange gift," I thought.

I slipped into the passenger seat and cradled the garments carefully on my lap. We drove in silence down a winding, single-lane road, coming to stop in front of a ramshackle medical clinic near the town of Radac. From the outside, it looked like the small building had seen better days. The interior confirmed this supposition. After we entered, I was shown to a changing room. I understood that I was meant to change into the surgeon's costume and began to get a bit concerned. When I emerged looking like a doctor, my grinning friend clapped his hands excitedly. He quickly led me down a short hallway to a dimly lit operating theatre.

That was when I first considered running away, but before I could work up the nerve, a door on the other side of the room opened. A nurse came in pushing a hospital bed on top of which lay a groaning patient (or victim?). The meek woman looked from her patient to me and nodded a small smile. Horrified, I was on the verge of fainting, when the door opened again and an imposing doctor marched toward me with his arm outstretched.

In one swift motion, he seemed to crush my hand and give me a jovial slap on the back. "Welcome friend!" he said with ebullience uncharacteristic of an operating room. "We are so happy to have you here today." I was somewhat surprised by the man's English skills. I'd been surrounded by poorly written textbooks for so long, that I had almost forgotten what flawless conjugation and sentence construction sounded like. I was jolted from my linguistic reverie with the next sentence, however.

"This man," said the doctor, stabbing his stubby finger in the direction of the sorry soul on the hospital bed, "is broken very badly. I am at a loss and would be glad to have your opinion as how best to proceed."

Before I go much further, I should say now that Kosovars are some of the warmest and friendliest people I have ever encountered. Never once did I cease to feel welcome in their country. In other words, I felt indebted to their hospitality. So maybe that explains my willingness to play along.

"My opinion?" I said. "I'm not sure what you mean."

"Of course! Forgive me—I should have explained the details of the case first. What is the scientific method without data?"

At that moment, I came to realize that I had not been brought to Kosovo to be an English teacher—that was just a tangential pursuit and opportunity for public service. Somehow, they were under the impression that I was a consulting surgeon. While the doctor explained the onset and progression of the symptoms, I untangled the course of events that had led me to this point. When I was first intercepted at the Gibraltar border, I had been wearing my second-hand boiler suit from the old ship's medic. When he crossed his heart, what I took for religious devotion was merely pantomime. He was tracing the red cross and I responded in kind, thereby sealing my fate.

As the symptoms and hypotheses mounted, I was at a loss. Though my medical knowledge was lacking, I did not want to let these kind people down.

"What do you think?"

"Well," I began, hoping for divine intervention. "The first thing I need to do is examine the patient."

As the panic rose in my chest, my prayed-for intervention came. For some reason, a recent reading came to mind—specifically a biography in the *Orion*'s library about a famous Russian concert whistler who had been recruited into the KGB. When he refused to carry through with his first assignment, they attempted to poison him with a dose of thallium (though some argue that the symptoms could just as easily have been induced by radioactive polonium). He was hospitalized, but the poison failed to prove lethal. Thankfully, the man had chronicled his symptoms and the progression of the poisoning in great detail. His dedication to science helped future doctors develop more effective treatments for a number of radiological sicknesses.

The patient before me seemed to be exhibiting a disturbingly similar pathology. With the doctor acting as translator, I proceeded on a line of questioning aimed at uncovering the root cause. Eventually, it came to light that the man was an engineer and had been bathing in a reactor cooling pond somewhere south of Minsk. Normally, these ponds are relatively safe (the people who recreate in the reservoirs along the Susquehanna are proof enough of this), however, it seems that this reactor had an almost undetectable leak.

Having pinpointed the cause, I recommended a course of anti-radiation drugs and assured the doctor that, based upon what I knew of radiation sickness, if it was exceptionally serious, the man would already be dead. There could be lingering impacts, but it would be hard to disentangle the effects of any single exposure from the cumulative effects of working in the industry. The concern that day—as it always is—was for the immediate odds for survival. As a layman, I rated those as fairly high.

Once I offered my assessment, the doctor seemed delighted. His impressive handlebar mustache twitched to and fro, a smile lit upon his lips, and he moved in to deliver a congratulatory clap on the back. He was nothing if not consistent, landing the blow on exactly the same spot he had earlier.

When I returned to my flat that evening, I was heady with adrenaline. I felt as if I'd truly accomplished something and made a difference. What's more, I had the hand-shaped bruise on my back to prove it. Many years later, I received a letter from the doctor indicating that our patient was still thriving and had not been sick since my consultation. He called it a "miracle." Even after a long career, this is one of the achievements of which I am most proud.

And now a quick note for my descendants. I hope that even the most unimaginative among you will realize that life is full of serendipities. Take, for example, my reading habit—something my mother always encouraged from a young age.

She would tell me that there were all sorts of important lessons to be learned if people would only read. "Reading may well save your life one day," she said. She was right, but off by an order. That day, it was not me, but someone else who was saved. I learned long ago to always listen to my mother. You would do well to learn that lesson, too.

5

*1984 SARAJEVO SKI JUMP COMPETITION —
Four years before Eddie the Eagle, there was
Gregor the Glider. What is seldom known, however, is that the success of Gregor the Glider can
actually be traced to a stand-in competitor...*

The day after doctoring, I half expected to wake up and see my smiling friend in the doorway, ready to send me back home. But when my eyes opened, all that was there to greet me was the pale light of a sun that had not yet risen above the mountains. It was morning east of the ridgeline, but merely pre-dawn in my hamlet. And so, I settled back into my routine. I gathered my things, went down to the schoolhouse, and taught my lessons.

If you must know, I was starting to get a little homesick. Yes, I was enjoying my European adventures, but after months of not knowing what would happen next, the normalcy of home sounded increasingly appealing. Even the most adventurous among us crave stability now and then. Fate, being the mischievous force that it is, decided to keep me in Yugoslavia a little longer.

A few days later, a local Gypsy child approached me as I was leaving school. Let me say here that the Roma are unfairly maligned throughout the world. Where they get their reputation for thieving and trickery is beyond me. True, there are pockets of dishonesty here and there, but the same can be said of any culture. Surely, some forgotten historian had encounters with a few bad apples, the story stuck, and persisted to this day. Some people even threaten their children with being "sold to the Gypsies." As is the case with all familial threats, the children feign terror for the sake of ritual. I, on the other hand, would relish the opportunity to live in Roma society. But the purpose of a memoir is not to set the historical record straight and right the wrongs of civilization.

The Gypsy child invited me to dinner at her nearby encampment. Taking it as a sign that I was having a positive impact as a teacher, I allowed myself to be led off into the Yugoslavian wilds. After an hour's walk through light snow, we came to a clearing with a large campfire and much revelry.

No sooner had we entered the group, than was I handed a steaming bowl of thick stew. I drew my spoon through the mixture, brimming with offal and other less-identifiable chunks, brought it to my lips, and chewed thoroughly. My face was all delight, but my mouth was flummoxed by the strange combination of flavors and textures. Thankfully, my time at sea had hardened my stomach. I did not want to insult my gracious hosts. Apparently, my act worked, because they loaded me up with a second helping as soon as I had finished the first.

When I finished that, everyone was duly impressed with my appetite. The women whistled encouragement and the men gave me a few boisterous huzzahs. I had passed my initiation into Gypsy culture. Next thing I knew, I was being whisked away on a post-supper constitutional. We trudged up a steep grade, heading toward the top of a long slope of fresh snow. The men carried long, thin birch planks over their shoulders. Despite their massive boots, they skirted the snow expertly—whereas I sank in to my knees with each step.

When we reached the top of the hill, the planks were stabbed into the snow in pairs like the pickets of an improvised garden fence. One of the men let out a blood-curdling whoop, grabbed his set of skis, balanced atop them and set off down the mountainside. He didn't carve the graceful S-turns I had been taught as a child in the Poconos. Instead, he charted a line straight down the mountain. I had been downhill skiing before, but never on skis like these.

At the bottom of the hill, when the man looked to be just a fraction of his original size, he went airborne. I hadn't noticed the jump that had been constructed at the slope's base. It then dawned on me—we weren't downhill skiing, we were ski jumping. My desire to avoid disappointing my hosts got the better of my fears once again, and after several men had gone, I took my turn.

The homemade skis had little in the way of bindings beyond a small leather strap. I laid the two planks before me and stepped onto them gingerly. Then, I slipped the straps up over top of my boots, jamming the frayed material through my laces. I slowly shifted my weight forward and rapidly accelerated down the hill. The wind whistling across my ears was pure exhilaration. I mimicked what I had seen before and made sure not to try carving any turns. I aimed straight for the jump at the bottom. It began to look more and more imposing the closer it got.

Momentum carried me up the ramp and sent me airborne at great height. The mechanics of skiborne flight were something that I had not previously considered. My center of gravity naturally shifted forward until my skis and body acted like a sail. At the apex, I lost my nerve, imagining being impaled by bits of splintered ski should my landing go awry. Discretion being the better part of valor, I dove out of the loose bindings as the ground raced up to greet me. Thankfully, my companions had piled soft snow high in the landing area.

I hit hard and gasped as the wind left my lungs, but those gathered round looked like they appreciated my effort.

In the midst of my oxygen-deprived stupor, I must have been scooped-up. My next memory is of being paraded through the forest on the shoulders of Gypsy men singing celebratory songs of conquest. They maintained their boisterous melodies all the way back to the encampment. I sat enthralled by the situation. The sun set amongst the birches, turning them to flame. Long shadows wove a mattress on the forest floor. The baritone verses played counterpoint to the dusky, eventide chorus of wrens. Darkness stretched a moth-eaten sheet tight across the sky. And I drank it all in.

As the evening descended, grotesque human shadows flickered against the wooded backdrop. Were the source of the shadows not such welcoming individuals, and I had happened upon the camp unexpectedly, I might have been afraid. But hospitality comes naturally to the Gypsies. Food and drink were kept in constant supply throughout the night. Stories were told of my heroics, complete with the requisite pratfalls. Even my shaky jump looked much more graceful when they related the tale.

Eventually, I gave my thanks and bid my adieus, slipping away as the bacchanal unfurled into the night. When I made it home to my hovel, I slept contentedly in undisturbed dreamlessness.

The very next morning, there was a knock on my door. I opened it to see Mr. Grins holding an envelope. He handed it over to me immediately. I fumbled with opening it and read the letter I found inside. At its top was an official looking seal. The signature scrawled across the bottom evinced no less pomp. What I gathered from the letter was thus:

A gentleman by the name of Gregor Ivayavich—a local hero from nearby Ukraine—had recently fallen ill. He had been slated to compete in the ski jump competition at the Sarajevo Olympics the next day. His illness prevented him from competing, but due to a paperwork mix-up, he was still required to present himself, lest the Soviet team suffer a stiff penalty.

Not wanting to damage its relations with a fellow socialist state, or risk tarnishing what had otherwise been a successful Olympics, the Yugoslav envoy had devised a plan. It would supply a look-alike so that the Olympic officials would be none the wiser. I had been nominated as a prime candidate to replace the erstwhile Ivayavich—the likeness was said to be striking.

It seems my reputation from the previous evening had already spread throughout the valley. In fact, the letter addressed me as a ski jumper of some esteem. Since I was in Yugoslavia on the basis of a misunderstanding, I gave in to fate and went along with the plan. As I've said time and again, I was treated so kindly while I was there that I didn't want to let my hosts down.

And so, I competed as Gregor Ivayavich. What's more surprising, however, is that I was able to do well enough to earn a bronze medal. It is amazing what proper bindings and a few test runs can do for the confidence. If you look at pictures of the medal ceremony, you'll see me there waving back. To think of the bloodshed and horrors that podium later endured in the Bosnian War makes my perfect moment of victory all the more precious.

Amid my intoxication from unexpected victory, my smiling friend materialized out of the crowd. I hated to leave the celebration and the camaraderie of the ski jumpers, but my friend had not led me astray before, so I followed him. In the car outside of the venue, he handed me another letter. Reading it, I learned that to complete the ruse of Gregor's participation, I would have to fly back to Ukraine. At that point, the Ukrainians would send me wherever I desired.

The end of my Balkan adventure was just as serendipitous as the beginning. I glanced into the back seat and saw my belongings there. My departure was to be immediate. I looked at my friend as we sped off toward the airport and noticed it was the first time he wasn't smiling. To this day, I'm not sure if the tears welling in his eyes were on account of the extreme cold or my leaving.

At the airport, he helped carry my bags to the Ukrainian plane, embraced me in a tight bear-hug, then turned on his heel and disappeared with his characteristic magician's ability.

When I got off the plane in Kiev, my competitive namesake was waiting for me at the bottom of the stairs. We didn't really look much alike after all. He was easily a foot taller and had to genuflect as I took the bronze medal from my neck and draped it 'round his. Gregor the Glider went on to win many more competitions, but that bronze was his only taste of Olympic glory.

I asked to be sent to St. Paul, Minnesota. My plan was to use my nautical skills to get on with a river barge company and float down the Mississippi to finally live out my Mark Twainsian fantasies. Either they didn't understand my request, or they didn't care. When I was handed my tickets at the airport, the final destination indicated Barcelona and included pre-paid taxi fare to Santa Pau. I shouldn't have been surprised—from Spain I came and to Spain I was destined to return.

6.

PIC DU MIDI, France — This famous observatory in the French Pyrenees dates to the 19th Century. In fact, it is the world's oldest, continuously operating mountaintop observatory. Many famous astronomical breakthroughs have their roots at the facility. Most recently, the work of Dr. Josephine Abatxa has gained notoriety. Interestingly, early in her career, she took on an apprentice...

As a child facing the black winter nights of Damascus, I used to imagine the view from the other end of the telescope. Somewhere, thousands of light-years away, circling one of those faint dots of light, was someone (or something) gazing through a telescope with equal curiosity. Perhaps one day we would unknowingly focus our telescopes upon each other and neither of us would be any the wiser to our fleeting moment of contact. At any time, there might be thousands, millions of worlds focused in on our own.

What might these beings look like? I had a picture book that posited a variety of hypothetical permutations. Most of them were comically grotesque. Watermelon-colored zeppelins on Jupiter, ice-skating green dinosaurs on Europa. My imagination was more influenced by the humanoid creatures I saw on sci-fi television programs. Different colors and appendages, but all discernibly familiar enough. I had never even considered the important prerequisite for telescopic exploration—eyes. I don't know why it took a nature special on cave animals for me to realize that our eyes might be unique. After all, there is an abundance of plant and fungal life here on Earth that thrives without the benefit of eyesight. What use does a cave shrimp have for a telescope? With these thoughts on my mind from a young age, I was predisposed to astronomical pursuits.

I give you this background only because of what happened when I landed in Barcelona. Life has a way of folding over on itself, doubling-back to bring everything into alignment.

My flight landed in the morning. After I collected my baggage, I emerged into the ground transportation area and immediately saw my name on a taxi placard. Somehow, despite butchering my destination, the Ukrainians had managed to pass on the spelling of my name flawlessly. Without any other plans, I figured I should see what Santa Pau had to offer. My weekend in La Garrotxa was a welcome respite. I climbed the volcano and saw the chapel nestled on the crater floor. I walked the Val de Bas as the sun delayed its setting, lingering on the tall grass lining the fields. The snow-etched Pyrenees were visible to the north, their saw-teeth separating me from the rest of the continent. I found a Roman stone bridge arching high over a deep pool and joined some locals in taking the plunge. In the course of the weekend, however, it became clear that employment options would be limited in this bucolic landscape, so I decided to head back to Barcelona and find a flight home.

I got back to the city in late afternoon, planning to go to the airport early the next morning to arrange my U.S. return. And so, with my remaining time, I found a hostel in the Bari Gothic, and explored the city. In and out of paper shops and cathedrals, I eventually found my way to Park Güell as night descended. For a long while, I stood gazing up at the barely visible Milky Way. Constellations drifting in and out of focus, the galaxy revealed itself to me in succeeding layers. From these depths, the occasional Centaurid made its entrance. For one brief shining moment, a remnant of the solar system's beginnings usurped the moon's role as lord of the skies.

"I prefer to think of the moon as a queen."

Startled, I realized that I had been reciting a running narration of my thoughts. Leaning on the railing not far from me was a fellow stargazer.

"You know," she said, nodding up at a particularly bright, particularly sustained shooting star, "this is how life begins... the great seeding of the universe."

"Wouldn't they actually have to make it through the atmospheric autoclave?"

"Fair enough, but the process is the same. I'm Josephine," she said with a smile. "You can call me Jo."

I tore my eyes from the scene unfolding overhead to size-up my unexpected companion. She was tall, but not lanky, academic, but not severe. Her long brown hair was gathered up in a tight bun at the top of her head, pierced by a pencil. She looked to be five to ten years older than me, which, at the time, seemed more consequential than it does now. Truthfully though, we were both quite young. As I made my assessments, I could feel her doing the same. The connection was instantaneous. I had never felt love blossom so quickly.

We spent the next three hours discussing cosmology and our favorite planetary bodies. You wouldn't think that astrophysics would be a hotbed for flirtation, but can you name another discipline so littered with the mythology of love? After all, some of the most massive asteroids we know are named Eros and Psyche. I came to learn that Jo was an astronomer who worked at a nearby observatory. She came to learn that I was planning to return to America the next day. Having need for a lab assistant (and wishing to delay my departure), she offered me the job and I accepted on the spot. The contract was sealed with a kiss so passionate, it could only be born of youthful indiscretion. She looked into my eyes, told me where to meet her the following morning, and disappeared into the night.

The next day, instead of going to the airport, I gathered my bags and walked down to the harborside park. I counted five date palms past the ferry ticket office and there on the bench was Josephine, sipping an espresso. She saw me, smiled, and rose to greet me with a kiss.

"Ready for an adventure?" she asked.

I was hardly given a chance to reply before she grabbed my hand and led me across the esplanade to her car, a tiny red Renault. We drove a meandering route through the countryside, the satisfied silence an accomplice to our blossoming love. In fact, it wasn't until we made it to Andorra that either of us dared to break the spell of quiet, but it was time for lunch and it would have been hard to order food without speaking.

Over Iberian ham sandwiches, we opened the floodgates on our life stories. From that point on, the remainder of the drive was filled with the exact opposite of the silence that had come before, yet we found it equally as pleasant.

Jo's Catalan grandmother—a schoolteacher in Andorra—had drawn her to the Pyrenees. Initially, after graduating with a degree in astrophysics, Jo thought she'd give up the researcher's life and become a tobacco farmer like her Catalan forbearers, but a flier seeking volunteers for the local astronomy club was all it took to sweep those thoughts aside.

The incestuous stargazer community being what it was, it wasn't long until Jo's credentials betrayed her and she was recruited to work at nearby Pic du Midi. Once there, she quickly ascended through the ranks. She was chief astrophysicist within two years. It seemed she had a knack for spying distant nebulae and new phenomena. When I joined her, the priority was creation of a pulsar catalogue. Telescope time was at a premium, so we needed to be precise and efficient.

My tasks were routine: scheduling time, programming the survey transects, and analyzing the collected data. Outliers and points of interest were flagged for review by Jo who did the theoretical heavy lifting. But even the mundanities of the science were suffused with romance. Jo named the lone binary pulsar pair we discovered the Abatxa-Brecht formation and the cosmological constant she calculated to explain its existence, P_{A-B}. Those were lusty days.

Outside of work, our love grew as we explored the high mountain valleys and dined on regional delicacies. In Mirepoix, we ate cassoulet. In Seu D'Urgell, we sampled the finest goat cheeses and tiny, tender olives so savory, they tasted as if they were soaked in the essence of pure flavor. Since my children and grandchildren are the only ones likely to read this, I'll spare you the more intimate details of our nights, but it suffices to say that they were pure bliss—a tangle of streetlights, laughter, and limbs intertwined.

In those days, I would have thought that nothing could alter the chemistry between us. Marriage and family seemed an inevitability. There was talk of soulmates and eternity. Like the black holes we occasionally pinpointed, everything seemed to converge and we were the center.

At work, Jo encouraged me to pursue my own research interests. One evening, when the telescopic schedule was unexpectedly light, on a whim, I spun the coordinate dials and took a photo. At breakpoints throughout the night, I took several more photos of the same region. At the end of the shift, I viewed my series of photo pairs, and there, against all odds, beyond any rational probability, glided a point of light. Chances are this was an already-discovered rock floating out through the asteroid belt.

With our night's observations complete, Jo and I went home for our customary cup of tea before collapsing into bed. As she put the kettle on, Jo asked if I had seen anything interesting through the telescope. I mentioned the asteroid.

"Were you able to make multiple readings?"

With a smile, I produced the notes from my pocket. "Excellent. Should be easy enough for Dr. Marsden at the Minor Planet Center to corroborate if it is listed."

"If it's not, I've already got a name in mind."

"Let's take it one step at a time."

She took the scrap of paper from the table and began her mental calculations just as the teapot raised its shrill, crescendoing alarm. But instead of turning off the burner, she let the whistle continue blaring and sat down.

"Do you know where this is heading?"

"I haven't had a chance to calculate yet. I wanted to make more observations, then take a look through the digital microscope." Jo's grasp of interstellar geometries was intuitive and far better than my own.

"Where?"

"Here."

"Earth?"

Her eyes gave the reply. "What name were you thinking?"

"Calypso."

"That one's already been taken," she said, failing to grasp my attempt at humor, since it was Calypso who delayed Odysseus' return home, just as Jo had delayed mine. "It will take some more measurements to be sure—refine the size and orbit—but that's what these rough observations tell me."

I must have looked scared, because she back-peddled some consolation. "I've seen dozens of these, and it's always been that once we have more data, it goes from a near-miss to a statistical improbability. We'll gather some more observations tomorrow."

The kettle stopped its whistling as the water boiled away. We turned off the burner and went to bed, only I did not sleep. I laid awake dreaming of calamity, each envisioned impact punctuated by one of Jo's understated snores. Eventually, exhaustion overcame me.

When I awoke, it was late in the morning. From the smell of fried ham and eggs, I could tell Jo was already up and in the kitchen. I stumbled out and offered a groggy greeting. In response, she handed me a plate heaped with the fruits of her labor. We enjoyed a quiet breakfast as if everything was normal. And to be sure, the handful of hours before returning to work were our last gasp of normalcy—for a while at least.

It was an afternoon trapped in amber. A walk through the town center and park. Fresh figs from the fruit stand. Fresh bread for the walk home. Our fingers woven like the basket that held the produce for our afternoon meal. It was perfection. A wake for the living world.

But, ignore it as we might, I still sensed doom on the horizon. Preoccupied with the coming apocalypse, I broke the spell and asked, "What do we do if the calculations show it is heading this way?"

I could tell Jo was a little annoyed with my doomsday mindset. "There is no playbook for this. Just eat your bread and stop worrying until we know more—it won't help."

"I know. But it doesn't make it any easier."

With that, we headed back home to get ready for the work ahead. We were not scheduled to go into the observatory at all, but Jo called around and was able to switch shifts with a colleague. She called ahead and made sure the night watchman would have the building unlocked for us. The bulk of our afternoon meal was left in the basket untouched.

Our usual work routine was thrown off, but we still had the normal tasks to attend to before we could gather more data on the object I saw the previous night. Nothing was as easy as before. Perhaps humanity's potential impending demise had thrown us out of sync such that we no longer shared a common language. Truth be told, though I knew something was amiss, I scarcely noticed. My waking dreams painted pictures of repeated impacts. Devastation cracking the world in two. Fire and brimstone like a puritan preacher of old. When I thought about the cataclysm, it wasn't humanity's extinction that disturbed me most—no, it was the destruction of the natural world. The mighty oaks. The striped maple. The insects that feed on their foliage and then die to form the soil for the plants' next generation. All the flora, fauna, and geological processes that have shaped the world. I couldn't bear to think of a universe without an apple tree or snapdragon. And so, with these thoughts forming the background noise, it is little wonder that I had limited energy for the maintenance of our relationship. Jo called it my "end-of-the-world syndrome." I preferred to think of it as empathy for the planet. If I'm honest, I found her dismissal of my concerns a bit hurtful. It's hard to be told that your thought process, however irrational, is non-productive.

Amidst our other tasks, we were able to make more readings. At the end of the night, we combined them with those from the previous evening and made our calculations. The larger data set refined what we knew about the object. It was half-a-mile wide and moving at a speed of 43,812 miles per hour. Its trajectory could use additional refinement, but more and more, looked like it was bound for an inevitable collision course with Earth in just over eleven years—one more broad arc around the sun and our orbits would intersect. Knowing this fact brought me a certain peace—it was uncertainty that had frightened me most. But now, I could begin planning for contingencies. The realization had a similar effect on Jo. She also remained calm, but with that calm came an unyielding focus on averting the catastrophe. Her every waking moment was obsessed with how to deflect the rock.

But that all came a bit later. We still had to go through the full verification and cataloguing process. As outside experts weighed in, the probability of impact did something never before seen in recorded history—it went up. It hit a five on the Tornio scale within a fortnight. The Minor Planet Observatory confirmed it was a new and Earth-threatening object.

We lived through some strange days before the public announcement. People lazing on park benches during lunch break, oblivious (admittedly, they did this even when they knew what was coming). If part of the joy of delayed gratification comes from anticipation, then the inverse is true for delayed destruction. It can cast a pall over any activity. But push that horizon far enough into the future, and it blends into a haze of uncertainty, too remote for human consciousness to fully comprehend. Eleven years must have been far enough, because most people went about their normal daily lives. Jobs were worked, bills were paid, and evenings continued to be spent in the comforting glow of the television. There seemed to be no change in routine at all. But the discovery muddled what had been Jo's and my otherwise agreeable existence. With her obsession with deflection, there was little time for pleasantries anymore. Each day would follow the same strict routine of data crunching and hypothesis testing. Theoretically, with as much lead time as we had, a small alteration to the asteroid's trajectory early on would have compounding effects such that we could steer it safely past the Earth.

The first plan the government panel proposed was, predictably, explosive assault. If we could launch a so-called "bunker-busting" nuclear weapon at it, we could break it into pieces small enough that they would either burn up in the atmosphere, or have their destructive potential significantly reduced. But the prospect of having irradiated debris "rain down o'er the Earth" was not an appealing one to the ranking committee member. For the first time since the Cold War began, nukes weren't the answer. Another suggestion that emerged was a mass-driver impact. Basically, if we just launched something really big, we could nudge the threat off course. The trick, in this case, was finding something heavy enough, and then accelerating it quickly enough, to incite a meaningful redirect. Something about the eccentricity of the orbit and its interaction with our own made it a herculean task. We just didn't have enough propulsive power available to effect a change.

A few days into the meeting, during a break in debating the merits of the newest theory—gravity towing—I wandered into a breakroom where two congressional interns were passing the time playing pool. I walked in just as the slighter of the two attempted a difficult combination. There, on the idealized space that was a billiard table, I saw the answer. If we couldn't redirect the asteroid on our own, maybe we could use what force we had available to reroute another object that could. As I went running off to find Jo, I heard the other intern shout "Slop—that's total bullshit!" I can only assume that his opponent's shot ended up in the pocket.

Breathless, I related my theory to Jo; she flipped through the orbital catalogue and found a candidate. The rest is history—all Newtonian orbital physics and ballistics. Odysseus eventually obliterated Calypso and life resumed its normal course on Earth. In the interim, Jo and I went our separate ways. It was a mutually agreed-upon parting, the Calypso incident having given each of us new perspective and direction. Jo went on to seek out and deflect dozens of earth-endangering asteroids. I went on to spend a summer in the same forests I lamented being threatened by the impact. She was an unparalleled cosmological pool shark and sent me careening on to my next adventure.

7

LARAMIE FOOTHILLS, Colorado – As the chief mountain-plains interface in Northern Colorado, the Laramie Foothills stretch eastward from the Rawah and Medicine Bow wilderness areas, along the Wyoming border, ending in a series of chalk bluffs. The area serves as a corridor for numerous wildlife populations: elk, antelope, and more find refuge here. It is also an important pathway for the annual migration of euxoa auxiliaris...

I returned home from my time overseas, having failed at love, but having fulfilled my commitment to the nautical life as set forth by Kings Point (at least from my perspective). I needed a change of pace, so I decided to follow my passion for the natural world and spend some time out West as a crew member in the Forest Service's summer work program. The program was extremely popular. By the time I got around to applying, the only position available was field entomologist.

The eastern forests have their cicadas, but those in the Mountain West experience a far more regular emergence—the miller moth, or *euxoa auxiliaris*. Each summer, they appear on the plains for a few short weeks of light-flitting bacchanalia, before flying high into the mountains to pollinate flowers and become bear food. Those lucky enough to survive eventually return to the plains to lay their eggs and die. I was tasked with charting the bounds of one of the insects' most important migration corridors in the Laramie Foothills.

While I waited for the official paperwork, I spent the intervening months at home with my parents. Though it had only been two short years since I'd last seen them, I could see the telltale beginnings of age take hold in the lines on their faces. I could hear it in the creaks in their joints when they stood up from the kitchen table. Other than those subtle signs, the routines were unchanged. The pancakes, the sports talk, the evening news, the dozing with the reading light on. It was the first time I'd lived at home without being a student—aside from early childhood, of course. This new position in life brought joy to the house chores. I raked leaves with gusto, pulled weeds for hours, and washed dishes nightly. Having no responsibilities of my own had paradoxically made me more dedicated to those of my parents. That is one of my most cherished years, all evening meals and firehall jubilees.

Eventually though, those blissful days and nights passed and became fused in the crucible of memory. One day, my mother came in from the mailbox, waving a letter in her hand. "James," she said, "it looks like the announcement may have come." Her voice was that mixture of pride, excitement, and sorrow that only a mother can muster. It was Good Friday. Easter had fallen exceptionally early that year, such that Ash Wednesday had preceded St. Valentine's. Given that our traditional family meal with all of the relatives was just two days away, I told my mother we would wait until after Easter to open it. The thought seemed to please her. She smiled and slipped the envelope into the entry hall writing desk. We went to mass that night and listened to the Passion. The fresh scent of palm fronds still hung in the church from the prior Sunday. The cock crowed thrice and the church bells rang in a somber eventide. We went home hungry, observing our family's traditional Good Friday fast. My parents respected most of the Vatican II reforms, but not those relating to Lenten sacrifice.

The rest of the family clan descended on Holy Saturday and we made our pilgrimage to St. Peter's Cathedral in Scranton for the Easter Vigil. Aunts, uncles, and cousins would come streaming in—some from Philadelphia, some from Poughkeepsie, and some from Allentown. We would all sleep under the same welcoming confines of my parents' roof. I was always shunted down into the basement with the other kids even though my preference was for the peace and quiet of an orderly bedtime. A large portion of the morning was devoted to people getting ready for mass. The crowded house demanded a strict shower schedule to accommodate the hot water heater. I spent the bulk of this time seated quietly at the kitchen table, ready to go in my periwinkle pinstripe suit. It was an ill-fitting hand-me-down from a cousin who was not quite my build. Nonetheless, I was repeatedly told how darling I was. When departure time finally arrived, the entire clan formed a five-car caravan and made the hour's drive to Scranton. During the long ritual of the mass, I spent most of the time gazing up at the enormous but distant murals painted on the ceiling, losing myself in the gold leaf framing the gospel stories.

By the time Easter Sunday arrived, so too had spring. The flowers burst their buds. The birds were singing frantic, desperate songs, bringing pleasant cacophony wherever they went. Dozens of plastic eggs were hidden around the yard, soaking up the sun, and melting the chocolate held inside. At midday, the family gathered for the traditional meal. The lamb always seemed so succulent after seven weeks without meat. The weekend thus over, prudence won out and I opened the letter. It seems I would be posted in a cabin just outside of Virginia Dale, Colorado.

I gathered my things and left Pennsylvania just as spring was hitting its stride. I arrived at my posting in Colorado where winter was still holding on. The parallax induced by a 1,600-mile flight made it feel as if I'd stepped into a time machine. The ramshackle appearance of Virginia Dale only heightened this sensation. To call it a town was generous. To give it a spot on the map may have been superfluous.

One weather-beaten, 1800s-era shack standing alongside a lovely stretch of highway was all there was. When I looked into the history of the place, I discovered that its heyday wasn't much different. As an overnight stop on the Overland Trail, morning would come and the stagecoaches would hastily rattle away. The settling dust and harsh sun would then bake Virginia Dale into focus. But like a potter's glaze in the kiln, one had the feeling that the town would have a different look when it came out the other side.

My Wild West rendering may make it seem as if I didn't enjoy myself. Truth be told, I found the landscape magical. Gigantic granite protrusions scattered amongst green valleys speckled with ponderosa pines. When the snows melted in the spring, the meltwater collected in depressions on the rock such that you never knew when you would stumble upon a crystal-clear pool. Raspberries often grew in the tiniest of cracks afforded by the rocks. When they were ripe, they were the sweetest, most flavorful I've ever tasted.

I made my way to the cabin in the back of a pickup truck, loaded with the season's supplies. Light snow flurries spiraled down from a multi-hued gray sky. Accompanying me in the pickup were the rest of the field crew. Three were up in the truck's cabin, and another sat in the back with me, leaning up against the rear window. Improbably, three of my compatriots were named Jeff, the other, a girl named Lourdes. To make it even more confusing, all of the Jeffs looked vaguely alike—I could hardly tell them apart. I suggested they go by Jeff 1, Jeff 2, and Jeff 3. Lourdes suggested we just use their middle names. They all seemed to prefer the latter option (even the one named Aberdashy), though in my heart, I still think of them as Jeffs 1 through 3. The pickup careened over the previous season's washboards—the road had not yet been re-graded for the spring. As we bounced along, Jeff 3 described his previous summer's employment in vivid, voluminous detail.

"Yep. Last season I was a fire spotter up in Oregon in the Gifford Pinchot. Pretty country, but I prefer roaming about more than sitting in a tower. You should've seen the storms that would come raging through. My tower got struck half-a-dozen times. Thank goodness the fella before me had insulated the sittin' stool. The lightning would singe the shingles and the thunder would be so loud my ears would ring for a few hours. Exciting stuff. You know where he got the glass coasters for the legs? Off an old fallen powerline. I appreciate a man who can put scrap to good use. As long as I stayed perched up on that stool, I was safe from electrocution. You know, there's a tower not too far away from here, up in the foothills off Deadman Road. Guess they named it after a guy without a glass-bottomed stool."

At this, Jeff 3 gave a hearty guffaw, having amused himself at his own wit. Before I could even respond, he launched back in.

"Yessir, I'm happy I'll be roaming the woods at ground-level this year. I'll leave the towers to Kerouac. *Dharma Bums* is what did it. I read it and thought the fire-spotter's life sounded glamorous, but it got to be like anything else. I've never had much of a thing for moths—I've always been a deer-stalking man myself—but, if they're the excuse that gets me out here, I'll take it. You look like a man of the same mind."

He'd been blathering so fluidly that it took me a few seconds to realize this was meant to be a question. Jeff 3 hadn't mastered upward inflection.

"Moths," he said, "you got a thing for them?"

"Not any more than the next guy I suppose. I'm here for the forest."

"Whammo. I knew it—we're kindred spirits. This is going to be a great summer."

Not wanting to run roughshod over the dreams of my loquacious friend, I simply smiled and let the bumps in the road convey a nod of approval.

To the southwest, it looked as if the Mummy Range was getting more than the few flurries we were seeing. I was just about to comment on it when the truck encountered a particularly deep washout. My head hit the truck window so hard it cracked. The window I mean, not my head. As I lost consciousness, my body slid deeper into the truck bed. The last thing I remember seeing was a matte-gray sky and a ponderosa pine. Everything tasted like butterscotch for a moment, then the world went dim.

The first thing I became aware of as I came to was Jeff 3's cheerful voice, laughing as he told the others of my plight. "You shoulda seen the look on his face. He was all starry-eyed and loopy looking. He'll be okay. I've seen much worse. Hell, I've had my own bell rung more than a time or two."

"He's waking up," said Lourdes.

"Hey buddy, you took a pretty nasty knock to the noggin... how many fingers do I have?"

I looked and was shocked to see only nine—the leftmost pinky apparently absent from Jeff 3's hand. Though I had to fight my natural instincts to just say "ten," my mother had taught me to always trust my vision. And so, my reply was a half-hearted "nine."

"See, he can't be that concussed if he can tell that!"

"Where did your other finger go?"

"I'm not quite sure. It's probably in the belly of some scavenging bird. Either that, or it's been broken down by whatever earthworm found it first."

I just looked at him, bewildered. Jeff 3 didn't even notice, but the natural inertia of his tongue carried him forward as he started unloading the gear from the pickup.

"You know, most people climb a volcano and their biggest fear is an eruption. Or some kind of poisonous outgassing. I hadn't even considered the more pedestrian dangers of rockfalls. Lava rocks are sharp as hell. One let loose there as I was clinging to the side of Mount Hood, came down on my hand, and all of a sudden, I saw rock and finger go flying past my face, tumbling down the mountainside. I will say that there are some benefits to razor-sharp rocks—the amputation was clean and quick. I lowered myself down to a ledge and wrapped my hand tight with an extra shirt. There really wasn't too much blood. It clotted up pretty quickly. I climbed down and looked for my finger a few minutes, but never found it. They stitched me up at a nearby clinic and it healed up real nice. If Django Reinhardt could play guitar with two fingers, I think I'll be fine with four."

In the time it took him to tell the story, Jeff 3 had already moved everything from the truck to a tidy grid on the ground. I hadn't even moved. Not wanting to be thought the weak one and make a bad first impression, I hopped out and assisted in shuttling the gear to the cabin. By the time we finished, the snow had stopped and night had fallen. We claimed our bunks, crawled in, and slept 'til morning.

Our first month there was full of preparations for the coming season. Setting up the transects, calibrating the sampling equipment, and getting a feel for the lay of the land. The plains-based crew along the Platte had reported an above-average number of army cutworms on the riverbanks and the migration peak in our area was projected to be in late June. Before we knew it, the swarm was upon us.

There were moths everywhere. Some living, some dead. Littering windowsills and staining walls. Floating in collected water and scattering when doors opened. Virginia Dale was just a stopover on their annual migration, but the millers looked like full-time residents. They spilled through the doorway by the dozens such that it was hard to remember a time before the all-pervasive staccato symphony of their wingbeats took hold. The sun would set, electric lights would come on, and the moths would flock.

It was a wild few weeks. We spent our days in solitude, walking miles, only to regroup each evening, physically exhausted, but craving human contact. We took turns cooking and cleaning. Those off duty for the night would sit in the kitchen anyway. Truth be told, there was nowhere else to sit inside the cabin. We'd share our days' adventures, drink our evening coffee, play cribbage, and sleep. I was in the best shape of my life and bounded up and down mountains with little care or effort.

It was a dry start to summer and, as a result, we were simultaneously tasked with fire-spotting. This was almost too much for Jeff 3 to handle.

"I thought I'd escaped that crap. Oh well, at least I'm not in a tower again. I swear to God, if they suggest that, I'm leaving."

At 10am on the Fourth of July, as moth season was reaching full crescendo, the summer monsoon fired up. The opening salvo came as a rainless thunderstorm. The forest came alive with arcs of electricity. From where our cabin was perched atop a rise, we had a commanding view of the surrounding landscape. I was wishing I had Jeff 3's insulated sitting stool as he began a running commentary on lightning strikes and forest fire management.

"Ooohie—we'll have to keep an eye on that hilltop out there. Smokey Bear would have us believe that most wildfires are human-caused and preventable. And sure, they are a proportion—and the ones that get all of the headlines, mind you. The press loves a story of human frailty. But in all actuality, the majority of wildland fires can be traced back to natural causes—usually lightning. It'll hit a tree, boil the sap, send bark flying, and fester there a few days until conditions are right for it to burst out. Then, if you're looking, you can see that telltale wisp of smoke curling up toward the heavens. It won't take more than a few hours at that point to create a real problem. Whadaya say you and I walk out that direction when the storm is done, Jimmy-boy?"

In the brief couple of months we had been living together, Jeff 3 had nicknamed everyone. I'm not even sure he remembered our real names anymore. I had never been known as "Jimmy" before and have not since.

"Sure. The stormy weather should suppress the moth activity today anyway." When the storm had passed, we grabbed our daypacks, some sandwiches for dinner, and struck out toward the spot where we had seen the big bolt strike.

I have always been amazed at how deceiving mountain distances can be. The hilltop we were heading toward seemed to be continually receding. A walk that, by our estimates, should have only taken a couple of hours, wound up taking five. Luckily, our persistence was rewarded with a bona fide pile of smoldering embers. We stamped them out, doused them with some water from our canteens, and mixed them all around just to be sure there was no chance of fire spreading. Work complete, we ate our dinner, looking east toward the windows of our cabin glinting back the late afternoon sun. A squirrel with a white-tipped tail came begging food, but we shooed it away. To the west, another storm cloud was building, threatening our return trip. Not wanting to get caught out in a thunderstorm, we scarfed-down our last bites, shouldered our bags and began the return journey. With any luck, we'd make better time retracing our route and be home before dusk became night.

About an hour in, an oversized raindrop—the first of the season—fell. More found their way through the tree canopy and splattered on our heads or exploded in little geysers all around us. Despite the prospect of getting soaked, Jeff 3 remained upbeat.

"Guess nature would've done our work for us anyway. It was a nice walk though. Good to feel rain on the skin again."

By the time we made it back to the cabin, darkness had already fallen and the rains had slowly grown in intensity. Just as the moth incursion reached its peak, the rains effectively wiped out the bulk of the generation we had been studying. Common conception has biblical floods pegged at six weeks in duration. It is surprising, what can happen then after only five days of steady rain. Entire mountainsides slough off, filling already brimming rivers and overtopping catchment spillways. Canyons channel torrents of pure destruction, which scour clean the banks. Homes, trees, and asphalt are deposited in tidal moraines. Eroded roadways leave "island" communities at the higher elevations. The muddy pools of water left behind take weeks to dry. The half-houses dangling over cut banks are often abandoned by their owners, the thought of repair and renovation too much to contemplate once the river has revealed its capacity for violence. Psychological scars like these linger long after the riverbank is recolonized by the willows and silver maples.

Our moth-work ended, the fellowship went its separate ways. Jeff 2 and Lourdes both needed more field experience for their graduate degrees, so they headed for an opportunity in the Wind Rivers. Jeff 1 had simply had enough and decided to go home to his parents' place in Eau Claire, Wisconsin. Jeff 3 and I, having nowhere better to be nor an overriding desire to leave, decided to stay and help with the cleanup and recovery efforts. As able-bodied young men, we went to the Red Cross center and quickly found new roles. I volunteered with rebuilding. Jeff 3 found a spot on a helicopter crew, assisting in the most remote areas. Like the New Deal-era work programs, people banded together and threw their backs into massive civil engineering projects. We helped build the infrastructure that would power the region's next generation.

One day, as I was coming to the work site, I made my customary stop at the state patrol checkpoint and struck up a conversation with the posted guard. While we caught up on the events of the past week, we could see a line of ancient cars wind their way up the narrow access road toward the cordon. I was saying my goodbyes just as the ragtag group of vehicles came to a stop. There were rusting microbuses, vintage pickups with wooden sideboards, and an assortment of other less-identifiable vehicles. Some looked as if they were held together by tape and twine. It was a miracle that they had made it this far. Nonetheless, all of them looked to have been freshly painted white. On them were hand-painted red crosses of various sizes and shapes.

My friend the patrolman turned to me and muttered, "Here we go." There had been reports throughout the flood-afflicted area of groups like this occasionally trying to bluff their way through the checkpoints. The patrolman told me that this sort of thing was common after natural disasters. For a variety of reasons—some nefarious, some voyeuristic, some genuine—people wanted through. Binoculars in hand, he called in the license plate from the lead car. "Just what I thought," he sighed, "Gypsies. Probably here for some sort of scavenging scam." He instinctively checked his sidearm, which made me nervous.

As I've said before, I have no idea why the Romani people are so maligned. My time with them in the Balkans had been nothing but positive. I said as much to the officer. He explained that there was a local population that ran several local psychic storefronts and had occasional run-ins with the law. His description of them seemed good-natured, yet wary. My experiences with these people had cultivated a sympathy for their plight and an understanding of how to reason with them, so I offered to help. There are so many things we take for granted in the west, but one of the most overlooked is sense of place. Space and property form the basis of much of our thinking. Those concepts mean little to a nation of nomads.

So when the leader approached, saying, "As the Red Cross, we must get through..." I simply smiled my reply. As he walked up to the barricade, keeping an eye on our reactions, I kept smiling. As he swung the gate open, I walked over to his truck, climbed into the driver's seat, and started it up. For each inch he lifted the gate, I backed the truck away a little further. Exasperated, he let the gate fall and I stopped his truck and climbed out. We walked toward one another with a knowing look and at five paces out, he began laughing hysterically. So did I. He slapped me on the back, gestured to the rest of his company, and they clambered back into their vehicles. He gave a whistle and the cars started up and began turning around.

"You, my friends," said the leader, "are good men." He seemed genuinely delighted by the turn of events and shook our hands vigorously. We all left the encounter the best of friends. In fact, as I spent more time with them over the course of the following year, Manfri, the leader, and I developed such a rapport that he tried to set me up with his daughter Lavina. Our engagement was brief, but even in saying this, I'm sure the rumors will spread. At least the truth is on the page.

And just so you know how it all ends, I worked with the rebuilding and recovery crew for another year. Lavina opened her own psychic practice, but quickly grew tired of my anti-nomadic proclivities and called it off. I wasn't all that broken up, save for the doubt her departure introduced: had she left because she wanted to, or because she had seen my life heading somewhere she didn't want to go? But those are questions we all ask, regardless of whether a psychic is involved.

8.

SS ATACAMA — A bullion ship that went miss-ing and was presumed lost at sea in 1858. No one knew its final resting place until the mem-oirs of Ray Callahan were published in the 1990s. It seems he undertook a recovery opera-tion on the vessel. This is all the more notable since he was the cousin of James Gordon Brecht, who happened to take part in the expedition...

My cousin Ray was larger than life. As such, all of the kids in the family lionized him. All of the adults held him in polite contempt. It was as if his mind and mentality were arrested at the precise moment of his thirteenth birthday—with all of the fearlessness and lack of judgment that comes with the age.

He was the one who hit sixty miles per hour on his brakeless ten-speed while flying down Conklin Hill Road. He was the one who bought us cigarettes and taught us how to brave the sixty-foot drop from the bridge to the river. He was also the only one in the family who had ever been to prison. I could never get a straight answer as to what he did—whether from him or the family—but it was enough to keep him locked up for a couple of years. When he got out, he went into the Marines and never looked back.

Later on, when he came to visit, he would appear first as a small dot overhead, then a parachute gliding gracefully down into the wide-open cornfield. He regaled us with his ta-les of underwater spelunking, his exploits as a stock car racer, and his encounters with famous personages. It was possible to talk to him for days and days and still learn something new every minute.

Around my twenty-sixth birthday, he came with a proposition: if I could help him with a small project, he would put in a good word with the chief curator at the Smithsonian in order to get me hired on. As you learned earlier, I have a special passion for museum work. Normally, the idea of a "collaboration" with Ray would have raised nothing but alarms in my mind, but the lure of the preeminent American museum was too strong to resist.

"Sure thing," I said, and Ray unloaded the details of his scheme. He recently learned of an overlooked blockade-running vessel that later became a bullion ship. After picking up a load of Chilean gold, it seemed this ship was never heard from again—officially, at least. Cousin Ray, through channels that weren't entirely clear to me, had learned the whereabouts of this sunken treasure—a secluded bay on Alejandro Selkirk Island. Though named for the castaway who inspired Robinson Crusoe, Ray assured me that we would not share the castaway's fate. It sounded like a grand adventure, but I questioned my role.

"Maritime law being what it is, we need a credentialed seaman with us to avoid any hassles from the local coast guard." Ray had gathered a trusted group of friends, but apparently, I was the only licensed merchant mariner he knew. I wasn't sure how my presence would counteract any problems, but agreed nonetheless. Chances were low we'd be intercepted.

We flew to San Diego, met up with the team's "logistics expert," Skull, and he drove us down through Baja to La Paz where we met the rest of the salvage crew. There was Toby "the Alchemist" Fieldman, who would be our chief metallurgist, Eddie "Bubbles" Montgomery, the dive and recovery expert, and the chief of security who needed no epithet other than his God-given name: Jake Steel.

We boarded a nondescript Panamanian-flagged cargo schooner in the harbor and heaved-off. Despite outward appearances, the small ship was sturdy and seaworthy. That said, crew quarters were tight. Three racks and five sailors meant we had to hot-bunk, sleeping in shifts. It was for the best, Ray assured us, since he wanted at least two people on watch at all times.

Ray charted a meandering course through the Gulf of California, avoiding the standard patrol routes. Once we breached out into the Pacific, the course was more straightforward—no one (or at least anyone of consequence), it seemed, was interested in Alejandro Selkirk.

We were a ragtag, yet well-oiled crew. Everyone knew their duties and all performed admirably. Really, there wasn't much to do but laze about on the deck or play canasta in the mess hall until we reached the island. Each crewman acclimated to his own unique rhythms. Jake Steel was meticulous and routinized. His body was a machine and he felt it his duty to keep it in perfect working order: 1,000 push-ups, pull-ups, and sit-ups daily. I had a feeling he could crush a man's skull with his bare hands. He looked as if he may have done it many times.

Toby took a different approach to our idle time. Instead of trying to chisel his physique, he simply sharpened the chisels he had brought with him. He also became the unofficial cook, able to transmute the most incredible flavors out of the simplest ingredients. These meals were a highlight every evening and helped mark the passage of time.

Knowing full well the frequent tedium of life at sea, I had brought a couple of large, impenetrable novels I'd been meaning to read, but had never had the gumption to begin in earnest. For some reason, I also took to writing letters—despite the fact that we planned no port calls in locales with reliable mail service. Nonetheless, I wrote a letter to Jo every day. With hindsight, it's easy to see this as a lovelorn response to the previous two years of my life. My mind knew the whys of our mutual parting, but my heart lagged behind like an orphan of faster-than-light travel. At the time, I thought of it as friendly staying-in-touch. How I would do so without ever sending a letter was beyond me. The act of writing was enough to forge a psychic connection. Even though I knew I would never send them, I imagined finding a mail slot in some tiny Latin-American backwater, and the letters taking years to reach her. Maybe she would even open one after I was long gone from this earth. Most of the letters began "Dearest Jo" and were more a stream-of-consciousness journal than anything else. As I wrote and rewrote each line, I imagined her reaction—smirk, smile, and tear-filled eye. At those moments, we were reunited. When I put the pen down, the bond dissolved in the spray coming over the ship's prow.

Three weeks of sailing brought Alejandro Selkirk in view. It was a welcome and rugged sight, all the more beautiful because of its isolation. Based on inside information, we knew Pinochet's navy wasn't scheduled to make a patrol for another month. Nonetheless, we had a lot of work to do in the meantime. The map detailing the wreck's location looked straight out of a pirate film—tattered, stained parchment with a red-brown "X" painted over the targeted bay.

We approached the island from the northeast, rounding it in a counter-clockwise fashion until we reached our destination on the southwest corner. A large, rocky peninsula jutted-out like an opposable thumb and we anchored behind it to take our refuge. Our schooner was obscured from all but those approaching from the southwest, which was unlikely given the fact that the major inhabited landmasses were to the east.

Eddie was suited-up and ready for a dive before we had even dropped anchor. As soon as we had, he was over the side and gone for over an hour as we set-up our floating camp. I was out swabbing the deck, with one eye toward the water, when I saw a hand on the gunwale. I dropped the mop and hurried over as the second hand heaved up a gold ingot. I couldn't contain myself and let out a joyful "whoop." The rest of the crew came over as I helped Eddie clamber aboard.

"Well that was fast," said Ray, flashing a devilish grin.

"There's a hell of a lot more down where that came from. Piles of bullion and some coinage too. The ship's gone to pieces, so there's a little maneuvering required, but it looks like it all will be accessible enough."

"Well then, let's get to work."

Ray and Skull suited up and joined in on the dive, Jake and I were in charge of shuttling the haul from the dinghy to the ship, and Toby oversaw "processing" and storage. Though we could get a pretty penny on the antiquities market, a load of ancient gold shows up and questions start to get asked. Ray wanted to avoid jurisdictional complications and claimant disputes, so he had devised an alternative plan. Toby would melt the gold down, pour it into molds the shape of large good-luck cats, and paint it yellow to make it look chintzy.

Though the final products didn't come with a waving arm, in all other respects, they were identical to those you'd find in Chinatown. It was the sheer artistry of an expert forger. If the initial calculations were correct, we would be left with four-dozen smiling felines once the melt-down was complete.

After ferrying the first two loads of gold from the dive site, we were waiting on-station when a large air bubble billowed up from below unexpectedly. The safety flags of all three divers vanished under the surface the next moment.

I can hardly describe the wave of fear and nausea that comes with the probable loss of a family member. That was the only time I ever saw Jake look helpless. Time stopped as I knelt staring into the water, hoping to catch a glimpse of any motion. A school of fish darted through, shimmering in the sun. But no divers. Contingency plans began racing through my mind. How would I break the news to the family? Thankfully, this downward spiral was soon interrupted by one, two heads appearing above the surface: Ray and Skull.

Ray shouted calmly (given the situation), "We need the crowbar and cutting torch—Eddie's leg is pinned." Being one to plan for all eventualities, this was gear that Skull had requisitioned and had handy in the dinghy. They swam over to us, grabbed the gear, and dove back down. After an hour, all three appeared at the surface, looking relieved. Ray and Skull helped Eddie aboard.

It seems that the bullion had buttressed the hull. When the gold was removed, it became unstable and collapsed, catching Eddie's leg. Surprisingly, though badly bruised and slightly cut-up, he escaped without any major or lasting injury.

With the dive team down its most productive man, the pace of recovery slowed. Ray and Skull continued as carefully as they could while we took Eddie back to the schooner. They called it quits at dusk, having gathered all of the easily accessible gold. We loaded the last of our haul on board and ate a quick meal. Everyone exhaled a sigh of relief. It had been a tense day.

After dinner, Toby went back to his smelting operation. I asked him if I could keep one of the few coins as a memento and he flipped it my way. The divers turned-in for some well-earned sleep. Jake and I were tasked with raising anchor and charting a homeward course. Ray thought the more distance between us and the wreck site, the better. He hated the thought of leaving any gold unclaimed but didn't want to push his luck in the gnarled mass of iron and pine.

We charted a course straight for Baja and sailed into the deepening night. When dawn broke to a wine-red sky, Ray and Skull took our place on watch. Ray didn't say a word, just winked and put his hand on my shoulder. I went down and clambered into one of the recently vacated bunks. It was still warm and smelled of seawater, but I fell into a deep sleep.

I awoke to the ship rolling and pitching violently. One second I was lying in bed, the next, I was lying on the wall. Before the room fully righted itself, I staggered toward the ladder that led to the bridge. A few tries and two bruised knees later, I made it topside to see a fearsome storm engulfing us. Waves were mountains towering over. I thought for sure our untimely demise was upon us, but Ray began barking orders and we all jumped to action. Hatches were battened and sails reduced to prevent too much strain on the masts. We hove to and rode out the worst. Though the ship was near vertical at points, she held together thanks to Ray's fearless command.

We thought the worst was over as we motored through calmer seas under cloudless skies, but that was when we caught sight of a flag on the horizon: the Mexican navy. The captain was eager to question our activities. It was not too often he encountered six gringos floating in the middle-of-nowhere Pacific. Though our loot had been obtained out of his jurisdiction in Chilean waters, we nonetheless wanted to avoid any discussions of provenance should our cargo be inspected. Chilean gold looks an awful lot like Mexican gold, after all.

As the patrol boat drew near, I knew my time had come—this is why I'd been hired-on. When they came alongside, Ray was preparing to step forward, but I gestured him to hold back and took his place. I stood amidships, looking up at the captain of the Mexican vessel. Though we were no more than ten yards apart, he insisted on speaking through a megaphone.

"*Buenos días. Me llamo Capitán Gilberto de León. ¿Puedo preguntarte que haces en estas aguas?*"

My rudimentary Spanish was riddled with Catalan, but I muddled through. I think he was asking our purpose and itinerary. I told him we were oceanographers like Jacques Cousteau, returning from the Galapagos. I invited the captain aboard to inspect our paperwork—which, I assured him, was in order—but he said there was no need.

"*Amigos de Jacques Cousteau son amigos de México.*"

I didn't bother to correct him that I had only invoked Cousteau's name for comparison's sake—it seemed like it was better to let the fortunate misunderstanding slide. As a good-faith gesture, I tossed over my merchant mariner's document in a small tube attached to a rope. Captain de Leon retrieved the tube and scrutinized the papers it held inside with a furrowed brow. I was worried he was going to take me up on my offer to inspect our cargo, but he eventually gave an approving, perfunctory nod, returned the papers, and bid us goodbye with a respectful salute.

"*Vaya con Dios*," he said as the patrol boat fired up its engines. "*Buscamos a un barco bregando en esta región. Si ves a cualquier cosa, por favor avísenos.*" With that, the Mexican ship sailed away.

I had expected a much bigger hassle, but the kindness of strangers prevailed as it had before in my life. Maybe in this instance it shouldn't have, with me being party to thievery. But no one was hurt by our actions and we were only looting gold that had already been stolen from its homeland. Rationalizations, I know, but they were the ones that sufficed for me.

A day or so later, we anchored off the Baja coast by Todos Santos, unloaded the schooner and traded the boat for an RV that Skull had arranged. We drove north and split the profits—$45,000 per person after expedition expenses had been accounted for. I had no need for so much money and donated the bulk of it to the Chilean Fund for Miners' Orphans. The rest of the group disbanded, dissolving into the crowds of Tijuana. Ray and I drove the RV back to Damascus and I prepared for my next adventure. Ray held up his end of the bargain and I dreamt of the days to come at the Smithsonian.

9.

SMITHSON & IAN's — A substantial global pharmaceutical conglomerate that existed during the late 20th and early 21st centuries. Most famous for its production of "the cure," the now ubiquitous anti-cancer drug. Once its patents expired, the company was unable to leverage its market dominance into a sustainable business strategy...

When I returned from my adventures in the southeastern Pacific, I endeavored to keep a dream journal, but found that I had neither the diligence nor the strength of will to maintain it properly. Certainly not as thoroughly as some of the cases I read about during my time at sea. One young woman in particular, suffering from some condition I can't remember, kept an extremely detailed log of her dreams as they came to her. I, on the other hand, managed daily updates for a week and increasingly intermittent updates over the course of a year. Gradually, the time between entries asymptotically approached infinity.

But as it just so happens, this period coincided with my start at Smithson & Ian's. Yes, you read that right. Apparently, Ray's wires and mine had gotten crossed at some point, because it wasn't with the Smithsonian that he put in a good word. Instead, it was with the Chief Cure-maker at Smithson & Ian's—a pharmaceutical research company. I suppose I should have asked Ray more questions at the outset (I did wonder how he had connections at the national museum), but the homophony led my ears to draw their own conclusions. Being that the proposed work seemed interesting and the pay was good, I decided to abandon my dreams of museum work. After all, growth opportunities for archivists are limited. I think the best way to explain what happened while I was at S&I is to start with one of my journal entries from the time:

> Last night, my sleeping moments were engulfed by a single, continuous dream.
>
> Somehow, I had unexpectedly been elected President. No one believed that a ballcap wearing kid could take the reins, but I stepped-in with aplomb. I knew that the first thing on the agenda was to define an open and engaging foreign policy, a course correction from those who had come before. And so, I met with a revolving cast of foreign dignitaries. I met the Russian president who greeted me with a vulgar postcard and a wink. We drank vodka and smoked filterless cigarettes.
>
> Soon, it became apparent that there was a plot afoot to violently depose me. I think it was my secretary of defense. I should've known better than to trust that haggard old man—he court-martialed his own son. We were in the briefing room and started hearing explosions outside. Men came in with their guns blazing. Bits of wall were flying everywhere just like in the movies. The perpetrator made a break for it. Despite being President, I had an alarming lack of security. When it was down to me and my sole bodyguard, we retreated downstairs.
>
> It was much more peaceful down there. We encountered some tourists and I suggested that they go explore a nearby monument. They sauntered off oblivious to the carnage around them, enjoying their vacation. I then met my doppelganger working at a computer terminal.

It came with the strange sensation of looking through a glassless mirror. The three of us cowered behind a desk. I knew that the only way forward was through destruction. "We're going to blow up the f***ing White House!"

Cut to an exterior shot of the building bursting apart in a great conflagration. Later on, in another briefing room, I sat with my bodyguard friend, and we laughed about our adventure.

A door slammed shut in the wind downstairs and I awoke. I laid my head down and was back in my motorcade. Being President was not so bad. Sure, there was the constant threat of thermonuclear holocaust and the interrupted sleep, but I had a calm self-confidence that I've never known in the waking world.

Why include an entry such as this? I think it is illustrative of my mental state around the time my research team helped discover the cure. Somehow, pervading my subconscious was the sense that I knew what I was doing. I suppose any researcher has to have a degree of self-assurance in order to chart a course into the unpredictable and often fruitless unknown, but as I said, the feeling I experienced was unlike any I'd known before.

My dreams became inspiration in the lab—abstract, metaphoric scripts of the steps I would need to take each day. Sometimes my dream interpretations resulted in seemingly nonsensical combinations of chemicals and processes, but who was I to argue? To outside observers, my decisions were arbitrary and bordering on the ridiculous. One incredulous colleague constantly harangued me: "Why on earth would you add that chemical to the mix? It has repeatedly been shown to be carcinogenic!"

At the end of the day, despite my colleagues' doubts, we were always one step closer. If you let the strangest of thoughts guide you, you will come across the strangest solutions. Our methods weren't pretty, but we had contributed to the eradication of cancer. People the world over were cured. There was an unexpected spike in the long-taboo arts of smoking and sunbathing. In fact, it seemed as if people were gleefully letting their skin burn—sunscreen sat untouched on pharmacy shelves everywhere.

Even in the midst of this success, my colleague was still skeptical. He had his doubts about my credentials. Perhaps it was scientific jealousy. I tried to tell him that the discovery was just as much his as it was mine. I was but part of a team. My serendipitous discovery of the final, key reagent was built on the foundation of his life's work. My platitudes were to no avail and did little to calm his doubts.

Several months later, after our breakthrough was being independently verified and fast-tracked through clinical trials, I found a mysterious envelope in my company mailbox. I opened the battered manila envelope to find a letter detailing my lack of credentials, along with a stack of my employment and university records. I knew this was the work of my colleague, so I calmly walked down to his office to discuss his intentions. I didn't want to deceive him, so acknowledged the truth of his findings upfront.

"I appreciate your forthrightness. Not that I have any intention of revealing this information to the public, but do you have any idea what would happen if someone looked into your background? All of our work would be discredited—spuriously, I might add—simply for the fact that you are not a research-degree-holding scientist. That would be a catastrophe—our work will help so many."

I agreed that this could be problematic.

"I hope you haven't interpreted my trepidation over the past months as being directed at your character or abilities. I'll admit, your methods are often unorthodox, but they consistently produce useful results. What I'm concerned about is public perception. It is half (or more) of the battle when it comes to new drug candidates. Any hint of unreliability and it will fail, no matter its scientific fortitude."

Seeing this side of my colleague gave me a whole new perspective. I felt childish for having viewed his doubts as jealousy. I suggested that my name be stricken from the records and that he take credit for the full discovery. At first, he refused to even consider the idea, but I argued that it was the only viable option. After a prolonged debate, my persuasive skills won out.

However, my colleague pledged some recompense—even though I insisted that none was necessary. He explained that he had connections at Brookhaven National Laboratory and could get me a position there. Not having a post-Smithson & Ian's plan, I humbly accepted his offer. And that is how I came to work in quantum mechanics.

10

*BROOKHAVEN NATIONAL LABORATORY —
Once known primarily as a nuclear energy research facility, it became one of the leading
centers for theoretical physics upon installation
of the Alternating Gradient Synchrotron in
1960. It was this very accelerator which paved
the way for the development of the Theory of
Everything...*

Given my entry-level credentials, I settled comfortably into a
position as lab tech in the particle physics department at
Brookhaven. Dr. Stanislav Routinev was head of the AGS
group and eased me into the morass of measurements and
calculations. He was very encouraging and claimed to be giving me the problems no one else could solve. In reality, I was
just a routine number cruncher. I got the work no one else
wanted because of its tedium. But I was happy to be employed
in a laboratory setting once again, associated with something
exciting. We were on the hunt for the building blocks of matter — the gluons responsible for the strong interactions
between quarks. In the process, we hoped to advance what
was known about string theory. Analyzing signatures on the
detector might have been tedious, but it seemed like we were
close to a breakthrough.

When Elmer Wittgensen beat us to the punch, it broke
Dr. Routinev's spirit. I've never seen a scientist so forlorn. Our
work turned from the exploratory to the task of independent
verification. And with that shift, my interest waned. It began
slowly at first. Five-minute daydreams. Brisk afternoon walks.
But soon, these demonstrated their elasticity, stretching ever-

longer. My walks became filled with tangential observations that captured my attention more thoroughly than my sense of responsibility to work. Almost no one else took a lunch break, but those interludes were my salvation.

After realizing the pattern I'd fallen into, feeling guilty, I limited my sojourns to hour-long lunchtime excursions. I was always precise with my time. If I left the office at 12:48, I would walk back through the door at 1:48. But having a clearer conscience didn't alleviate the main issue: the work was boring.

All of that changed when Dr. Routinev suddenly became reenergized. He kept suggesting that perhaps Dr. Wittgensen had missed something. That we could take his findings and extend them in exciting ways that no one seemed to be considering. The theoretical discussion was all well beyond me. All I knew is that there was a hum of activity in the lab again. I was given calculations to make and charged with the transcription of several proofs. It was still boring, but at least there was a point to it all.

Nonetheless, I continued to struggle with concentration. In the afternoon, the sun would hit the west side of the concrete high-rise where I worked. As it warmed, insects would ride the thermals up to my fifth-floor window. They would flit about, backlit by golden light. If the temperature was comfortable, I would open my window, which would inevitably act as a scupper, collecting all comers and funneling them inside. To brighten my office, I had removed the screen. My investment in natural light yielded seasonal returns in wasps and boxelder bugs.

When I tired of my calculations, I would turn and gaze at the bugs' balletic displays in the setting sun. When I would turn back to the page, the numbers and symbols would take on a life of their own, swarming and swirling in dyslexic bliss. The sensation was always fleeting, but when the motion stopped, I was never sure the coefficients were in the same places in which they started.

When I showed my proofs to Dr. Routinev, he at first questioned my ability to transcribe accurately. In an attempt to show me how meaningful a small error could be, he took one of my "unfortunately configured" equations and furiously tore through a sample calculation. The result was better than he expected, so, flustered, he tried again with another of my errors. Once again, he produced a shockingly precise result.

"Are you some kind of undercover physicist sent by Smithson & Ian's to mock me?"

"No."

"Well then, I applaud your refinements. Truly ingenious."

I explained how it was only an accident of fate—boxelder bugs in the sun and the swarms of variables on the page. He laughed and called it a Newtonian moment—inspiration from the natural world—but I certainly don't deserve to be counted in Newton's company. I had only gotten lucky. My sun-flecked daydreams were meant to be distraction, not a model for quantum mechanics.

As our Theory of Everything took shape and autumn merged into winter, my momentary scientific inspiration abandoned me. Boredom returned.

To disrupt the humdrum, I tried to reinvigorate my inquisitive instincts outside of the office. For instance, on my route home from the lab, there was a building shaped like a duck. Not anatomically representative, mind you, more like an oversized toy pining for an oversized bathtub. I stopped there one evening to see what it housed. Surprisingly (or perhaps not surprisingly), it sold a variety of poultry products. I had expected more of a souvenir shop. I wanted to send a postcard to my mother, but the only ones I could find said "New Yordk." And she, being grammatically attuned, would have been disappointed with my choice. That this excursion was a highlight of my week should have been a sign that particle physics wasn't for me. At the beginning of my employment, I hardly noticed the creature-shaped building, yet by the end, it was a siren calling me in.

Each lunch break found me battling it out with the clock. When my sixty minutes of freedom expired, panic would overtake me. I had taken to using the time to write a novel. I would sit silently mulling my place, trying to grasp the loose threads from the day before, and before I knew it, I would only have fifteen minutes remaining. When you factor in the time it took to walk back to the office, I was left with ten minutes of writing time. But I made the most of those ten minutes.

My sluggish synapses would suddenly begin to flare, my fingers flail, and my creativity find its flair. For the briefest of moments every day, I found myself master of my domain, words flowing without much effort. The staccato nature of these bursts of writing caused my novel to proceed in fits and starts. It took years—over a thousand lunch breaks—to cobble it all together, but eventually, I finished.

I shopped my manuscript around until I found a small publisher who offered to print a modest run. With that, I was satisfied. But somehow, the book began circulating in the most unexpected places. By the time the publisher ran the second printing, the critics were praising my disjointed fluidity. It was hailed as the Great American novel come at last. And that is how I left my job in particle physics to become an author.

11.

ST. SEBASTIAN PRESS – A boutique publishing house that existed during the mid- to late-20th century. In its first few decades of existence, it was not known for having anything more than a mediocre stable of authors. Nor did it have any particularly popular published works to its name. That all changed with the arrival of James Gordon Brecht's Arrows of Fortune...

Being labeled the next great author was not all it was cracked up to be. Writing, unlike other popular arts, does not make one instantly recognizable. I had made a fatal mistake by insisting that my novel's dust jacket contain no picture of my face. Instead, I had the photographer take a still of the back of my head. Afterward, I tried to rationalize it with a clever explanation—I wanted to give readers a chance to imagine me as one of my own characters—really though, it was just a lark. If you haven't noticed yet, I sometimes let whim be the guiding force in my life. This choice, however, left me with none of the attendant perks of fame. No preferential seating when walking in to get restaurant reservations. No free drinks. No VIP treatment at all. I didn't even have to deal with the blessed hassle of the unexpected autograph. No one recognized me. I was ordinary.

During my six-month speaking tour, I had the habit of wandering out into the crowd before I spoke and striking up conversations about myself.

"What did you think of his novel?"

"What do you think he looks like?"

"Don't you think he's a little overrated?"

When these questions failed to elicit much more than niceties, I would occasionally resort to rumormongering.

"I've heard he's really a billionaire playboy."

"I've heard he wears shoes to bed."

To this day, some of these rumors still circulate, even amongst my own family. Regardless, the odd thing was, once I took the podium, I don't believe a single person recognized me from our previous conversations. Thank heavens my book had made an impression, because it turned out that I was completely unmemorable.

The buzz continued to build throughout that year. I graduated from bookstores to late-night shows and college commencements. It all got to be a little much. I think that's when the pressure first began to build. The reading public prefers not to dwell on momentary success unless that success is your one-and-only effort. Instead, the public wants to know what's next. I ended up promising everyone who asked that there would be more to come. I was no Harper Lee.

The publisher rejoiced. I began writing between stops on my speaking tour, and by year's end, had another manuscript. The second novel came much more quickly than the first.

Unfortunately, unbeknownst to me, I was stricken with the sophomore slump. I became so obsessed with plotting, that manuscript number two became nothing more than a "choose your own adventure" novel. Characterization, setting, and descriptive imagery all went by the wayside thanks to my maniacal fixation. When I turned in my final draft, the publisher simply laughed.

"We can't publish this—what happened to your remarkable gift?"

"I'm not sure," I said.

"Well, I've seen this happen to all too many young authors. They reach their peak with their first novel. I chalk it up to a combination of naiveté and unspoilt inspiration. When they are fitted with the yoke of expectation, the words wither."

"What do you recommend?"

"Isolation. Nothing breeds creativity so much as time alone. I have a friend in British Columbia who provides room and board to artists in need. You get a cabin on a mountainside, a desk by a window, and hot meals delivered to your door twice daily—all free of charge."

"And what's in it for your friend?"

"She believes in the healing power of art. I think she fancies herself a modern-day patron. But don't worry, she doesn't dictate any bounds on the work she commissions."

"I'm not sure that I believe you."

"As a matter of fact, I've already called her and she is expecting you by the end of the week."

"How did you know I would be in need of her help?"

"I knew it from the first moment I met you—you don't look like an artist. There was no other possible result for your second effort."

Apparently, there were forces beyond my comprehension at work. As I've done so many times in the past, I gave in to fate. I gathered my few belongings and flew to Vancouver. Lady Emelina Bauhaus had a car waiting for me there and I was driven directly up the Sea to Sky Highway. We turned south at Lillooet Lake, made our way along the east shore until turning into a dead-end valley near Priory Peak. My cabin was situated at the base of Meditation Mountain. The names all seemed a little too contrived given the artistic vision quest

I was sent to embark upon, but it was just an accident of geography.

Aside from a slightly larger cabin guarding the valley entrance, there seemed to be no other sign of human habitation in this pristine nook in the mountains. The driver deposited me at my A-frame without uttering a word the entire trip. The cabin was small, but well-appointed. I set about arranging my belongings and organizing my writing desk. It had been a long day of travel, most of which was spent sitting, so I decided to explore my surroundings. I climbed partway up the ridge to a nameless bench lake. The waters in that region, charged with glacial flour, have a most peculiar hue—azure, cerulean, aquamarine, turquoise, blue-gray—I haven't heard a description that captures it accurately.

By the time I had finished contemplating the lake, the valley had become a luminous reservoir, filled with the setting sun. The red-orange glow worked its way up the mountainsides, leaving twilight in its wake. Night doesn't rush itself at those latitudes, but I decided I had better make my way back to the cabin before darkness fell. Upon my return, I found a foil-wrapped dinner—still hot—waiting on my doorstep. I took it inside and devoured it ravenously. Exhaustion overtook me soon thereafter and I climbed up the ladder to the sleeping loft and collapsed into bed, swallowed in eiderdown.

I awoke in the morning, took a frigid shower that felt piped in straight from the lake I had seen the previous day, got dressed, and opened the door to step outside and breathe-deep the fresh mountain air. To my surprise, there was another piping-hot, foil-wrapped plate waiting for me. There is nothing more luxurious than an unexpected hot breakfast. I ate huckleberry pancakes on the front steps, let my thoughts wander across the landscape before me, and went back in to start my writing.

Somehow, after only a day at this idyllic little retreat, my writing was already flowing more freely. The first sentence came quickly: "We are all prisoners to our situation and station in life." And so did those that followed. I wrote for five hours without even realizing it. The momentum built in the following days. I hit upon increasingly lengthy flows, punctuated only by the buzzing of black flies, chirping of birds, and my morning and evening meals. By the end of the week, I managed a twelve-hour marathon session.

Happy with the week's progress, I indulged in a weekend off. On Saturday, I climbed Meditation Mountain. I had gotten an early enough start that I was able to spend several hours at the top enjoying the view. After that, the name seemed far more appropriate. On Sunday, I walked out to Lake Lillooet and took a brisk swim. Its name, however, remained impervious to enhancement. Nearby, I found a small shoreline lean-to with a handful of wooden canoes arrayed on a rack. Next to them was a sign that said, "Free to use if you treat with care." I grabbed a set of oars, put a boat in the water, and paddled around the south end, by the lake's outlet. Fish rose to greet the oars' eddies. Some appeared as a hump of a back and large dorsal fin, others were mere minnows. The mountains rising sharply around the water gave me the impression that I was tootling about on the bottom of a well. An afternoon squall blew through as I made my way back to shore. Little whitecaps rose on the lake's surface as I was pelted with sleet. By the time I'd beached the canoe and was pulling it ashore, the storm was already passed. Such are mountain storms in the summertime.

The entire time I spent in the valley's isolated splendor, I never saw another soul. Clearly, there was someone about, what with the daily meals and free watercraft. Who that person was shall remain a mystery. I like to think that it was Lady Bauhaus herself keeping watchful eye over my progress, acting as unseen muse. As for the lack of people in the valley, I assumed it was just the offseason. My productive streak continued and, by summer's end, I had not one, but two manuscripts complete. One was a time-travelling tale interlaced with a rumination on the record collections of our fathers, the other was a man-versus-nature-type survival story in the spirit of Jack London. After another few months of editing, they became *A Family Record* and *The Mountain's Roots*, respectively.

No sooner had I straightened the stacks of paper for my two manuscripts, than did I hear a knock on the door. It was the driver, come to fetch me. It was good timing too, because at that moment, the first autumn snow started spiraling down over the evergreens. As much as I had enjoyed my solitude, the thought of spending the winter snowed-in was not an appealing one. The trip back to the airport was just as silent as the one that had brought me to my overlooked Eden.

The next day, I walked into my publisher's office and deposited the two manuscripts in a triumphant "whumph" on his desk. He smiled, picked up the first, and read the opening paragraph. "This is more like it—I knew some time away would do you good. How do you feel?"

"Fantastic!" which was true at the time. The novels were published three months apart. I was hailed as a wunderkind returned. The near-simultaneous release was called a "coup of juxtaposition" by the critical press. Wide acclaim returned, as did I, to the author talk circuit. For the first few months, everything was fine. With a book for each hand, no one dared ask what was coming next. At least until an event in Chattanooga that following spring. This query unleashed what some outside observers might classify as a minor nervous breakdown. Really though, what followed was a conscious decision. The question of what was next made me reflect on all that I had written up to that point. Surely, it was feasible to create a unifying work—to make it seem as if the three novels I had thus far written were all part of a larger, overarching plan. The protagonist from *The Mountain's Roots* shared certain traits with the lead characters from *Arrows of Fortune*. What's more, the personal history woven into *A Family Record* was echoed in each of my other novels.

Nevertheless, manufacturing an interlacing novelistic experience where none had existed before is perilous work. Maybe if I had set about to do it from the outset it would have been easier. Retroactive stitching took hold in my mind. I began to see connections where none existed and lost myself in blissful paranoia for a few months. When I finally recognized the tailspin into which I'd entered, I knew that there were only two choices. I could either keep hurtling down the rabbit hole to see where it all would end, or I could abandon the project, and with it, my career as a writer. For sanity's sake, I chose the latter.

The experience of feeling my mind begin to fray was an unsettling one. I needed time away and a place to lose myself in other pursuits. And that is how I came to work in a bakery.

*MONASTERY OF CHRIST IN THE DESERT —
Founded in 1964, this Benedictine enclave is situated in a large wilderness area near Santa Fe,
New Mexico. Though it is now known primarily
as the only monastic brewery in the United
States, it once housed an impressive bread bakery that was famous in the region...*

I returned home as lost children always do. My parents welcomed me with open arms. My mother made up my bed, my
father baked a pie. The years since I had last been home
seemed to have stooped their bodies further, but their spirits
were still lively. They were glad to have me for a visit. We sat
on the porch watching midsummer thunderstorms and fire-
flies, ate our nightly dessert, and made the rounds to their
usual haunts. I hadn't been to mass in years but accompanied
them weekly.

On the 23rd Sunday of Ordinary Time, we went down
to the church hall for post-mass coffee and donuts. I took the
weekly bulletin from the usher (Mrs. Dorothy Jensen to be exact) and flipped through it, eating a bismarck while my
parents made small talk with the rest of the congregation. The
raspberry jelly oozed out and dribbled down my wrist as it did
when I was a child. But I read on, oblivious. Perhaps it was the
influence of having recently lived under Priory Peak, but when
I saw a help wanted ad from a monastery in New Mexico, I
was intrigued:

> *The Monastery of Christ in the Desert is seeking
> a hardworking young man willing to commit
> three years of service to the monastic bakery.*

Catholic preferred, but all men of decent character will be considered.

Here, I saw an opportunity to live the ascetic life I longed for without taking any formal vows. When we got home, I telephoned the number listed and spoke with the woman who answered. It turned out that though the monks were not part of a silent order, they still largely chose to observe silence, so they had an answering service handle their calls. I explained that I'd seen the advertisement in the church bulletin, described my background and desire for the position, and was given the job without any questions asked. It was both a good omen and a good first impression. Like me, the monks liked their verbal communications to be as efficient as possible. I was told to report to the monastery in two weeks' time—I would be apprenticing under Father Bricazzi.

My parents were happy that I had found a job within the faith, but sad that I would once again be venturing off into the western wastes. Their temperaments were much better suited for the rhythms and distances of the east. By now though, they were used to my unexpectedly itinerant lifestyle. They drove me to Newark, where I caught my flight to Albuquerque (connecting through Chicago and Denver). On the flight, as the landscape out the window gradually turned from green to brown to rust, the distance between my home and me was emphasized.

My welcome at the monastery eased my first-ever sense of homesickness. The sharp, hollow clack of the metal knocker was answered with a creak as the big wooden door swung open. Behind it stood the living incarnation of Friar Tuck—a brown-robed, rope-belted, balding mound of a man, he knew my name before I could speak.

"Welcome Master Brecht, I am Father Bricazzi. Let me show you to your room."

The silence of the hall was a physical sensation unlike any I had felt before or since. Not the silence of empty spaces nor the silence of a church at midday prayer, nor even the silence of a library. This silence was more than that. It was a third person walking down the hallway with us. I felt as if I had been transported back to the Middle Ages.

I disturbed the tranquility with a question that had been burning in my mind since I had left New Jersey. "What need do you have for an apprentice who has no intention of staying beyond the three-year commitment? Surely, it would be better to train one of your younger brothers in Christ, more devoted to the order."

Fr. Bricazzi smiled knowingly. "Perhaps you misunderstand your role here."

The panicked reaction that rose in my gut was soon dispelled. "The question, more appropriately, is what do you need with an apprenticeship? This opening is not the product of any need on our part, but the need of those drawn to it. I for one, love baking bread. It's an art that is too quickly dying in the U.S. today. If I can pass some of this knowledge on to you, I will be happy."

The silence elbowed its way between us again while I mulled over his response. All that was audible was the shuffle of our feet down the hallway and the background hum of our circulatory systems in our ears. We came to the room that would be my chamber and it was empty save for a cot, small chest of drawers, and candle on the wall. It was just as I had hoped.

As Fr. Bricazzi was getting ready to take his leave of me, I heard my voice say "Peace," without having planned to do so. The friendly abbot smiled and said, "And peace be with you." That's not what I had meant. I thought about correcting him and explaining that it was "peace" I was looking for in my apprenticeship, not "peace" I was granting at that moment, but his interpretation was so genuine that it seemed a shame to upend it. "I will let you get settled now and will come back to fetch you in a few hours for a tour and our evening meal."

No sooner had he gone than did I lay down and weep. My pillow was quickly soaked with tears of relief. After sacrificing myself many times over on the altar of creativity, here was a place where I would know my horizon line. The monastery walls would define my bounds. My uncertainty evaporated and I was looking forward to the time ahead when I would lose myself in learning a trade. I was lost in reflection when Fr. Bricazzi knocked gently. We walked quietly down the hallways with silence in tow. When we spoke, it was in hushed tones.

"Traditionally, the monks of Christ in the Desert only speak if absolutely necessary. Clearly, when someone new arrives, an abnormal amount speech is required to introduce our customs and conduct any associated training. Though there are no formal vows of silence, we ask that you follow the spirit of this tradition as well. You are also welcome to come to morning and evening prayers—whether to take part or just to listen."

Fr. Bricazzi led me through the labyrinth of halls, pointing out the dining room, the washrooms, the library, and the provisions storeroom. We circled back around to the kitchen to complete our tour. It was massive, but not ostentatious. There were two large wood-fired ovens, an industrial eight-burner gas range, and an assortment of sinks and cabinetry. In an adjoining room was a small brewing system. Fr. Bricazzi explained everything once in exhaustive detail and told me to feel free to ask later if I had any questions. The rest of my training would be conducted—as much as feasible—in silence. "You will be surprised by how much a person can communicate with a look and a gesture." Though some might have viewed a silent training regimen as an inconvenience, I looked at it as a welcome challenge. In my time as an author, I'd well learned that language too often clutters things up. That my apprenticeship would be tactile, devoid of linguistic ambiguities, was refreshing.

Having had the tour, silence stepped in and acted as our intermediary for the rest of my time there. I began baking the next morning. For the first couple of weeks, my alarm was a soft knock on my bedchamber door. Then, my ears became attuned to the shuffle of feet passing by, until at last, my body was locked into a rhythm. The work was hard and the learning curve was steep. Until this point in my life, the only baking I had done was as assistant to my mother during Christmas cookie season. I had certainly never attempted bread. But by year's end, I knew my ryes from my sourdoughs, the intricacies of milling grain, and the scientific precision of moisture and temperature control in the proofing and baking phases.

Once I had the basic knowledge, Fr. Bricazzi began instructing me in the artistry of the trade. Scoring the dough to produce baked-in designs. A brush of egg for a shiny finish. When my mastery of bread-baking met his approval, we turned our attention to pastries. Fruit tarts, cream puffs, and anise cookies. Contrella, contessa, lebkuchen, and more. Laboring in silence brought me into communion with work in a way I had never experienced before. A proper loaf of bread or carefully finished pastry was more than a scrumptious treat—it was an extension of myself. But unlike my previous pursuits, my well of enthusiasm never seemed to run dry. I was tired at the end of the day but fulfilled. There was never the feeling that I would have rather devoted my time to something else.

Silence is a wonderful teacher, but also the trickster ally of time. Before I knew it, my three years at Christ in the Desert were up. At the risk of this account turning into a baker's training manual, I have decided to forego many of the tales from that period. As I never set foot outside of the compound during my stay, all of my adventures had to do with baking or the requisitioning of supplies. If you want those kinds of details, you can just turn to the family cookbook.

When I left the brotherhood, I decided to put my newfound baking skills to use and started a bakery. You should know that, like being a mariner, baking runs in the family. My grandfather on my father's side ran a pastry shop in Philadelphia. It was closed before I ever had a chance to visit, but a few of the recipes had been passed down. These became the signature items at the new Brecht Bakery. Word of mouth helped usher the establishment to success. Apparently, old-world techniques were still appreciated in the era of convenience. First, it was the buzz of the block, then our southside neighborhood. Soon, people came from across the city to sample our marbled rye and German cookies. When the first person arrived from New York and reported a cabbie raving about it, I knew we had found our niche. And when the Pope showed up unannounced one morning, as part of his American tour, that was the metaphorical icing on the metaphorical cake.

Every morning—especially on weekends—the line wound out the door and down the block. For as long as they were able, my parents made the weekly three-hour trek down from Damascus. They had always made a habit of Sunday drives. The fact that my bakery was close enough to visit sweetened the deal. I would set aside their favorites—my father, the nurnberger, my mother, the shortbread, and for both, a loaf of Swedish rye to take home. They would arrive, I would leave the store in the hands of my trusty employees, and we would walk to Mifflin Square to eat the picnic lunch they had packed. Being of hardy German stock, they continued this tradition well into their nineties. And when they could no longer drive, I reversed the tradition and drove up to Damascus to make the weekly delivery. I've always been happiest when keeping to a routine.

Years down the line, when my own apprentice was ready, I sold the bakery to him. It made it easier to know that it was in good hands. In monastic tradition, he thanked me in silence.

Of course, I've left out a great deal of my story. Amongst all the time growing the bakery, I met my lovely wife and we started our family. They took up much of the slack time outside of work. Honestly, I probably should have devoted more time to family life in those days, but we were happy nonetheless. Monday was my day of rest at the bakery and so we made the most of it with hikes in the Poconos and walks through Fairmount Park. We lived a modest, contented life.

When the kids were grown and the bakery sold, my nervous energy needed an outlet, so I took a job as a bus driver. And it's a job I still have to this day. The monotony and peaceful rhythms suit me well. I spend the day smiling at people and watching the world go by.

I think back to all of the times during my life's journey when before me appeared a vision of my future self—the shuffling gait, the stooped back, the graying pompadour. Surely, I would fare better than that, I thought. But those are youthful thoughts. Eventually gravity wins, pulling us back to earth. Until then, you'll find me on the Snyder Avenue bus every morning.

13.

I add this sentence simply for the benefit of the triskaideka-phobics in my family. Thirteen is only a number. There is no need to be afraid. Harmony.

Part 3: An Interlude

つ

He looked over the words he had just written, satisfied that no one would pay heed to his opening enjoinder.

❊

He read the greats, only finding inspiration in their thrall. "I am a charlatan," he thought. "No ideas to my name and reliant upon the dead or the soon-to-be for what words I can muster."

❋

He had completely lost count of the chapter numbers. In a fit of madness, he decided he would begin using symbols instead. "Perhaps I should go back and replace the placeholders I began with?" That thought, like all of language, was but a passing fancy. It soon receded into the ether.

His mind full of worry, he dreamt of great calamities. The Hudson froze in an instant. Aircraft carriers were beached somewhere near Poughkeepsie, torn asunder by the heaving ice. A landscape full of empty metal carcasses belching smoke into the night.

☉

He approached each spurt of writing as an exercise in predestination. A puzzle for which he would dutifully assemble the pieces, having no idea of the final picture until it resolved itself. It all depended on that first piece, the keystone with which all others interlocked.

➤

One of his great-grandfather's most precious memories and famous accomplishments was being called in by the local surgeon for advice. He had read widely in the field of medicine, you see, and his opinion was respected by all doctors he encountered. He peered into the chest cavity, made his recommendation, and walked out to a chorus of applause. He had saved the day yet again. Doctoring tired him though, so he became a sewing machine salesman. It was much more suited to his temperament.

♪

[The original manuscript was unreadable at this point.]

✲

"Inspiration always strikes when I can least afford it," he thought. "What am I supposed to do when I'm swept away in the middle of the grocery store?"

Everything was all wrong. This was not how writing a novel was supposed to be.

♩

Perhaps he would self-publish. Then they might label it "vanity." Isn't every author's work a vain exercise? How then, could this be any different?

Outside, the children screamed as if they were being run over in the street. Inside, his heart beat still.

"I should do something better with my time than just spending the whole day thinking."

♠

He checked his page count and felt the blood drain from his head as if his brain were being juiced. "Six pages? That's all I have to show for years of toil?"

✳

To write, he simply imagined famous actors saying his lines.

≈

He had read that the young find it fashionable to preoccupy themselves in the dustbin of history. Here, they content themselves to live their days in bohemian squalor. Their only cares revolve around their own hermetic worlds. They ponder questions like:

What is the best and happiest way of being?

Why don't more people choose the sunshine over the office block?

Who might want to fuck me?

In this condition, they blissfully wallow until their health or their social group fails. Then they reluctantly trudge into the halls of business, the autoclave of society. Resistance was indeed futile. We would all be assimilated.

Had he been assimilated? It is hard to say. He took comfort in knowing he could never be a sell-out, since no one was buying what he had on offer.

�

He looked around and wondered where his sandwich had gone. No doubt that ravenous, repugnant creature he called his pet had stolen it away.

The mangy feline was nowhere to be seen. Probably off gobbling what it could, inhaling what it could not. He stood up in a fury and realized the sandwich had been in his pocket the whole time.

Relieved at having found it, he sat back down to write.

◣

His room was lined with sticky notes and scraps of paper taped to the walls. East, as the direction of the sunrise, served as the home for his unused ideas. As he incorporated them into his work, they were transferred to the north wall to live the remainder of their days as a dusty memorial to fleeting moments of inspiration.

Why the north wall? For one, it was the direction of his imagination. For another, it was obscured from view by his open front door, thus preventing delivery drivers and traveling salespeople from thinking he was crazy.

Unfortunately for him, six had declared itself his number. (Though he did have a special place in his heart for the number five.) Every time he looked at a clock, he saw the fiendish minute hand hanging there at the bottom of the hour, and when it broached this milestone, the hour would drop like ripened fruit to the ground, slowly rotting.

"Someday, I will make a clock-face without a bottom," he thought. Three through nine at first quaked, but, on second thought, laughed mockingly at the plan. Try as he may, he could not banish time from his existence.

From that moment on, he resolved to live outside of time. Time, likewise, resolved to live outside of him. Nothing had changed, but he felt immeasurably better. What marvelous sleight of hand!

He had never read nor written the sixth chapter of any work of fiction. (Let's be honest—he had never written a work of fiction that contained chapters. But for now, that's beside the point.) In his mind, it was where authors typically ran out of ideas. He decided he would save all of his worst ideas for his own chapter six, if he ever made it that far.

He was thinking about the many numbers between five and seven when his thoughts were interrupted once again by a hemorrhage of rain falling from clear blue skies.

℮

He felt like a cheat. He was simply copying and pasting his old words in order to keep the momentum going.

One, two, buckle my shoe.

ꝺ

Sometimes all he wanted was to be left alone.

ϑ

All of a sudden, it seemed like someone else was adding words to his opus. He would open the document to find sections he had no memory of.

"Are these the first signs of an impending psychotic break?" he wondered. But he noticed none of the other hallmarks, so he favored the invisible author explanation instead. Besides, he had too much to write to deal with psychosis.

ʎ

It had been too long since he had last written. But the floodwaters raged everywhere, so he had something of an excuse.

⌂

They labored throughout the best hours of the day. By its end, they had removed every tree on the property. Only the stumps remained. Each axe-fall and rev of the chainsaw broke his heart. The legacy of the disbanded fraternity continues.

⌀

He hoped he was close enough to steal a wifi signal. He didn't want to have to hear nearby pedestrians' idle prattle or look too closely at the building's bricks. The signal came through, but so did the prattle.

::

He found a better place to write. But, being self-conscious about doing anything more than contemplate when in a place of worship, his productivity plummeted. Thus, though the building was consistently empty, he sat just outside in all types of weather, hunched-over and writing. He would take a break, put his notebook away, and go inside to warm up. Then, when inspiration would once again strike, he would step outside into the bitter winds of the Great Plains.

He lived in constant fear of someone coming around the corner and interrupting him. This was his space and he was in no mood to share.

Have you guessed where he is yet? If you have, please don't tell anyone else. It is better to remain a secret.

ɣ

He was fascinated by blank, white expanses. He hoped to leave several in his book, like this:

Part 4: A Scrap Heap

1.

Back before the Impact, lots of people wrote a lot of schlock, imagining asteroids ploughing into the planet. The ways we'd deflect them. The ways we'd cope if they made it through our defenses. This was considered entertainment. There was a "post-apocalyptic" genre. And while this encompassed more than simply orbital transgressions, meteors were a popular subset of this type of fiction. "Civilization-ending" became an astrometric size distinction. People, it seems, can't help themselves when it comes to pseudo-science—they eat it up like scavenging birds picking at a carcass.

Then, a mountain of iron and iridium came hurtling toward us from the black depths of space. We had only a few weeks' warning. Scientists calculated trajectories, factoring in the whims of orbital mechanics and tidal forces. There was nothing to be done. Gravity always wins.

The reality of a meteor impact is far less glamorous than popular culture would have you believe. The aforementioned rock wasn't big enough to wipe us out, just big enough to do some serious damage. It hit smack in the middle of the Indian subcontinent. Being one of the more population-dense places on the planet, you can imagine the consequences. Several hundred million—maybe even a billion—people died on impact. Another billion or two died from the food shortages.[1] Like that, in the matter of a year, one-third of the human population was extinguished.

---

[1] Admittedly, no one has conducted a meaningful census in the interim, so the numbers I'm quoting could be wildly inaccurate.

Post-apocalyptic fiction always turned to the tried-and-true trope of people going all uncivilized on one another and getting murderous over food and water. The truth is, that didn't happen when the apocalypse actually came. I've found that, on the whole, people unite after disasters. When homes and livelihoods are destroyed, clubs and cudgels aren't the most effective implements of survival. Deep down, we all understand that biology does a pretty good job at killing us off as it is. None of this is to say that life post-Impact has been a cooperative cakewalk, just that an asteroid is a problem bigger than all of us.

The worst of the dust wafted through the atmosphere for the better part of a decade. While it was not enough to choke out the sun completely or eradicate significant swaths of the flora and fauna on earth, there was a pronounced cooling effect. Combined with the reduction in available sunlight, the productivity of many plant species was adversely impacted. Instead of dying, they meekly clung to survival. The places where meaningful agriculture was possible shifted toward the equator. With our breadbaskets faltering, and given the prevalence of deserts in the tropics, arable land was at a premium. What little cropland we had would have been hard-pressed to feed us all.

Our only hope were the economies of scale that come with banding together for survival. We in the resource-rich north leaned on technology, built our LED-lit, wind-powered greenhouses, and soldiered on. Elsewhere, those without our resources chiseled their hardscrabble living out of the land. There were mass-exoduses as cities de-urbanized to adjust to the post-Impact limits of sustainable existence. Farms were reclaimed and once again began teaching the harsh lessons of survival. The densest urban cores persisted, but only in a diminished state, limping along as centers of trade and commerce. All of this is to say that, outside of the immediate impact zone, life was merely a grayer, dingier, slightly more ramshackle version of its former self.

There were reputed to be, however, small, unperturbed oases of green scattered across the oceans, owing to the vagaries of the rivers of wind flowing overhead. Though their usual supply lines were interrupted—the mainland had enough to worry about, after all—the people on these islands were cut from a hardy, self-reliant stock. To them, the disappearance of the monthly quota of bananas and postal offerings was not a significant concern. They simply turned their backs to the wind and made do with what they had. The gardeners among them saved their seeds and coaxed sustenance from native species. The shepherds kept on as they had for centuries, minding their grazing lands and culling their herds as necessary. This was the way people had survived in these places for generations and will continue to do so for generations more.[2]

But now I'm growing tired, so I shall resume this tale tomorrow.

---

[2] In all honesty, I have not seen these lands firsthand (or even pictures of them). I am simply relating what I have heard. There is some debate as to whether or not these island refuges actually exist. Some go so far as to claim that their existence is physically impossible. Others take it as a matter of faith. One wonders, whether the emergence of these tales, particularly those of remote Atlantic islands, is merely a form a wishful thinking—a rekindling of the Antillian mythos. Whatever the case, it is nice to believe that normality persists somewhere.

2.

Yesterday's talk of death and destruction left a foul taste in my mouth. It all seems to have lodged in the back of my throat and festered while I slept. Now I've gone all mucousy, beset by a möbian thirst. The more I drink, the thirstier I get.

It reminds me of the trials of Allison Lexington. Back in the days when exploration had evolved to the point of hobby—a list of more and more outlandish things that had yet to be done—she decided that she would be the first to walk the breadth of the Sahara, from west to east, by herself.

When she set out, she was laden with the necessary gear. She charted a circuitous course from oasis to oasis, precisely requisitioning her water and food accordingly. When she made it to the first oasis, she found it dry (or rather never found it at all). As a result, she was forced to drink her own urine to survive.

By the time she made it to her next scheduled oasis, she was severely dehydrated and hallucinatory. One sip of the muddy water and she passed out. A concerned Tuareg guide found her shortly after and immediately transported her to the nearest infirmary.

When she regained consciousness, she learned that her kidneys were failing and that she would henceforth need regular dialysis treatments. When asked what she was doing out in the desert in the first place, she explained her trek and goal to be the first to traverse the Sahara. The doctor laughed.

"You would not be the first."

Crestfallen, she asked how far she had gotten.

"Ninety-eight kilometers. It has been a harsh year in the desert."

A lifetime of dialysis and she had not even crossed the century mark. Years later, when interviewed about her mental state after missing the first oasis, the frail Ms. Lexington explained her drive to march forward. Drinking one's own urine is palatable if there is the promise of fresh water around the corner. They say that death by dehydration is one of the more peaceful ways to go.

When I was young, I dealt with a different kind of thirst. Knowledge and learning were my obsessions. Books were my canteen. In the eighth grade, I read Asimov's *Foundation*. I was swept up in the idea of archivist-as-hero, never really doubting the resilience of our current knowledge stores against any similar calamity. Maybe that is why I have taken on this task. Archiving the memories of impact.

3.

Up until the newscasts were trumpeting humanity's impending demise, I hadn't thought much about space. I'd read my share of science fiction, but when it came to the realities of an endless universe, celestial mechanics, and eventual heat death, I figured my mental energy was better spent on the quotidian concerns of immediate existence.

In those days, it was easy to ignore what lay beyond the sky. During the day, we could see the sun and, occasionally, the moon. At night, we could see the moon, and occasionally, if we were lucky, the brightest of the stars and planets. We had built ourselves a protective cocoon of light, oblivious to (or perhaps willfully trying to obscure) the vast expanse that spiraled into nothingness above our heads.

The first reports trickled out. We'd seen this kind of thing before. The astronomers would make their observations, crunch the numbers, and tell us that there was no real chance of impact. The initial discovery was always more exciting than the calculated reality.

The object in question was 921 meters across. More measurements were needed, but initial calculations showed a small, but significant chance for impact. We ignored the news. Within a week, all earthly telescopes were focused on this one celestial body and the odds of impact were revised upward. Soon, collision became a certainty. This was upsetting to say the least.

Furious, the Italians expedited litigation against their scientists for failing to warn humanity in time.[3] Instead of the customary manslaughter convictions, however, the solicitors argued the impending impact was nothing short of premeditated murder. To be sure, the wheels were set in motion long ago. While the rest of the world prepared for the worst, one country relished its revenge. The accused scientists were convicted and hung from the Senate building for all to see. The Vatican called for calm, but the mob could not be sated. From science, we expect perfection. Yet despite all of the revelations of string theory, we failed when it came to anticipating the simplest of trajectories.

Early on, the chorus of those advocating a ballistic intervention swelled. After all, humanity had mastered ballistics long ago, able to shoot pigeons (clay and otherwise) out of the

[3] They have a history of doing so—from the L'Aquila earthquake of 2009 to the unexpected awakening of Vesuvius in 2027.

sky since we had invented gunpowder. Those with nuclear arsenals pondered whether it would be better to unleash them on the rock or save them to unleash on each other. Eventually, the concerns of earthly contamination won out. There are rumors that a solitary soul stood in the way of our radioactive future. The order had been given. And the hand hovering over the button wavered. Archibald Jones is a true hero. He would have been court-martialed if he had not asphyxiated himself in his garage first.

Instead of nukes, we launched a few dozen of the largest rockets we could find, simply hoping to deflect the meteor slightly. Like bugs on a windshield they withered and the threat drew ever closer.

4.

I'd like to stop here for a moment and consider the physics of a comet hitting a planet. The talking heads equated the odds of impact to trying to hit a bullet with another bullet. This was entirely wrong. Instead, imagine hitting a bowling ball with a grain of sand. Now imagine trying to do the same thing with a handful of sand. The Oort Cloud was that handful, the sun the siren drawing the comets in. A collision seems much more likely when you think about it that way.

What no one had previously discussed (outside of the halls of geophysical academe) was the potential for an abrupt change in the Earth's rotation after an impact. Most people know that a day is not exactly twenty-four hours in length. Nor is a year a perfect 365 days. That's why we have leap years and leap seconds. Nonetheless, having spun so many globes growing up, people had woeful misperceptions about the

Earth and its axis. Our planet is not a perfect sphere. It is an oblong ellipsoid, fat around the middle like most of us when we reach middle age. We should have expected a jiggle every so often.

In the grand scheme of things, the resultant 8.3-second shift in our rotational period might not seem all that consequential. But little changes add up. Over the course of a year, an eight-second shift brings fifty new minutes winking into existence. Fifty minutes that we did not previously have available to us. While this was a nice thought for both the slothful and productivity-minded among us, it gave the orbital mechanists conniption fits. If not adjusted for, the systems we'd been so carefully honing for generations would slowly drift out of sync with reality. All at once, we no longer lived in a Gregorian world.[4]

Thus, a corrective factor was introduced for all calculations both temporal and galactic.[5] While the world was mathematically different, life on the ground proceeded at much the same pace. Sure, there were the privations of post-Impact life, but we quickly grew used to them. The bread lines, the water rations, the soot-obscured sun, we were like Londoners in the Battle of Britain. We soldiered on while the dust in the atmosphere kept our windows blacked out.

---

[4] Not that these sorts of shifts were entirely unprecedented. Large earthquakes had previously been observed to alter our rotational values.

[5] If not accounted for, the change in rotation would have sent transport and supply rockets careening past their destinations. A few seconds of difference here can translate to millions of kilometers in the far depths of space.

5.

Let me be upfront when I tell you that I harbor no delusions that I'm going to stave off 10,000 years of barbarism by writing this. I am no Asimovian encyclopedist. Truth is, I have been commissioned by the local library to collect, organize, and codify our post-Impact history. Somehow, it takes the written record to make something real in the eyes of bureaucracy. While that project is all well and good, officialdom dictates the inclusion of certain facts and stories and the elision of others. If the project were my own, I would include it all. The "kitchen-sink approach," as they used to say. That's why I have taken to writing this—a secret, parallel document to ease my conscience. Will anyone read it? Doubtful. Unless, of course, I'm branded as a dissident and the inspectors who come to kick down my door find this under the floorboards. Maybe instead, I'll die a peaceful, early death from silicosis, having inhaled more than my fair share of atmospheric dust. And when my friends sort through my meager belongings, they will find this and share it with the world. Chances are, if you are reading this, the latter has happened.

There are those who would have you believe that there is no possible future where either of these scenarios could occur. That the world is on an irrevocable downward run. Yes, some of the major settlements have been failing, whether through resource strain, poor planning, or straight-up sedition. But does that mean the rest will fall? I doubt it.

At least we have not yet had to resort to cannibalism like they did in the Martian colonies. As Earth's own destruction loomed, resupplying those intrepid pioneers became an afterthought. Overlooked by their usual support systems, the settlers of the red planet did not have the luxury of falling back on the land (as their terrestrial brethren were able to do). There had been no meaningful terraforming completed. The biospheres produced enough to supplement a diet, but not enough to sustain a population. Thus, when their stores ran dry, nature ran its course.

I can only imagine what it must have been like. No one thought to inform the Martians about the Impact—everyone here was too preoccupied with survival. For a while, the Martians would have been blissfully unaware of their predicament. Life would have continued at the usual pace, the usual foods consumed, the usual squabbles aired out amongst rivals.

But when the weeks passed and the dropships failed to appear, the panic must have begun to build. Repeated attempts to contact the home base—each one more frantic than the last—must have failed.[6] Little did the Martians know that the dedicated terrestrial staff only admitted defeat and abandoned their posts to be with their families when the inbound meteor obliterated the communications relay satellite. It has been said that knowing what is coming breeds far more fear than not knowing at all. The Martians might be the exception to this rule. Thus, where the Impact united the citizens of Earth through the crucible of common struggle, it tore the Martian society asunder.

Some placed their faith in the futile attempts to hail mission control. Others placed their faith in the power of hoarding, for a short time, becoming black-market kingpins.

---

[6] There is no record of these missed communications, so this is embellishment on my part. It is easy enough to imagine, however.

But even the best-stocked larders run dry with time. In the final days, there was murder, wailing, and gnashing of teeth. To the victors went the final scraps of bread. And when the bread was gone, they ate their dead. Imagine fighting for survival so hard that your prize is a mouthful of your friend's flesh.

Woe be to the pioneers in this world (or on others).

6.

I mentioned before that no one had considered the rotational effects of an impact. This is not to say there weren't a host of other fears under consideration in the days leading up to our meteoric encounter. There was initially fear that, along with the more obvious repercussions of impact—localized destruction, soot in the atmosphere, etc.—the meteor would usher in an era of heightened volcanism, that the crust would fracture and lava would come welling up.

This failed to occur. True, there were a few geothermal disruptions that may have been triggered by the tectonic changes wrought by impact.[7] Impressive steam explosions around the lakes in the Yellowstone caldera, disruptions in the geyser fields of Kamchatka, increased stratovolcano activity in the Andes—none of these proved too devastating. After

---

[7] Some seismologists have pointed to the unprecedented wavelengths detected on seismographs around the world (both P-waves and S-waves, and, more locally, the surface waves) as proof of causation. Indeed, the seisms were so significant as to have rendered inoperable the vast majority of recording equipment at the time, deforming the miniscule pendulums on which their operation depended. Nonetheless, since there was a (sometimes years) lag between impact and eruption, debate persists.

all, there was so much debris already in the air; a little more did not significantly compound the problem.

Nevertheless, there were lots of people getting worked up about different types of volcanic destruction. As if we needed more to lament. I read a story around that time that explained the sadness surrounding the loss of a stone tree. Back in the early days of Yellowstone as a national park, there were several standing petrified trees. Souvenir seekers being what they are, all but one of these rocky trunks were eventually chipped apart and slipped into visitors' pockets. One gentleman (I cannot for the life of me remember his name) was horrified at the plundering and so worked to erect a fence around the last surviving specimen. The Park Service agreed and thenceforth, the fossilized trunk would be preserved for future generations.

At some point after the Impact, a sinkhole opened up beneath the former tree and it collapsed to the bottom, shattering.[8] Geologists around the world were heartbroken—after all, a standing petrified tree is a rare thing. I never understood it as much of a loss. There are entire stone forests standing underground, waiting to emerge when the waters wash the silt and sediment away.

7.

Another phenomenon that entered the public's imagination at the time was the creation of new lands. There had been so

---

[8] If you look at the former location of the petrified tree, you will see that it is well outside of the Yellowstone caldera. As such, I am of the mindset that the sinkhole and the Impact are unconnected. But then again, I am not an expert in the morphology of sinkholes.

much destruction wrought by the Impact, that creation was a novel counterpoint. Island-birthing was a well-documented phenomenon in the journals of plate-tectonicists, but for some reason, when it came to the general populace, volcanic processes stole the limelight. Everyone eagerly awaited the day they could visit Lōʻihi, the newest of the Hawaiian Islands, willfully overlooking the fact that it wouldn't broach the waves for tens of thousands of years. Building something lasting with magma takes millennia, after all. Given the prevalence of islandic fixation, it is surprising that more people didn't pay attention to the other ways islands can be born—particularly, the suddenness with which they can appear after earthquakes.[9]

On the vast, comparatively shallow continental shelves around the planet, sizeable new landmasses appeared. In the disarray following impact, governments were overwhelmed with relief efforts and overlooked their usual inclinations toward gobbling up unclaimed lands—if only to expand their territorial waters. The hesitation was a boon to would-be nation builders, and for a while, we witnessed the most prolific period of nation-formation history has ever seen. By some counts, hundreds of new nations staked their claims among the international community.[10] Surprisingly, the bulk of these

---

[9] Perhaps the previous instances were quickly forgotten due to their transience. In the decades leading up to the Impact, earthquake-triggered islands had repeatedly risen out of the ocean south of Pakistan where there had previously been none the day before. These islands however, were primarily agglomerations of mud and loose sediment. They lasted just days to months before the oceans reclaimed them.

[10] Strictly speaking, not all of these were technically new. Many claimants were micronations that had long harbored dreams of independence, but

claims went uncontested. The nouveau-landed liked to point to it as not only de facto recognition of their legitimacy, but also as further evidence of the impotence of the old "meganations." Perhaps, the established nations put up no fight because they didn't care—seeing the specks of land as the resourceless money-sinks that they were.

For a number of months, it looked like the micronationalists would have the last laugh. Private investors flocked to their shores. Flurries of building began. But gradually—quickly on a geologic timescale—the islands began to dissolve. Their hastily built casinos and prefab high-rises began calving into the sea at an alarming rate.[11] Some tried to stave off their inevitable demise with seawalls, but it was of no use. Once reality set in, the great exodus began and one-by-one, the micronations blinked out of existence.

This created something of a problem for those who had renounced their previous citizenships in favor of newly fashionable micronationalities. Suddenly without country, these people became caught in bureaucratic limbo. Some countries refused them access altogether, others slotted them into the decades-long queues for immigration and naturalization.

---

lacked the territorial resources necessary to make much of themselves. The Dominion of Melchizedek, Sealand, Marduk, and more all rose from the ashes of their previous failed experiments to claim new spits of land. Such is the insatiable thirst for personal fiefdoms.

[11] My use of the iceberg metaphor is intentional here. Like the same flows that doomed the Titanic, the detritus of the short-lived construction boom endangered international shipping. Great tangled masses of steel and buoyant concrete (which had initially been hailed as a miracle product for seaside construction) tumbled through the ocean currents, puncturing any hulls unfortunate enough to intersect with their course.

Gina Teleman, one of the leaders of the "rights for the nation-less" movement (herself a one-time resident of the ill-fated Georgetonia colony), was once quoted as saying: "To punish those who yearn for a brighter future is disappointing, but it is a common recurrence in human society. What is most disgraceful is bringing that retribution to bear on those who had no choice but to be born into our ephemeral nations." Thanks to her eloquent words, most of the remaining countries on the planet granted amnesty to the few hundred children unlucky enough to be born to nonexistent nations. Their parents were left to live off the land in the abandoned spaces of this earth. Such are the stakes for the dreamers among us.

8.

There are those who would rather a document like this focus on the gruesome, gritty details of the Impact itself. The sweeping, broad brushstrokes with which I have described the Impact won't be enough to sate their appetites for destruction. Anecdotes about changes in the Earth's rotation, toppled petrified trees, and ephemeral islands only go so far. So, for the sake of the sadists among you, here is some real human tragedy.

Though the meteor hit India, since China is shielded by the towering Himalayas, it would be easy to assume that the People's Republic was able to escape no worse than the rest of us. That assumption would be wrong. While it is true that they didn't suffer much in the way of the direct debris and ejecta that decimated the subcontinental region, it is important to remember that in the 20th and 21st centuries, the Chinese became enamored with water. They blocked valleys to create massive reservoirs. They used that water to generate hydro-power and green their arid interior, building a "great green wall" stretching through the Gobi. In the late 21st century, the Central Party proclaimed victory over the ravages of rivers. People no longer needed to live with the hassles of seasonal flooding—every river in the country's borders had been tamed.

This hydrologic miracle was hailed as a triumph around the world. Every country hoped to emulate the Chinese success. The weakness in the plan was exposed by the Impact. Due to the peculiarities of the network of tectonic faults in the region, the huge reservoirs acted as liquid amplifiers for the resultant seismic waves that propagated through the Earth's crust.[12] As the precise resonant frequencies were achieved, dams liquefied and sloughed away. Given the population concentrated in the river deltas and floodplains of the Yangtze, Yellow, and Pearl rivers, the benefits of any advanced warning were cancelled out by insufficient transportation infrastructure. The cars clogging the roadways were all swept to sea.

Even today, every so often, it is not uncommon for Chinese autos to wash up on our shores, with skeletons at the wheel. Some susquecentarians in China, old enough to remember the Three Gorges in their unflooded glory, say it is

---

[12] Though this story is repeated time and again, I have yet to find a scientific analysis of the exact tectonic mechanisms that drove this phenomenon. What we know is that dams for reservoirs over a certain size threshold failed. The intricacies probably matter little to you the reader. They matter even less to the scores of people swept away in the great floods.

just their ancestors finally exacting their revenge. The flooded became the flooders and in doing so, re-inherited the earth.

9.

I would be remiss, if, in writing about great floods, I omitted what is reputed to be the largest flood in recorded history. One so massive it earned capital letters for its name: The Great Inundation.

There was a time in the late 20th century when great deluge theories abounded for the Mediterranean and Black Seas. Archaeologists posited that these basins had been cut off from their mother oceans during the last ice age, and at some point, sea-level rise found the weak elevational link on their perimeters and brought them back into the hydrologic fold. Many scientists scoffed at the idea of dramatic, catastrophic inundation. Changes like that are liable to be gradual, they argued. Humanity was privy to a firsthand test of the idea thanks to the effects of global warming. Those who argued against deluge theories had their victory. All that was witnessed was the relentless slow expansion of the oceans—there was never a mad, thunderous rushing and gushing. What's more, the lack of definitive geological evidence saw the theory wither and fade into obscurity.

Only one anthropologist kept the idea alive in the second half of the 21st century—Dr. Reinhold Gutsendang. He had carefully secured tenure before embarking on his quixotic quest. Peers viewed him as a pariah or worse. The general population paid him no mind. In the first weeks after the Impact, when he was frail of health and lying on his deathbed, Dr. Gutsendang was finally vindicated.

East Africa's proximity to the impact site had brought about some startling regional effects.[13] Word is that a new sea was born in the Great Rift Valley over the course of two weeks. A biblical-scale flood swept in through a gap that had opened in the Afar Triangle when the Somalian Plate finally broke free from the Nubian. The fertile land and lakes that had dotted the fault were quickly overcome with saltwater, creating a long, narrow finger of ocean that stretched south to Tanzania. Many people who lived in the region were swept away in their sleep, unaware that the ocean had come calling.[14] Those left on the banks of the Rift helped usher in a Messianic revival, claiming the Old Testament God had returned. And who could argue with them?

On his deathbed, Dr. Gutsendang heard the news and shed a single tear. With his final breath, he exhaled his victor's speech: "I wish I'd been wrong."

---

[13] It has been theorized that though the asteroid was not big enough to punch through the Earth's crust, it had enough mass to cause some of the surrounding plates to buckle. Like the shell of a stubborn hard-boiled egg, the crust flexed and cracked, but still adhered. To be sure, the relatively small Indian Plate experienced the worst fracturing. Adjoining plates suddenly had pressure upon them relieved and got to live out their tectonic fantasies. The Arabian Plate curled up on its western edge, making the Persian Gulf landlocked. The nascent Somalian Plate slipped eastward to fill the gap, enlarging the East African Rift in the process.

[14] Given the poverty of the region and the basic survival challenges facing the rest of the world, the story of the Rift Sea only received passing mention from Western media.

10.

With the face of the Earth being remade by new lands and seas, and a twenty-fold increase in atmospheric particulate matter, it is perhaps not surprising that global weather patterns changed rather abruptly. It wasn't so much a randomization as an amplification.[15] Places that previously received rain received more; the previously arid places grew drier. Those locations in the Goldilocks zone of neither too much nor too little often tipped one of the two directions. Moderation seemed to have been spurned in favor of excess. Cascadia won the climatological lottery in this sense. Since the Pacific Northwest was by and large a wet region, the average annual rainfall increased by 50 percent. Luckily, our rains come in steady waves off the Pacific instead of intense monsoonal bursts. Thus, they haven't wreaked the same havoc as their counterpart storms streaming off the Gulf of Mexico.[16]

To capitalize on the increased liquid bounty, the Cascadian government—much against the wishes of the ecotopists who felt as if the country's founding principles were

---

[15] A number of theories have been posited—many of the same ones trotted out for the climatological impacts of global warming—but since there is little consensus (and even less published on the topic to date), I have simply decided to present the reality without delving into its underlying causes.

[16] Since the Impact, there have been at least a dozen 5,000-year event floods in the corridor stretching from Denver to Houston, and many more 500 and 1,000-year events. Casualties, of both property and human life, have reportedly been high. Some hydrologists have suggested that the flood scale needs to be recalibrated for the new normal. Skeptical meteorologists are resistant to the idea and still expect the climate to settle back into its pre-Impact patterns. Nonetheless, FEMA and the Army Corps of Engineers are busy resurveying floodplains in the American west.

being betrayed—commissioned new reservoirs along the spine of the Cascades to irrigate the agricultural lands in their rain-shadow. Without this water, the Walla Walla valley and Columbia plateau would become untenable. Other locations do not have the luxury of an ample water supply abutting fertile farmland. Just look at what used to be America's wheat belt for an example of what can happen when irrigation falters—everything west of Iowa is now just dryland beset by an unslakable thirst.[17]

As the west emptied out in the Great Drying (another phenomenon that has merited capital letters), there were still the intrepid optimists who believed they could find secluded oases in which to start their lives over. This led to a new era of wagon trains. One of the chief proponents of this was the Reverend Devonshire Lewis. His plan was to take a small band of followers out into the Nevadan hinterlands and establish a small colony. He was sure he could find a spring or construct a rain catchment system that would store all of the water that would be needed. His merry band disappeared into the shimmering waves of heat west of the Bonneville Salt Flats and was not heard from again. Several years later, a passing prospector found him and the rest of his unfortunate band desiccated and

---

[17] While it is true that the Rockies still act as a "water tower" for much of the West, river flows across the region have dropped precipitously from what was considered normal when the Colorado River Compact was signed. If the dryland farmers of the Great Plains took what they needed to sustain their practice, the major rivers would have been mere trickles by the time they joined with the Mississippi. Wells were not an option either as much of the Ogallala Aquifer had been pumped dry as global warming stressed the water supply. As such, most of those who worked marginal land chose to walk away from their farms in search of greener, wetter pastures.

mummified in the desert. Rev. Lewis was clutching a scrap of parchment in his hands with the following prayer written on it:

> *Lord, spare me from the farms of the Great Basin. A speck. A circle of green in an expanse of nothingness. But the salvation of the Sierra Nevada looms up ahead. Bury me not on the Bonneville Salt Flats. They give more water to prisoners—and I took tithes for this. Reno is an abomination.*

No one was really surprised by the discovery. I like to think that his spirit went on exploring the western wastes, the landscapes of our imagination. He's out there somewhere, populating our dreams with mirages of waterholes.

11.

Consecutive anecdotes about floods and deserts might give the wrong impression. Yes, there are still a variety of biomes across the planet and temperatures fluctuate depending upon location. We are not just outposts in a godforsaken wasteland, after all. It's just that, in the places where much of the population has concentrated itself, it's a half-dozen degrees cooler than it used to be. That might not sound like a lot, but it does leave a psychological scar. I remember how the heat used to be so ungodly in the mid-latitudes. Now, we cling to every ray of sun like it may be our last. Ninety-degree days are all but unheard of anymore.[18]

---

[18] Of course, I assume it remains fairly warm around the equator. Without a reliable network of weather stations, I can only accurately report the temperature in my current location in Cascadia.

Though metric measurements of distance, weight, and volume won out with the remaining populace for standardization's sake, temperature systems have thankfully reverted to the more pleasing Fahrenheit scale. While centigrade might make logical sense in a scientific realm, Fahrenheit has far more resolution for the physical reality of human bodies—we can register temperature variations that fail to make a dent in centigrade.[19]

To counter the colder temperatures, most remaining cities have taken lessons from Reykjavik and turned to geothermal heat exchangers. Of course, not everyone has the abundance of volcanism and near-surface thermal features, so many settlements tend to cluster around available heat sources. The native cultures are still willing to brave the elements with their traditional methods, but, on the whole, humanity has become soft. There are no polar explorers among us, no mountaineers.

The tales we grew up with surrounding the last gasp of Earth-exploration focused our wanderlust on the unexplored heavens. People were content that we knew everything we needed to know about our home. While I won't argue the importance of interplanetary exploration, particularly in light of recent events, space explorers are entirely dependent on technology. Frontierspeople of yesteryear relied instead on their wits and biological adaptability. Where the former have taken us to Mars and beyond, the latter had the everyday survival skills that would have been useful when a meteor comes a-

---

[19] Excepting decimals, which are an entirely unintuitive and ridiculous option in my opinion. Seemingly, the remainder of humanity agrees.

visiting. Put the Impact a few centuries earlier, and we might have actually coped better.

12.

The Impact threw us all out of our normal routines. Things we had taken for granted like the ready availability of food and energy were less dependable. Being able to pop down to the corner market to pick up a banana for tomorrow's lunch was no longer a guarantee. It is easy to dwell on the Impact's impacts, the negative consequences—I've been doing it for the bulk of this project. So let's shift gears for a moment and consider the positives.

I realize that it's probably neither popular nor kosher to talk about the "benefits" of murderous, havoc-wreaking meteor impacts. But I'll leave tact to the ethicists. My goal is to chronicle life after the Impact, and so chronicle I shall—warts and all. In any event, there were several unanticipated—and dare I say, welcome—consequences of Earth's galactic encounter. For one, disease and infection rates dropped exponentially. There simply was not the concentration of human hosts left to sustain many of our common maladies and thus, without that critical mass, viral and bacterial populations plummeted in regions around the globe.[20] These sorts of statistics are always a double-edged sword. True, there was a smaller proportion of the population infected with disease at

---

[20] It has since been suggested that celestial impacts have played a vital evolutionary role in this regard. They act as cosmic inoculants, sweeping through every several thousand years, forcing disease populations into hibernation and allowing life to proliferate unhindered for a time. Whether or not this is the case is hard to say—viruses don't leave behind fossil records.

any given time, but there were also several billion fewer people living on the planet.

I have already touched briefly on another collateral benefit of the Impact—namely, the resultant dust's counteraction of global warming. But there was more going on in the atmosphere than we initially realized. After the impact, global CO_2 concentrations fell precipitously. This is especially counterintuitive given the decrease in vegetative production that came with the partially obscured sun. Add to that the volcanic outputs, and, if anything, one would think that the concentration of insulating gases would increase. But readings were corroborated at measuring stations around the world.

One leading scientist suggested that the meteor had triggered a kind of "forced sequestration" where molten debris ejected by the Impact acted like billions of scrubbers, absorbing the heavier greenhouse gasses, solidifying, then falling back to earth. Another suggested that the initial shockwave cascaded through the atmosphere, imparting so much energy that a daisy chain of CO_2 split into its less-harmful constituent parts. Other, more fringe thinkers, argued that the carbon dioxide was selectively bled-off into space from the upper atmosphere.

While the atmospheric chemistry behind the change is unclear, current air measurements speak for themselves—we are back at a pre-industrial equilibrium. The absence of the long-departed Arctic sea-ice, coupled with increased atmospheric particulate matter, its associated cooling, and the now de-greenhouse-gasified climate was all that was needed to jumpstart increased rates of snowfall. Since the ocean's ability to retain residual heat exceeds that of solid earth, in the storms rolling off the Arctic Ocean we see warm waters feeding the beginnings of new glaciers throughout the northern hemisphere. People have taken to calling this era the "new ice age." Some have even gone so far as to call it a step forward for sustainable climate moderation—a much-needed recharge of Earth's air conditioner.

Nonetheless, we have a long way to go until we see the glaciers gobbling up our homes. Even the earliest recorded civilizations in the Indus valley only go back 8,000 years. If the climate scientists are correct, the ramifications of the Impact will linger longer than civilized humanity has existed on the planet. These are sobering thoughts.

Faced with ungraspable timescales, there are some who suggest geo-engineering to counteract any possibility of glacial growth. For instance, in New Miami, the Greenhouse Party has secured a dominant position. They advocate intentional and sustained emission of greenhouse gasses in order to counteract excessive cooling. You would think with the city's troubled history that its citizens would welcome a reversal in global warming and the attendant reduction in sea level it would bring.[21] Instead, they seem to have forgotten their origins, having made a clean break with their now-submerged

---

[21] As sea levels rose in fits and starts in the mid-21st century, coastlines were redrawn. Low-lying population centers took a variety of tacks to address the issue of habitability. Some dissolved as their populations migrated inland toward opportunity and higher ground. Others, inspired by the Dutch, built elaborate protective structures to keep themselves dry. This, of course, led to some notable and horrendous accidents like the failure of the seawall at Yokohama. As walls grow higher and the quantity of ocean being kept out increases, failure becomes something of an inevitability. The third option, which proved popular, was for endangered cities to be granted new charters on "empty" land elsewhere. Thus, New Miami (and Florida) was given a

homeland. It is as if the suggestion of re-emergent land is an affront to their entire self-conception. I think there may also be some mover's fatigue involved. Uprooting and reestablishing an entire city takes its toll on the inhabitants. No wonder they wouldn't want to consider doing it again.

There is one story I heard from the Greenhouse camp that stands out. An especially zealous acolyte named John Ramsey, so incensed by the thought of a cooling climate, devised a personal protest to counteract it. Mr. Ramsey was a high school chemistry teacher and volunteer firefighter in Youngstown, Ohio. He was also an amateur historian who documented coal mining disasters. One of his particular interests was the Centralia mine fire that caused entire towns to be abandoned. What's more, he knew that coal seam fires could burn for centuries and were a measurable emitter of atmospheric CO_2 and other greenhouse gasses.

Putting all of this knowledge together, he mapped the major coal deposits of the United States and went to work setting them alight. By the time Ramsey was caught, he had worked his way west to the Southern Illinois coalfields. Though he was tried, convicted, and sentenced to life in an environmental services labor camp, the damage was already done. One man had ignited 30% of the U.S. bituminous coal reserves. There are similar stories of people trying the same tactic with oil wells. One Canadian activist planned to set the Alberta tar sands on fire but was stymied when she realized

---

small, District of Columbia-sized plot of land in the Ozarks. It was a unique way for much of the Floridian population to learn firsthand the brutal lessons of the Trail of Tears.

that there was no easy way to induce ignition in the cold, wet north.

These fanatics envisioned a continent blazing bright like the North Dakota natural gas wells of old. During the fracking boom of the early 21st century, the inky midnight of that state was transformed into a perma-dusk by the ever-blooming industrial lights and gas flares. The light pollution was so impressive, it was visible from space. But nature always regains the upper hand—when the natural gas market crashed, she was content to return that stretch of country to the blackness from which it came.

In the end, the efforts of anyone who would seek to burn our way out of an ice age are futile. I've heard it said by prominent climatologist Samantha Cardaway that even if all of the fossil fuel reserves were set alight, the upward trajectory of the Earth's albedo accompanying the "new ice age" would negate any gains. What's more, we can't afford to spare the few natural resources we have access to for such purposes. If we burn it all in-situ, what will we warm our homes and power our fragile infrastructure with? Who will keep lit the flame of humanity?

But I digress. I was telling you about the unanticipated benefits of impact so that I could finally tell you about the impact site itself. It's best to keep a balance of emotions so the reader neither gets too confident nor too despondent.

13.

Thousands of years ago, North America was dominated by freshwater lakes of far greater scale than we have today. Immense lakes with names like Bonneville and Agassiz.[22] As temperatures at the end of the last ice age rose, these lakes swelled. Eventually the icy dams holding them back gave way and their frigid waters burst forth, flowing over the continent to find the sea. In their wake, they scoured canyons and deposited sediments. Bonneville, in particular, is responsible for having carved the Snake and Columbia River gorges and created the fertile farmland we now enjoy in Cascadia.

We like to think of geography as a slow process, but there are times, like glacial outburst floods, when its forces act abruptly. The Impact brought this fact into sharp resolution.

As ground zero, the Indian subcontinent became a vast wasteland overnight. A thick layer of molten rock and ash blanketed everything for hundreds of kilometers. The Himalayas acted like a planetary smokestack, channeling the

---

[22] These lakes are said to have held more freshwater than all of the current lakes of the world combined. Whether or not this is true, I cannot say for sure. Some have linked their draining to the demise of the Clovis people. The argument goes that the Clovis culture's subsistence living depended upon the lakes. When they drained in massive outburst floods, the proto-civilization collapsed. And yet, those floods provided the nutrients for our crops today. One civilization fades and another clings to their detritus. Of course, there is another theory that the Clovis people met their demise at the hands of a meteor burst that ignited all of the forests of North America in a great conflagration. Though that too would enrich our soils, I think it is too dark a thought given our recent history with space rocks.

northern arc of the debris-filled shockwave high into the upper atmosphere.[23] The Indian Ocean absorbed much of the fallout from southern arc. The quick influx of minerals led to massive algal blooms that meandered throughout the South Pacific on the prevailing currents, fouling desalination systems as they went. Sydney is said to have been without fresh water for three weeks. The algae grew in thick mats and choked the city's intakes. What little water did make it through was laced with toxins declared a threat to public health. What the well-intentioned city officials overlooked was how the lack of drinking water would only exacerbate the impact-induced asthma epidemic sweeping the city. Hydration was critical to the mucous production necessary to filter out the dust. Thousands succumbed to coughing attacks before water service was reinstated.

But we shouldn't get sidetracked with oceanic concerns. Back to the impact site. Previously, exclusion zones around places like Chernobyl or other nuclear disasters had fear of radiation keeping people out. At the Indian Crater, people stayed out because there was nothing left. Not even enough to sustain a subsistence living. And where subsistence is impossible, business is unlikely to follow.

There was one notable exception. When meteors strike the surface of the Earth, the energies, as should now be quite evident, are enormous. Some of the byproducts of extreme

---

[23] It is unclear just how high the material went. Certainly higher than any previous event in human history. Calculations have demonstrated that the momentum would have brought the ejecta close to escape velocity, but how much (if any) Earth-born material is now floating through space is impossible to quantify. It is heartening to think that the Impact's destruction could result in Earth having provided the seed for new life on other planets.

heat and pressure are diamonds and other precious stones. On top of that, asteroids in general—and ours was no different in this regard—are concentrated reservoirs of precious metals and other exotic elements. To mineral speculators, this potential bounty was too much to ignore. Hundreds of mining companies were hurriedly established.[24] Borrowing the tricks learned from the asteroid-mining consortiums of the late 21st century, they perfected their surveying and extraction techniques.

Recovery was no small task, since the most valuable shock-morphic minerals were either within or below the brecciated lens—a continuous layer of hardened rock that had been shattered and then fused due to the high temperatures of impact. To break through this layer is exhausting and tedious work if undertaken by hand. It even takes its toll on large excavation equipment. The Indian Crater, no man's land that it was, was not an easy place in which to work. It was hard enough to get gargantuan machinery there, let alone effect repairs when that machinery inevitably broke down. As such, most of the work was undertaken by teams of semi-skilled demolition experts. The work was dangerous, but the payoffs were substantial.[25] The first crews focused their efforts on the central rebounded cone, using the logic that it absorbed the

---

[24] To say there was no one and no business outside of the rare earths miners might not be entirely accurate. What better hiding place for bandits, pirates, and other lawless folk? Piracy in the Indian Ocean is reputed to be a particular problem. Many have attributed it to the lack of effective post-Impact governments in the region. I prefer to think of it as a quirk of our new geography. The asteroid created an abundance of places to hide.

[25] Exact statistics are hard to come by, but it is rumored that anywhere between 500 and 1,500 miners lost their lives working in the pit.

most force, and thus should have had the highest likelihood for precious stones. To be sure, the volume of diamonds and shocked quartz coming out of the area was reportedly quite high. Rather than compete with the clamor within the crater, the next wave of prospectors to arrive focused their efforts on the periphery. Instead of laboring to break through the breccia, they simply went to work gathering the exotic-rich ejecta around the crater. Several fortunes were made on the resulting hauls of iridium. The speculative frenzy wound down, however, once it was realized that there was significantly less demand for these materials in the post-Impact world. There were very few viable jewelers or electronics makers left in need of gems and rare earths. The low prices brought on by the market glut made the manufactures happy and the disaster profiteers extremely sad. Soon, the crater was left empty once again.[26]

14.

Years later, at the behest of the astrophysicists, we turned our attention back to the heavens. None of us had considered that these sorts of impacts often come in waves spewed from the Kuiper belt. Surely one calamity is enough for a civilization to endure. The specter of another impact loomed large. Most people did not have much faith that we would even be able to identify the potential threats anyway. After all, our track record was none too good.

---

[26] It would be easier if we just lived on Saturn, where it is said to rain diamonds.

The scientists and governments promised that success was all but assured if we just focused our resources and made a concerted effort. Most countered: If it was so easy, why had we failed to do so in the past? The official answer: The threat was never taken "seriously."

There were those vociferously opposed to renewed sky surveys, afraid of what we would find. If destruction was coming, why spoil our peace of mind? Others were afraid that we would find nothing and still be destroyed. Isn't a false sense of security worse than none at all? Most reasonable people dismissed these notions as pure poppycock.[27]

Though the cross-examination and rebuttals continued apace for months, the great asteroid survey began in surreptitious earnest. At that time, the ground-based telescopes were still incapacitated by the dust swirling through the upper atmosphere.[28] The existing orbital observatories worked in tandem with a motley array of former spy satellites and earth-observation platforms to create a composite search grid scouring the solar system.

The months passed and the catalog of near-earth objects grew. We waited with bated breath, but none of them seemed to pose much of a threat. Each rock slotted into the "miss" category bolstered our confidence and increased our sense of security. The all clear was soon sounded. Normalcy (albeit post-Impact normalcy) was once again on the rise.

---

[27] Though I believe that many secretly wondered if the skeptics were really that far off.

[28] One pleasant, if unanticipated side effect, was that the stars twinkled with newfound vigor like beautiful, distant strobe lights.

That was when they first detected the Swarm.

15.

Hubris. It must be inescapable. Humanity's one universally magnificent character flaw. I've been doing a lot of reading in the months leading up to this project. While hubris has not been the primary focus of my research, it has infused every page I've read. Whether the heroes of classic literature or the scientists of the modern journals, it is our nature to always assume we are in control. To always assume that we know best. And yet, the countervailing forces of fate always seem to intervene.

My father once told me the tale of the greatest boxer in history. He would take on all-comers, bashing their faces to a bloody pulp, leaving nothing but their concussed brains rattling around in their skulls. When he was born, his mother consulted a local soothsayer who prophesied his unbeatable streak. Like the Witch King of Angmar, he would fall to no man.[29]

At the height of his career, in the prime of his age, he had money, fame, and power. He lived without fear of defeat. For most, it was an honor just to be knocked unconscious by his gigantic fists.

This boxer was famous for his fastidiousness. He was always well-dressed, articulate, and compassionate. He only allowed himself one vice: smoking a pipe. Paradoxically,

---

[29] Most clever people surmised he would be humbled by a woman (or some sort of boxing kangaroo).

though the outcome of each fight was essentially predetermined, his nerves always swelled the night before. Thus, he would take his pipe in hand and calmly puff his cares away. On the night before what would have been his biggest bout yet, he was particularly agitated. His pipe never left his hand. Eventually, exhaustion overcomes us all. He fell asleep, his still-smoldering pipe fell from his hand, and flames quickly engulfed the room. The coroners said he was still sleeping as he burned to death. Even reduced to ashes, he remained undefeated.

I never liked boxing anyway. It is a brutal, barbaric sport. Like the boxer, we thought the worst had come and we had conquered it. We were foolish enough to proclaim our renewed supremacy despite being utterly humbled only a few years before.

16.

The first reports of the Swarm were enough to bring even the most optimistic to tears. There seemed to be a large cluster of trans-Neptunian objects bearing down on Earth. The trajectory of the mass (initial observations were unable to discern more than the vague outline of the grouping) indicated a potential collision in four months' time. How many objects constituted the group, how many of them were in the impact window, and their individual masses and compositions were all unknown.

At the first mention of a new round of impacts, alarm reverberated throughout the populace. The more dramatic claimed the end was nigh (for a second time). The pragmatists weren't worried since we had already survived one salvo. At least we had a longer lead-time. Soon the panic transmuted itself into preparedness. Communities began stockpiling food and resource stores to weather the initial disruptions and supplement any ongoing shortages. On the whole, people worked together, digging in for the trials to come.

The advance warning gave scientists time to refine their calculations. What had initially been an amorphous mass was slowly brought into resolution. There were thirty-three objects in all, ranging in size from a few tens of meters to a few hundred. Thankfully, all were smaller than the initial meteor. At most, they would level a mid-sized city.

We even calculated reasonably precise impact zones. Any in those regions were evacuated ahead of time and settled in the predetermined "safe enclaves." Some people refused to go and, like those who refused to leave Mt. St. Helens, found their final resting places buried under hot ash.

I have always thought the word "swarm" was something of a misnomer. Say "swarm" and I picture a tightly packed group of objects with both organization and intent. "The Swarm" was more like a celestial conga line stretched over thousands of kilometers.[30] As its parts came into contact with the earth, our rotation would ensure everyone between the 44th parallel north and 10th parallel south had a chance to

---

[30] Some hypothesized, that like Shoemaker-Levy before it, the Swarm had begun its life as a larger asteroid and had been torn asunder by the massive tidal forces of Jupiter. This seems unlikely, however. If the object got close enough to be shattered, the gravitational pull would have been strong enough to attract the shards to a gaseous demise. There is a reason, after all, that Jupiter has been likened to the solar system's vacuum cleaner.

score a direct hit. I've heard that pictures of the aftermath reveal a Morse Code-like scar. But I'm not aware of anyone who has taken the time to decode its communique.

17.

I've heard it said that somewhere in the depths of the Amazonian jungle, there exists a tribe as yet unspoilt by modern society. And there, the local shaman concocts the same cures and potions that have been handed down for millennia. Poultice after poultice, his people are healed of the usual maladies.

Western pharmacology has long coveted these miracle jungle cures. In fact, several of these unique plants have been exploited over the years. Your cholesterol medicine? It comes from a canopy-growing epiphyte. Virility pills? These too have their genesis in the ever-reproducing jungle. And so, we've slowly worked our way in from the fringes. Environmentalists used to bemoan the destruction of the rainforest, wondering what medical marvels were lost in the process. All of this without recognizing the wealth that still existed.

When news of the second wave of impending impacts broke, many anthropologists were concerned. They argued that we owed it to the Amazonians to warn them of the danger and spirit them away to the safe zones. While the ethics of this course of action were heavily debated, the plight of the "noble savage" always plays well on the heartstrings of the industrialized citizenry. Soon there were small gatherings of protesters outside the Brazilian and Peruvian embassies. "Save the innocents" was their marshalling cry. They gathered donations for a few weeks and mounted a "rescue" operation. Though the group was not government-sanctioned, there was no government opposing it either. Governments had bigger problems on their minds.

The group's preparations were met with a great media hubbub. Film crews gathered as the would-be rescuers marched into the jungle. The popularity of the mission was chalked up to "Swarm fatigue"—people were glad to see a human-interest story dominate the news cycle for once. As many hastily planned endeavors go, the rescue mission faltered. Soon a new story dominated the airwaves—it was time to rescue the rescuers. Two of the initial six disappeared immediately, most likely eaten by jaguars or overcome by some unexpectedly poisonous amphibian. The remaining four took to their radios to plea for assistance. Recordings of their last transmissions were replayed over and over for the global audience. Their mournful, sobbing wails were mesmerizingly cathartic. They vocalized what we, the impact-desensitized, could not. A small team of Ecuadorian paramilitary operatives attempted a last-ditch rescue, but to no avail. The jungle overgrowth stood in monotonous silence.

What seemed to be lost in this whole escapade was the nature of the natives. Dr. Xavier Hopper, one of the only dissenting anthropologists at the time, argued that a rescue was reckless. The "civilized" always went into these situations thinking they had something to teach, ever the heroes. We failed to realize that magic and the supernatural are part of these tribes' daily existence. As such, it's likely that they would understand great fireballs in the sky far better than we, equipped with empirical rationalism, ever could.

18.

Our misunderstanding of these tribes reminds me of how the ancient Greeks stood in awe of the Mycenaeans. In their minds, the Mycenaeans were a race of giant cyclopes, capable of hefting giant stones and smashing men with a single blow. Modern society has similarly stood in awe of the resilience of the Pyramids of Giza and the Roman Aqueducts.[31] How could these technological simpletons build something so enduring? We so easily forget that there has always been someone who has come before us. Knowledge, unlike genetic heritage, does not flow down through the generations.

This is all to preface the most recent of civilization's contributions to monumental construction. Initially, when word spread of the impending impact, the Azerbaijani government sprang into action. At that point, no one knew exactly where the rock would hit, but scientific consensus was that it would be somewhere around the equatorial margins. Many of those in the tropics were already predisposed to fatalistic responses, so they resigned themselves to whatever might come. There was no point in preparing for the future if they would be instantaneously obliterated anyway. Extra-tropical populations decided to give survival a fighting chance and laid in their provisions for the trials ahead. Azerbaijan decided it would make its stand on the Khazar Islands and opened a refugee center there.

---

[31] It is true that acid rain and human mischievousness have taken their toll on some of these landmarks—Napoleon's use of the Sphinx for target practice mirrors the North African Alliance's sniper mounts on the pyramid walls—but, for the most part, they remain imposing.

When the islands were first constructed in early 21st century, they were a haven for the super-rich.[32] For nearly a hundred years, the quirks of geography insulated an aristocratic micro-culture in middle-Asia. Flats and fortunes were handed down from generation to generation. When the rare residence came onto the market thanks to dead-end family-lines, it was put to auction, soliciting great bidding wars.[33] The claimants would begin new dynasties. No one paid much attention to the phenomenon. With the immense expanse of the Caspian to the East and sandwiched between the Greater and Lesser Caucasus, the islands and the abutting lowlands provided welcoming shelter. Political boundaries only intensified the isolationism that geography had kick-started.[34]

The opulent society's central idol was the Azerbaijan Tower—the tallest building ever constructed—a stocky yet soaring edifice. Soon after its construction, humanity reached its vertical limit and abandoned its attempts to meld heaven and earth.[35] Thus, the tower stood as a tangible reminder of

---

[32] The islands even entered the popular imagination as shorthand for ostentatious wealth. "Retire to Khazar" became an aspirational slogan.

[33] In fact, the highest price ever recorded for a domicile (on a per-square-meter-basis) came from one of these auctions in the Khazar Islands—$2.8 billion for a 220 square-meter condo in the great tower.

[34] The unfriendly New Russian Empire along the coast to the north was complemented by the rough-around-the-edges Free Persia to the south. The border guards were fierce and few dared the land approach from either direction.

[35] The Megalith in Tokyo was, for a brief moment, a taller structure. Media reports of its opening day depicted hordes of people in the street celebrating their great achievement. Three short months later, countless people were lost when the structure buckled and collapsed under its own weight. Conservative estimates put the loss of life at 14,000. After that, the stigma

the limits of our architectural defiance. It was revered all the more because of that fact. And so, when the government requisitioned the tower and surrounding buildings as a refugee center, the aristocrats were predictably upset. However, sensing that public sentiment could quickly turn on them, a few of that society's leading socialites began sloganeering, "There is room for all in God's Tower." The move was hailed as a model of utopian idealism and was one of the few bright points in the days leading up to the Impact.

Less is known about what happened next. It is hard to sort through the rumors of food shortages and anoxic events. What is known is that the Volga rerouted itself to join the Don and empty into the Sea of Azov. With the Caspian's inflow severely reduced, the Khazars soon ceased to be islands.[36] Newly exposed sands and Impact particulates whipped themselves into storms that sandblasted the tower's once gleaming facade. The glass became pitted and opaque, some of it even fracturing and falling away. Each pane of glass that fell was a

---

against hyper-skyscrapers was too much for structural engineers to overcome. We contented ourselves with hundred-story and smaller buildings, having concluded that such heights were enough.

[36] It is predicted that the Caspian's waterline will stabilize at 30 meters lower than its historic average. Many of the port cities have already been left high and dry. The region had lived through the evaporation of the Aral Sea a century and a half before and the legends of its terrible consequences persisted as a warning. Ghost towns. Faltering crops. Toxic dust storms. With a cultural memory like that, no one wanted to test the limits of the far larger Caspian basin.

blow to the Azerbaijani psyche. The losses mounted and residents began to flee toward the rumors of more stable and accommodating climates in continental Europe.[37]

Aside from a few squatters barely eking out an existence, all that is left of the once mighty refuge is the tower's hulking carcass of steel and shattered glass. Generations into the future, what will people think when they come across the spire glistening kilometers from the Caspian shoreline? A new Mycenae, I'd imagine—complete with giants able to accomplish what should have been impossible.

19.

Science had brought us so many great advances in the years leading up to the Impact. But when it spectacularly failed us by first allowing the scourge of climate change and then, the asteroid, large portions of the population began questioning its worth. These were of the same caste of society who had challenged heliocentrism and spurned vaccination. It is tempting to label them luddites, but it would be incorrect since they embraced other technological innovations like electricity and the automobile. No, this was a group of people whose interactions with science had to conform to their predetermined conception of the world. As uninformed mobs tend to do, they turned to arson as the great adjudicator. Some

---

[37] However sad this end might be, it seems poetic for a people who eradicated the Caspian tiger. Just as human pressures pushed that population to extinction, Mother Nature nudged humanity in the same direction.

of the world's most prominent laboratories were lost as a result. CERN, Brookhaven, Chongqing National, and more all turned to ash.

When the first reporters arrived at the Franco-Helvetian border to assess the destruction at CERN, they found a smoldering scar where a monument to science once stood. Dr. Jacob Lebowitz, director of the facility at the time, was found wandering through the wreckage, tears streaming down his soot-smeared face. The footage was haunting. He looked as if he were stumbling through a graveyard, unable to find the family stone. At several points, he stooped to scoop up the ashes into a small jar. Thenceforth, it sat on his office shelf, labeled: The Strata of Destruction.

One of the CERN researchers who made her way to Cascadia in the aftermath said she thought Dr. Lebowitz kept it as a reminder of the sacrifices of science. I prefer to think that he just hadn't found the right place to scatter the ashes yet.

When the torch-wielding groups ran out of particle physics labs to destroy, they attempted storming the CDC and other bio-containment facilities. Thankfully, these were far better equipped to deal with onslaughts, having been built to withstand hurricanes and nuclear impacts. The waves broke upon the biolabs' battlements. Heaven knows what terrors would have been unleashed on the world if the mobs had successfully penetrated the quarantines. Smallpox, ancient mega-viruses collected from the thawing tundra, some more insidious plague? For the time being, we don't have to worry. Once the groups were rebuffed, they lost their missionary zeal and science again held sway with the masses.

20.

In the aftermath of the second round of impacts, countless people came out of the woodwork offering their new manifestos for our earthly lives. Hindsight prophesiers and would-be cultists attracted sizable followings in the larger cities. The Coviden Collecture was one of the most prominent. Led by former biotech CEO, Graham Coviden, the Collecture espoused a return to our ancestral, subsistence-living roots. Soon the river valleys surrounding Pittsburgh were overrun with desperate idealists, sowing their crops, and banking their harvest in Coviden's central warehouses so foodstuffs could be doled out equitably. The experiment didn't last the year. A grain elevator in the Strip District exploded, leveling a full city block, including the neighboring Collecture storage building. The year's stockpile was reduced to smoldering rubble in a matter of moments, and the starving contributors relearned the harsh lessons of their collectivist forbearers: utopian visions only last as long as they keep people well fed. Another generation now knows that the only thing that follows the plow is furrows.[38] Starvation is reportedly a painful way to go.

---

[38] Compared to the nouveau-homesteaders on the abandoned prairies of North America, however, the Covidens had it easy. The Homestead Act of 2123 reopened vast swaths of land that had been abandoned by its owners after the successive calamities of the Great Drying and the Impact. In an unprecedented move, all standing landowners in these zones had their titles revoked. If they wanted their land back, they were welcome to take part in the various races held to stake claims to the new 500-acre parcels that had been established.

Many in this new wave of homesteaders had grossly underestimated the hardships they were about to endure. With the aquifers long-since pumped dry on the Great Plains, they had to rely solely on surface water and

When land-based subsistence living flamed out, attentions shifted to the ocean as the new frontier. The mariner's life promised freedom from the oppression of terra firma. This was, of course, too good to be true, but for a time, the idea proved alluring to the woebegone Covidens and backwater bureaucrats flooding international shipping lanes in search of a brighter future. At least as opposed to starvation, the mariner has the option of a relatively quick and peaceful drowning.

21.

Certain corners of the industry thrived with the influx of land-lubbers. Perhaps owing to the influence of Melville on the American subconscious, whaling once again came into fashion.[39] The ever-expanding oceans seemed to contain more

---

rain catchment. Deprived of rain and homegrown food sources, a good number turned to the only options in relative abundance, prairie dogs and rattlesnakes. When those populations crashed, so did the human ones depending on them.

   While the overall population declined, not every community withered and died. Some people are even reported to have created flourishing little oases just like Rev. Devonshire Lewis had hoped to do in the Great Basin. Anything is possible.

[39] By the mid-21st century, whaling had all but been abolished for the sake of preserving the population. Even longtime holdouts like the Norwegians and the Japanese eventually relented under sustained pressure and sanctions from the global community. The Icelanders were the lone exception, but given the harsh conditions they had to endure in the North Atlantic (and the low number of whales they took each year), they were granted an exemption. The population rebounded to new heights within four decades, but there was no clamor to renew the hunts—people had grown accustomed to viewing whales as benevolent kings of the sea, not a resource to be harvested.

whales each year. The blooms of plankton enabled by global warming, combined with the ocean fertilizing that accompanied the Impacts, created the perfect conditions for a population explosion. Whale sightings became a common occurrence. Protected breeding grounds became choked with baleen and blowholes. In these circumstances, the taboo on whaling was easily overcome. Everyone, it seemed, was an Ahab at heart.

Several whaling hubs sprang up along the Pacific coastline. Sitka was home base for those patrolling the great Alaskan arc, Hoquiam the Cascadian coast, San Francisco handled California and the Baja lagoons. There was a gap in the mid latitudes, but Valparaiso took charge of the majority of the South American coast, while Deception Island was resurrected as the peaceful anchorage for Tierra del Fuego and the Antarctic Peninsula.[40] Each of these bases not only provided the basic foodstuffs, munitions, and ample portside relaxation, but also housed massive whale processing facilities. No part of the felled creatures went to waste. Massive cauldrons bubbled away to process the blubber and oil. The meat was salt-cured or frozen and became a commonplace staple among the coastal set.

Most people steered clear of the whaling districts because of the intense smells emanating therewithin. Putrid may be a kind word to describe them. The unique geography of Deception Island, in particular, allowed the odor to collect

---

[40] To be sure, whaling operations are reputed to have been established along other coastlines—notably in the Russian High Arctic and South Africa, but at the risk of reading like a catalogue of points of whaling interest, I have chosen not to include them. It suffices to say that whaling had returned in as widespread a fashion as was possible for post-Impacts society.

in the old volcano's caldera. That said, photos show many sailors enjoying soaks in the beachside hot springs behind the Deception processing plant. It goes to show that people will put up with a great deal just to feel a little warmth.

This period of cetacean fecundity was not meant to last. As happens with most unmanaged bouts of resource harvesting, the take was unsustainable and the population plummeted. Some mariners still cling doggedly to the harpoon as their "livelihood," but they are few and far between. They stop in port with tales of fleeting sightings and white whales, but rarely do they have anything to show for their voyages. Without the critical mass to sustain the industry, whaling bases closed, though the stench remains, ready to concentrate again when the next great whaling renaissance occurs.

22.

Wind. That crudest of earthly elements. Invisible and all-moving. Humanity's great tormentor.[41] Were it not for wind, the oceans would only gently slosh around, governed by tidal forces. Wind, however, whips waters into a frenzy, birthing seething troughs and crests that obliterate one another. And

---

[41] Though life owes a debt to wind, it is the natural element whose beneficial effects are least immediately apparent. There are stories of countless pioneers on the Great Plains going crazy from a combination of the vast expanses and the omnipresent wind. Whether the same is true on the Siberian steppe or the barren wastes of Iceland (reputedly one of the windiest places on earth), I am uncertain. Those landscapes have more than wind trying to obliterate settlers.

it is the mariner's plight to chart daily courses through this maelstrom.

The post-Impacts shipping world, denuded of satellite-based tracking, saw a renaissance of time-tested navigation methods. Nautical museums were looted of their sextants and astrolabes. The historical artifacts, still in perfect working order due to their simplicity, allowed the ragged remnants of international trade to continue apace. Sailors became astronomers once again, able to name any constellation in the night sky. With the resiliency of astronomical navigation, it is hard to imagine why anyone completely abandoned it in the first place.

The long-dormant knowledge of ocean currents and wind patterns also percolated back up from its ancestral hiding places. These features were of little concern before the Impacts, aside from their efficiency-boosting (or efficiency-hindering) propensities. Bunker oil was plentiful in those days—burning more only cost marginally extra, so people had stopped paying attention to nature's carbon-free propellants. Much of the world's energy infrastructure was fractured when the meteor hit. With the resulting fuel shortages, some shipping companies resorted to improvised sailing vessels.[42] Ships motored only when absolutely necessary.

---

[42] It should be clarified that the fuel shortages were not entirely the result of damaged pipelines. Some previously successful oil fields lost production capacity and new fields sprang up in unexpected places. If you think of the earth's crust like a giant sponge, the force of the Impact was such that the sponge was wrung out. The reservoirs of liquids—water included—flowed from newly constricted areas to more amenable voids. This was how Texas and Oklahoma lost their centrality in the American energy markets. The oil

As the shipping industry regressed technologically, a whole new generation of cartographers came into existence. Instead of Geophysical Information Systems and satellite-enabled mapping, tried and true surveyors' tools came to the fore. Pen and paper were the medium of choice.

All ships began to employ navigation officers whose job it was to chart courses the old-fashioned way. Maps were slid under glass tops and wax pencils smeared lines from port to port. The Navigation Officer held the power to send the ship through the roughest of seas or calmest of waters. On the off chance a navigational error crept in, he apologized profusely and donated that day's pay to the rest of the crew. When paychecks are on the line, it is amazing how accurate we can be. Because of this, some have claimed that, even with its technological disadvantages, modern shipping functions with fewer delays than its pre-Impacts predecessors.

Any navigator will tell you that there is only one constant at sea, the randomness of wind. Those who can chart a steady course through the chaos are viewed as a class apart. Now when asked what they want to be when they grow up, children don't fall back on the once standard tropes of firefighter or astronaut—instead, they longingly say "navigator."

23.

Just as a great wave of disillusionment brought scores of people to the sea, the natural sloshing of human hopes brought

---

that had pooled in those basins shifted north and east toward Arkansas, Louisiana, and Tennessee. The New Floridians were especially happy, since one of the biggest of the new pools appeared beneath their plot in the Ozarks.

them back to shore when the sea served up disappointment. Some tried to avoid the sad truth for as long as possible—not everyone was made for ship life. They bounced around between crew assignments over the span of months or years, but always eventually returned to solid ground. Other, wiser, people gave up more quickly or never set foot on a ship at all.

But the ocean still holds a powerful allure. It is the source of some of our most enduring myths. Its endless expanse is the release-valve for humanity's landlocked imagination, promising freedom and opportunity. In the post-Impacts world, I have heard countless tales of people taking to the sea in search of escape—a chance to answer to no one. The most notable in our corner of the ocean is the famed pirate of the Pacific Northwest—known by the epithet of "Lord Eagle." Like all good enigmas, the origin of Lord Eagle is shrouded in mystery. His penchant for wearing a face-obscuring Nuxalk eagle mask led to all sorts of rumors regarding his origin. Some say he was a submariner from Bremerton, others, the last warrior from Bella Coola. More probably, he was a fisherman turned privateer. What made Lord Eagle unique were his methods. Where most post-Impacts piracy was perpetrated by groups of loosely affiliated plunderers, Lord Eagle always worked alone. Moreover, he defended his territory fiercely. After the first few challengers were found lashed to totem poles, adrift at sea, spouting terrified tales of the Lord Eagle, other pirates began giving his territory a wide berth.

In his own way, Lord Eagle was defending an important portion of the Cascadian coast from large-scale pirate incursions. He became a swashbuckling hero who captured our imaginations. Books and comic strips were written detailing his exploits, so desperate were we for a positive story. As you might expect, these tended toward oversimplification, glorifying the good while eliding the unsavory bits. Few, if any, saw Lord Eagle's actions for what they were—a protection racket. He funded his defensive campaign from fees levied on our merchant vessels.[43]

Eventually, like all heroes, Lord Eagle sailed off into the sunset, never to be heard from again. The new golden age of piracy waned as the remnant governments organized more effective patrols. Some claim he is still out there, on the vast expanse of ocean, searching for his next coastline to assist. Hope springs eternal.

24.

It's all well and good to record the unfiltered consequences of the Impacts—the ecological, the political, the societal, the personal. But for this account to be of any use to anyone, I should pay more attention to the lessons of history: to understand where you are and where you're going, you need to know where you've been. So then, on to the Cascadian question.

Though some will point to the Impacts as what made Cascadia possible, the nation's origins can be traced almost a decade prior. As the 21st century came to a close, the world was poised on the knife-edge of destruction. When China fulfilled its promise and became the leading power in the world, Western confidence was shaken. This led to a great deal of

---

[43] Some have argued that Lord Eagle's fees were entirely reasonable—so reasonable, in fact, that it is conceivable he was a hope-generating propagandic creation of the maternalist Cascadian government. There is no proof of this however.

soul searching and an equal amount of soul crushing. The European Union, which had always had an inferiority complex, consumed itself from the inside out and dissolved. Instead of forming smaller regional leagues, as many surmised would be the case, or worse, paving way for a new bloom of ultra-nationalism, the entire area reverted to something harkening back to its feudal past. Local affiliations soon subsumed the countries that had once housed them. The Basques, the Occitans, the clans of Scotland. Europe's increasingly impenetrable isolationism earned it the nickname of the "Locked Continent." In other, less euphemistic quarters, it was called the "Lost Continent."

With the collapse of the European order (and its attendant markets), China plugged the gap with its own populace. Where it had before been manufacturing goods to send to the West, most of those goods were now sold to the consumers it had been so carefully hoarding and cultivating. This was a shock to the Americans. They had thus far avoided the worst of the consequences that came with the European dissolution by keeping their citizens relatively fat and happy. But when their pipeline of consumables was suddenly constricted, the lack of native industrial production capacity was felt most acutely.

On top of the economic chaos, the symptoms of global warming were beginning to overwhelm our capability to deal with them. Some countries responded by creating focal regions and investing in a more "sustainable" path. Some regions responded instead by creating new countries.

This is how Cascadia came to be. Displeased with the intractable nature of the Canadian and U.S. governments, British Columbia, Washington, Oregon, Northern California,

Idaho, Western Montana and Alberta simply declared their independence and seceded. Inspired by their European contemporaries, the Cascadian secessionists argued that their survival was threatened under the status quo—local sovereignty was the only viable remedy.

You can imagine the repercussions of such an assertion. Secession had not been attempted since the Civil War or the Quebecois Uprising of 2083, both of which had come with disastrous consequences.[44] The world waited with bated breath. Would North America rend itself apart? The media did its Pavlovian best, salivating at every hint of potential conflict. Soon, pundits assured us, neighbor would take up arms against neighbor and lives would be destroyed.

Just as the situation looked as if it would come to a violent head—American and Canadian troops ringed the border—the meteor was discovered. Suddenly, border disputes seemed rather petty in comparison.[45] Those stationed

---

[44] Certainly, in terms of lives lost, the American Civil War was a far greater disaster than the Quebecois Uprising. However, where the former had the greater body count, the latter resulted in an unparalleled brain-drain. So many francophones, feeling unwanted in Canada chose to emigrate to the linguistic motherland. Some only went as far as Saint Pierre and Miquelon (its population tripled almost overnight), but most returned to continental France. Quebec witnessed a precipitous population decline of nearly 75% in the five years following the Uprising.

[45] While the meteor was an obvious factor in Cascadia's secessionary success, political scientists have wondered whether there might be more to the story—namely nuclear missile silos. While the new nation had little in the way of a standing army, it did wield the vestigial military might of its forbearers: nuclear subs in Bremerton, ICBMs near Great Falls. Given the pacifist leanings of Cascadia's founders, the use of these weapons were never once threatened. That didn't stop those in the U.S. and Canada from imagining the horrific outcomes should the arsenal be unleashed.

on the frontlines rushed home to be with their families and the matter was settled. Cascadia joined the ranks of the league of nations.

In its infancy, the newly birthed country bore many of the hallmarks of the ecotopia envisioned by some of the movement's founding ideologues in the 1970s.[46] Localism in food production and governance. Harmonious returns to ruralism attuned to the local ecology. A rejection of needless technology. Flourishing harbors of creativity.

As happens with all idealized systems put into practice, however, the everyday grievances of humanity begin to take their toll. Social efficiencies decay and settle into a less-than-ideal equilibrium. Whether the Bolsheviks, the Americans, or the Romans, no social order has proved immune to eventual

---

[46] It should be noted, however, that the movement summarily rejected the "Doug" flag designed by Alexander Baretich. Instead, they settled upon a design unlike any other flag in the world—brown polka dots on a magenta t-shirt with a white line snaking its way through. Instead of trying to pick a design imbued with meaning, they picked one specifically because it was meaning-devoid. Glenora Youngwood, the nation's first elected leader described it as follows: "Everyone knows that the sea and sky are blue. Look around and you cannot help but see a tree. This landscape is a living emblem and coat of arms. Our flag represents a harsh break from past ways of being and that is all."

Of course, communication scholars took it upon themselves to analyze the implicit meanings in the imagery and found a wealth of available interpretations. One feminist scholar hailed it as a brave leap forward: the dots representing individuality, the white line, peaceful adaptability, and the magenta background an outright abandonment of the male-dominated forms of government that had come before. Another saw a representation of the transgressions of the impure against the pure and the impossible task of separating the two. Most people simply saw it as avant-garde and took to wearing its soft organic bamboo material over their torsos wherever they went.

atrophy. Sure, it takes varying lengths of time, and the equilibria reached are of varying degrees of satisfactoriness, but all trend in the same direction. Cascadia has been no different.

The Impact made our weaknesses glaringly apparent. The scale of the disaster was beyond what local governments could handle. What's more, the carefully cultivated luddism exemplified by so much of the population depended, in large part, on the very technologies they eschewed. When these faltered because of the electromagnetic disturbances accompanying the Impact, communities were forced to revert to their more primitive tendencies. It is easy to embrace nature and live "off-grid" when you've got a state-of-the-art city as a backstop. Broke your hand? Run to the outpatient clinic. Crops failed? Run to the grocery store. Suffer a massive EMP? There's nowhere to run. What had seemed a utopia was revealed to be small bands of woefully prepared dreamers without a clue about the basic arts of survival. Turns out, we were no less tribal than European city-statists.

The Montanan prefecture calved away and united with Alberta, preferring a more isolated form of independence. Idaho, not wanting to be left out, charted its own course as well, fragmenting into eighteen "townships" with lots of barren land in-between. While the remaining elements of Cascadia stuck together, some communities fared better than others. These were the ones that had managed to attract the craftspeople who kept civilization's ancestral knowledge alive. Huddled around the Puget Sound, the green cities of Cascadia became the new hub of North American industry and were held up as a safe haven for all.

25

As the U.S. port situated across the bay from the southern border of Cascadia, San Francisco assumed a new role. It had always been a melting pot and crossroads. But now, it was primarily a gateway for U.S. emigrants. The Golden Gate Bridge straddled the water, and with it, the gulf between the American Dream and its heir-apparent. This was a blow to the American consciousness. People had become so used to the clamor of those wanting to be let in that when the flows reversed, they sat in denial.[47]

The saying goes that post-Impacts San Francisco was much like gold rush-era San Francisco. It had completely lost its air of snobbish refinement. In its place, an unfettered eclecticism arose. Some would argue that San Francisco had always been a harbor of bohemian instinct, but starting in the early 21st century, that spirit was subsumed by technocrats and cyborgian fashion. Even the plentiful homeless were addicted to technology.[48] The asteroid was a great technological equalizer. Its EMP eviscerated magnetic storage and its physical force severed many of the important links in the great web

---

[47] There are, of course, no official census numbers to confirm or deny this trend. Anecdotal evidence of people leaving the U.S. abounds, but bearing in mind that these stories circulate primarily in Cascadia, it does cast doubt on their veracity. The relationship between mother country and secessionist is always a tenuous one, prone to jealousy and ridicule.

[48] In fact, where previous growth-spurts in the homeless population were attributed to the excesses of drink and drugs, many of the new generation were addicts of a different nature—tech addicts used to the constant connection supplied by the Bay Area's free wifi. When the internet's architecture imploded in the months after the Impact, these addicts went into withdrawal, ever on the lookout for their next fix.

of wires encircling the planet—undersea landslides and tectonic fracturing being the two main culprits. With survival being the main concern, restoration of the global network was not deemed a priority. As such, those who had previously amassed their influence because of technological dominance fell back to earth to take their places among the nameless masses.

Surprisingly, a few of these asocial-types went on to forge viable second careers. Frank Loveless became a restaurateur and Giovanni Buscemi was reborn as the nouveau-beat author "John Smith." Like Kerouac before him, John Smith became the voice for an entire generation of disaffected youth. His first and most widely read novel, *San Andreas*, was lauded as a guidebook for living a fulfilling life in post-Impacts San Francisco. While I've never been a big believer in the philosophical underpinnings of the nouveau-beat movement, Smith's descriptions of San Francisco were spot-on:

> *The fog rolled in over the dying city. San Francisco seemed to be waiting hopefully for this angel of mercy to swoop in and extinguish the evening with a suffocator's flair.*
>
> *I was in a surly mood. It seemed there was no silence in downtown's concrete canyons. The cables trenched into the street continuously groaned as they made their Sisyphean circuit. The old men in Chinatown staggered along, wailing at random intervals. Screeching, enormous flocks of wild parrots deafened those unfortunate enough to get within earshot.*[49]

---

[49] The flocks were originally composed of orphaned pets, released into the wild when their masters had grown tired of them. Lucky for the birds, the

Maybe my displeasure stemmed from my nausea. The air was thick with the cologne of businessmen and the gaudy perfume of low-rent hookers. To this cocktail, the sobering scents of diesel exhaust, old beer, and decomposing trash were added to create the city's signature odor. I trudged uphill through the stifling smells and made my way to Grace Cathedral. There, I found my solace. My nausea dissipated and peace returned.

I skirted the edge of the labyrinth in favor of the spartan pleasures of the pew. Suspended from the ceiling, slender ribbons of blue and green hung down, catching the light from the spotlights and stained-glass windows high above. It looked like the rays of heaven. I lost myself in contemplation. Someone was practicing organ in the auxiliary chapel.

The story of how John Smith's books were published is of particular note. With mass-market electronic publishing a shambles, everyone feared that our literary heritage was lost forever. Certainly, a goodly number of libraries had abandoned physical collections entirely, re-branding themselves as gathering spaces and "information hubs." When the electronic cataclysm hit, these buildings lost their purpose. The

---

sea-moderated climate and abundant city food supplies allowed them to prosper all year long. Once a novelty, by 2025, these birds had multiplied to the point where they outcompeted and displaced the pigeons. When one enterprising audiologist recorded their collective cacophony at 113 decibels, the birds were declared a public nuisance and menace to the eardrums of all city dwellers. By that point, it was too late—there was no reversing the problem. Telegraph Hill was abandoned. The flock could be culled, but not eradicated. To this day, San Franciscans carry foam ear plugs with them whenever they venture outside.

few outposts that remained owed their existence to the intransigence of the Librarians and Archivists for Physical Publishing and Storage (LAPPS). Though their membership was low, they had the financial resources of a reclusive billionaire supporting their mission.[50] And so, throughout the 21st century, LAPPS began purchasing and preserving the collections of closing libraries. They were branded anachronists and worse but pursued their mission with unflappable grace. Along with physical collections, LAPPS also prioritized the preservation of printing presses as print shops went out of business around the world. These century-old machines were restored and strategically situated across the country. The occasional literary purist would run a hundred copies of a novel for friends and family, but the presses were otherwise underutilized.

After the Impacts, however, LAPPS was hailed as one of the saviors of civilization. Its presses began to hum nearly continuously. John Smith availed himself of the sole Californian press—Golden Gate Textery in San Francisco, making an optimistic print run of 1,000 copies. *San Andreas* was available in every corner of the city and throughout the Bay Area, but beyond that, only traveled elsewhere thanks to the migratory whims of humanity.

The same was true of other local publishing operations. National distribution gave way to localized publishing ecosystems. New ideas would occasionally transcend geography, but

---

[50] In an ironic twist of fate, it has been suggested that this unknown billionaire made his or her fortune as a technologist. Whether or not this is true will never be known, but if it was, it should have been a warning for all of the fervent electronic encyclopedists.

these instances were as rare as the emergence of new species. Take away easy travel and immediate connection and it is amazing how quickly we all diverge. But just as has been recorded on countless islands, certain evolutionary convergences are bound to occur. *San Andreas* bore a striking similarity to *Three Rivers* by Benedict Penn, which in turn shared themes and styles with Jean Boulanger's Quebecois masterpiece *La Manic*.[51] I like to think of it as proof of the universality of good ideas.

26.

Cascadia's unique founding principles attracted a broad array of idealists. Libertarians and anarcho-syndicalists, humanists and eco-zealots—many joined the immigration queues. Only the lucky few made it through due to the strict immigration and screening quotas of their would-be homeland. San Francisco, being the Cascadian limbo, thus became a hotbed for angry activists and passionate proselytizers. No longer was it just the technocrats who held sway. The streets were littered with eco-zealot fliers about the Great Pacific Garbage Patch, showing thousands of Olympic-size swimming pools full of debris for scale. Street-corner preachers described entire islands of trash, trotting out images of football fields for reference. Other infographics were drawn, showing trash

---

[51] Some scholars have suggested that these share enough literary hallmarks that they may have been written by the same author. It was sort of a reverse-Shakespeare paradox—homogeneity of ideas suggesting sole authorship. While Shakespeare was long ago proven to have been three people: Francis Bacon, Christopher Marlowe, and Edward de Vere, no one has yet been able to bring the nouveau-beat trinity together in a single person.

stretching to the sun and diagrams of hikers trekking across the ocean. The illustrations assured us that it would one day be possible to walk to Hawaii.

I must give them credit for their imagination. It's as if these terraformic Pollyannas believe that humanity, despite being laid low, has the ability to birth continents out of empty sea. Alas, since much of our manufacturing base was obliterated, we no longer churn out disposable plastics in ocean-filling quantities. The upper water column of the Pacific contains only the slowly degrading remnants of our former glory, bobbing up and down for eternity.

I've often wondered why no one has paid a similar amount of attention to the garbage floating in other bodies of water. Back before the Impacts, there were countless campaigns to clean the Pacific. Meanwhile, the Sargasso Sea languished. Maybe the singular focus has something to do with our monumental obsessions. Only the biggest is the most relevant. Once eclipsed in size, all others in a category are relegated to the dustbin of memory. Who even remembers the Singer Building skyscraper? Within sixty years, the people of New York held it in such contempt that they razed it. This is how we treat the victorious. Fame for a year, then the onward march to oblivion.

Despite what the trash pamphlets might tell you, the oceanic gyres and the garbage patches they covet are not unique. We are all swept up in the great whirlpools of humanity, waiting to be pulverized and polished into perfect indivisible spheres.

27.

And so, the hopeful migrated toward the northwestern promised land. Whether they made it across the borders or languished in San Francisco printing pamphlets, they all held the same belief in the incorruptible supremacy of the Cascadian ideal—it was humanity's last best hope. Nothing could shake their faith in its virtues or motivations. We had failed before, but finally, we had come up with something lasting—a way of being that would help us band together and prosper. But it hasn't made us any smarter or more clairvoyant.

After all, evidence of previous impacts had long been documented. If we had only seen our planetary pockmarks for the warnings they were. If we had only started our scanning and defense efforts earlier. If satellites zooming out of the solar system hadn't perturbed the orbit of that rock in the Kuiper Belt. It is easy to get caught up in a game of "what ifs," but a game of chance seems a more appropriate metaphor. Stone. Paper. Scissors. Stone beats all. What warnings do we still overlook?

The same forces that had created Lake Manicouagan, the Prescott Crater, and set Tunguska aflame are no longer the thing of scientific scenario. One of humanity's great weaknesses is its perception of time. The past is of little concern to the masses. Events whose cycles exceed generations (and civilizations for that matter) are beyond our comprehension. If our genes only encoded cultural memory in the same way they encode hair color and cancer.

But maybe there is reason for hope. There is a story I once heard about a Russian blessed (or cursed as the case may be) with a perfect memory. Every instant of every day, every fleeting fact, every inconsequential name and date—all of it was locked permanently in his mind. More impressively, this man could recall the information at will. As you might expect, he became something of a curiosity. He went on the lecture circuit, taking questions from all manner of audiences.

Gradually though, the gift became a burden. His thoughts, cacophonous. No longer was he able to disentangle and filter his memories. Every word spoken, every inquiry, triggered an avalanche of thoughts that overwhelmed his senses. Try as he may, he could never forget, never expunge the data from his mental inventory. Eventually, he had a nervous breakdown and was taken away to a secluded spot in the taiga where he was allowed to live out the remainder of his days in silence. There is no record of him after this point. But we can rest assured that he remembered every detail nonetheless.

Now, I've taken up his mantle in an effort to be the memory of civilization. Projects like mine—commissioned by the Victoria Library to write, edit, and curate the official encyclopedia for the People's Republic of Cascadia—will only get us so far. Government oversight and bureaucratic meddling will no doubt make sure I get the "facts" straight. You will probably read how Cascadia triumphed, while the rest of the world faltered.

Denis Diderot, father of the modern encyclopedia, faced the same challenges. When the church took offense, work on his *Encyclopédie* went underground. When the pressure continued, his friends deserted him. Eventually, only he was left to write and assemble the sum of human knowledge. He worked tirelessly, writing and self-printing by candlelight until his eyesight was effectively gone. After twenty years, he triumphantly delivered his last volume to the bookseller. The bookseller, unbeknownst to Diderot, cut out those segments he thought would be most troubling for the church and monarchy. Thankfully, his vision gone, Diderot never got to see his crowning achievement cut to ribbons. Fate is occasionally kind, it seems.[52]

Luckily, I've also been writing this, my own account of life post Impact. It may not be widely read (or read at all for that matter), but it is the truth as I experienced it. Even if I were able to aggregate all of the facts and my words made it through the official review unscathed, I'm not sure that my personal filters are good enough to ensure 100% accuracy. I'm tempted, at times, to alter history, and leave my mark on the record of our days. To add heroes who overcame all challenges that confronted them. Someone who defeated an asteroid. Stories and characters from a world unlike ours. I'm only hoping that when I do, I'll have chosen the articles of least import to the powers that be. Maybe, thinking that astronomy could not possibly be a harbor for the subversive, they'll not be reading too carefully and my elaborations will slip through. You will know them when you read them.

I only hope there are other encyclopedists out there tasked with identical missions. The more there are of us, the more likely we are to succeed. Lord knows the history I've

---

[52] This story may be apocryphal. I was unable to find actual proof or corroboration of the tale. That said, I thought it provided a nice counterpoint to the work I've been doing. Moreover, it alleviated the pressure I had put on myself. There can never be a definitive version of events. We all become editors as we read. Even the most well-researched documents, untouched by official edits, will be parsed and compartmentalized by the reader. The only narratives of events that matter are the ones in our own minds.

written has its discrepancies, intentional and otherwise. If we combined the best fictions from every sanctioned document, we might have a history worth aspiring to.

John G. Bailey
Victoria, Cascadia
May 2146

Part 5: A Coda

5

He was certain that he only needed four parts to complete the novel. His editors informed him that he was mistaken. And so, to spite them, he added five more. Moreover, they said that the voices of the first two narrators were altogether too similar.

"They're the same," he thought, "because I only have one voice."

◼

If he was going to finish his novel this year, he would have to vastly increase his daily output. He remembered his writing professor saying, "238 words per day does not a novel make."

His words were like molasses creeping across the highway.

↑

Three, four, 1,000 words more.

"Maybe I'm already done with this blasted novel," he thought. "My words are written somewhere. Surely, during my lifetime, I've written 10,000 sentences worth reading. All I need to do now is collect and assemble them."

Somehow, that proposition seemed a whole lot more appealing.

6

Somewhere in the middle of it all, he lost steam. Whether it was because he bought a house or because his ideas no longer invigorated him, the end result was the same. He would go days without thinking of a useful or interesting phrase.

He'd once read that writing was a matter of practice—the more one spent time writing, the more the words would naturally flow out. He disagreed. His words were finite in number. The more he wasted on idle banter and discussion in the course of a day, the less he could get onto the page.

"Have I peaked already?" he asked the fox-tailed squirrel, which promptly bolted for the treetops.

Disheartenment is the writer's lot.

ש

He wondered how long he had been writing in earnest. The answer: three months. Ten thousand words in three months. It felt like a lot, but he was sure his efforts would feel like a failure by the year's end.

צ

The weight of the bureacracy became almost too much to bear. Moreover, he couldn't even spell the word correctly.

ק

"Three copies? In three formats? And they are not all the same?" The editor's incredulity filled the room with a palpable fragrance. It smelled like an office urinal left unflushed over the weekend. Acrid but human. "Who do you expect to merge them all together?"

And so, the transcription began. Word by word he would assemble the remainder. He was sure he would never write again after this. After all, these were a lifetime of words. If they ever built a monument to inefficiency, he was sure to be enshrined.

פ

Everyone wanted the one thing he did not have: time. Well, truth be told, he had the same amount of time as everyone else, he just guarded it greedily. An eye for an eye, a tick for a tock. No one would steal his time away.

At least the apportionment of time was somewhat under his control. The other thing that people wanted was talent. It came and went like winds in the doldrums. He spent his creative life marooned with Saint Peter and Saint Paul.

❦

His publishers repeatedly told him that the quickest way through a novel was from beginning to end. He informed them of another option—to skip to the last chapter. He hoped his readers would not do so, for then they would learn he had been plotting against them.

∞

On his bike ride into work, a small insect had flown straight into his eye. Given the mucousy substrate, the bug stuck as if his eye were flypaper. He winked for an entire day, but the mote would not come out. Instead, he imagined it was boring straight through his cornea, back toward his brain.

Once there, he was sure it would rob him of all his inspiration. And left without any more ideas, his novel would be abruptly finished. He must hurry. There was no time to waste any longer.

➤

A new apartment building rose gleaming on the corner in the November sun. They were offering a 200-year lease to the local fraternity. Either they had great faith in the durability of modern construction or were taking advantage of humanity's secret dreams of immortality. Whatever the case, the fraternity rejoiced.

♦

He decided that he would make his name as an impression-ist—his writing a swirl of nostalgia and vagary.

"So you're an impressionist?"

"Yes," he said, pleased that someone was paying atten-tion.

"Can you do the President for me?"

Despite the misunderstanding, he didn't want to let his adoring fan down. Thus, he attempted a muddled interpreta-tion of the President's diction. The result was ham-fisted. His fan looked at him with growing disdain.

Back to the drawing board.

♦

That was the evening he learned about the plight of the Amer-ican chestnut tree.

"But where will the village smithy stand?" he wondered mournfully.

♦

No matter what he was writing, he was always distracted by the next project on the horizon. Thus, from his perspective, it felt like he was writing five novels at once. At 250 words per day, five novels fail to progress. To make matters worse, he couldn't even remember where he had left off.

♦

There comes a time in every novel when the author's initial wave of euphoria dissolves into confusion. This is one of those times. Note the flaccid, struggling language. Note the aimless plotting. "Perhaps it's being done for effect," thinks the reader. "Perhaps, there is some meaning."

"No, these are just my linguistic death throes," says the author.

✦

Counterintuitive as it may seem, his spirits were lifted by the thought of the accent grave. Instead of a guide to pronunciation indicating proper syllabic stress, he imagined a tiny textual coffin. The other, weeping accents in attendance had realized their mortality. Where does an accent go when it dies? The accent grave.

◓

He was disconsolate. Despondent. Depressed. Discomfited. First, they cut a hole in his door, then they cut a hole in his wall.

"Everyone loves windows!"

Not everyone, apparently. The march of progress continued its asymptotic approach toward voyeurism. He would never be alone again.

⬢

Through the door, it sounded like people were making love. He had no love left so he was glad someone was making more. Nonetheless, it was hard to concentrate and he had so much writing left to do. His linguistic flow interrupted, he closed his notebook. The sound stopped but he did not feel like writing anymore.

◕

Clearly, they had no regard for his health. Asbestos dust and paint fumes filled his office. He was given little recourse but to feel light-headed and weak-chested.

✦

He looked out across the social trails weaving their way through the esplanade. All he could think of at that moment were the game trails from his woodland youth. "We are all just beasts bent on survival," he thought.

In what appeared to him to be a futile effort, a woman crisscrossed the lawn, picking up the yellow fallen leaves from the American elms, a gleaming bouquet of autumnal decay. All that is gold inevitably becomes desiccated brown.

In another month, there wouldn't be a leaf left. For now, let us live with our fantasies of evergreen arbors.

♠

Seventy words away from 25,000, he wondered what it would feel like to cross that barrier. Would he know which word it was? Would everything feel different? He wrote this section to find out. Word 25,000 passed without the slightest sense of accomplishment. Ask him again when he hits the halfway mark.

♫

This part of the novel didn't sit well with test audiences and is slated for removal.

♟

He spent the morning laboring to transcribe his dreams. There was something about an elevator in a grand subway terminal. And something about being forbidden from death until a preordained travel itinerary was complete.

It all sounded much less intriguing in the morning sun. Everything had seemed so fully formed while he was asleep, but each waking moment brought further dissolution. At

7:48am, he gripped his pen and let the words flow. By 8:30am, he was mourning the loss of his best ideas yet. Novel #3 was stillborn. And he hadn't even finished Novel #1.

✖

He had written more times than he had exercised this month. And though he preferred calisthenics for their adaptable portability, he had only managed to exercise three times in the past thirty days.

He had just completed a large project. The project was someone else's, but it felt good nonetheless. He hoped that it would provide him with a creative boost. If only he could devote as much energy to his projects as he did to others'. If he did, this would be more than some idle pastime.

✦

He did feel bad about writing on the company dollar. But, technically, they also paid him while he sat on the toilet after his morning coffee, so clearly, they were not overly concerned with how he used their funding.

♣

There was a time when he was filled with winsome aviator dreams. A ferocious bout of turbulence brought him to grips with his mortality and he kept his feet firmly attached to the ground from that moment forward.

♈

The squirrel with the fox's tale reappeared. It seemed to have been shadowing him for the past several weeks.

"Might I simply be seeing similar squirrels?" he wondered. "Certainly, this one creature cannot be following me around town."

Then again, how many squirrels with ruddy auburn tails tipped in white could there possibly be? In his thirty plus years of existence, he had never seen one until a few weeks ago. The rodent came toward him, sniffing about for food, looking tentative. Then, without warning, it bounded toward the dying walnut tree and clambered up to gnaw on the season's last nuts.

☼

He was beginning to lose his handle on what he had written up to this point. It used to be easy enough to keep in his head, but now he had thoughts scattered on scraps of paper throughout his daily life. How would he ever organize them all? He decided to assemble it all into one binder so that he could cut and paste accordingly. The materiality of his work brought him joy. With a little bit of string and glue, he could chart the narrative flow. When he saw it all before him, he cut this section out and moved it to its present location.

🏹

Someday, he would be finished. For now, he would have to console himself with a glass of water and a bag of cheap pretzels. Salt and hydration were his favorite feedback loop.

✄

He wondered if there was a way to game the system. "If I could find a way to add words without it taking so much effort, so much time—that would be fantastic. I could write an accidental novel."

He had forgotten (or failed to realize), however—as per our previous discussions—that all novels are accidental. No

one in their right mind would embark on the endeavor intentionally.

❧

All around him, trees were dying. The walnuts by the chapel
succumbed to thousand cankers disease. The pine-covered
Rockies were ravaged by the mountain pine beetle. Ash trees
of all types were bored by emerald beetles. Someday the blight
would quietly take his beloved apple tree. The sound of chain-
saws and wood-chippers stole the spotlight in the summer
symphony.

❧

He would forget all he had written up to this point, erase everything, and start over. In gothic script, he scrawled the line:

Turn back the pages if you
dare, dear reader, and find
only blank pages staring
back at you. Hopefully,
you memorized your favorite
passage.

∴

He had become so fixated upon his word count recently, that
he had failed to keep track of their quality. His Dickensian at-
titude was unfounded. He was not being paid by the word. In
fact, he was not being paid at all. Each passing page simply
provided another bit of kindling for the fire.

He dreamed that he had gone to the movies instead of work. Time kept slipping by despite his best intentions to earn an honest day's pay.

The alarm disturbed his slumber. He put on his clothes and went to work dejectedly.

Part 6: A Question

Introductory Comments

Annabelle Laetner was tired of life. Not in a suicidal way, mind you, she was merely frustrated by the humdrum stability of her world. There was no turmoil or trauma. No historic happenings or financial failings. No cataclysm, no foreboding. In a word, her life, and the world she lived in, was completely and utterly boring.

However, one day, she awoke to find the world transformed. Adventure, mystery, uncertainty—each day was brimming with the unknown. This is not the type of transformation you and I have ever experienced. Yes, you've no doubt at one point gone to sleep and awoken to find that a bomb has gone off somewhere and changed the tenor of the political conversation. Or, you might learn that someone you care about has been stricken with a horrible disease. However surprising these events might seem, they all have their antecedents—unassuming happenstances in chain reaction, slowly lumbering toward inevitable outcomes. Our human hubris leads us to believe we have a firm grip on cause and effect. But, being the magnificent character flaw that it is, it simultaneously papers-over our panoptic deficiencies. If we are not witness to each step in a causal chain, we are quick to posit ludicrous irrationalisms.

But in Ms. Laetner's case, perhaps the irrational is the best explanation. Rather than being subjected to an exterior event that changed her life, her *life* changed and events around her adapted accordingly. Now normally, the convention in the telling of these sorts of tales is to save the big reveal for the end. The young Kansan never actually went over the rainbow; she was unconscious in her bed the whole time. The young Briton never actually chased after a white rabbit but was instead dozing in the garden. I'm afraid I must depart from convention in this case. You see, Bella (her friends called her this) had fallen into what's now known as a "lucid coma." I believe it is important that you have all the facts at the outset, since they are what make the account that follows all the more remarkable. For while the unconscious mind is capable of great feats in fiction, real-world examples of its fecundity are painfully rare. But before we get to the wondrousness of it all, let me provide some context.

Young Bella was born into a rather common family. Her parents, William and Priscilla Laetner had agreed at their nuptials to produce the two children mandated by the state. In return, the family's needs were provided for—useful education for the children, meaningful employment for the adults. They were given a small parcel of land and a cottage in which to enjoy their days. Such are the perks of the landed gentry. Bella's older brother—by only a year and a half, she would remind you—was a prodigious athlete and an invariable pest, but their relationship was no more fraught than most brothers and sisters. In fact, you might go so far as to call them close.

Annabelle followed a more intellectual path, equally adept with complex equations as she was with the written word. As a result, she lived what most would consider an interior life and during her childhood made each moment part of a grander, overarching fantasy. Her mother always told her she spent too much time daydreaming. Bella believed daydreams were the necessary spice for a needlessly regimented world. Humanity had settled for the predictable, but Bella knew that beyond the fences and under the pavements lay nature's disorder, simmering away and looking for every opportunity to seep out.

And seep out it did. Her coma descended unexpectedly, disrupting the usual order. This is the part of the story, dear reader, that is the trickiest to adequately flesh-out. Bella's catatonic transcriptions had not yet begun—or rather, she had not yet been properly equipped to make them. So what we have to rely on here are secondhand memories. Even though these come directly from Ms. Laetner, a good researcher must always consider the veracity and reliability of their sources. How much trust should be granted to a brain that is obviously keen to play tricks on its master? Is what she remembers from this early period the actual dream narrative, or is it somehow adulterated? It is hard to say. While there are some extant discontinuities, I have to say that the stories I've been able to gather all feel part of a unified whole. The storyline and subjects evolve, yes, but the narrator remains the fulcrum around which everything rotates. And you do not simply have to rely on my word in this regard—the experts all more or less agree.

You see, much later, after having emerged from her coma, Bella became a prized research subject for neuroscientists. The many sessions she endured produced reams of interview transcripts. The findings were of great interest within the research community but were not much more than a passing curiosity to those outside the field. Dr. Nasim Predroyovich, a neuroscientist at First Health Priority Hospital, called Bella's coma journals "the most coherent snapshot we have available of the human subconscious." In an effort to assess the consistency of Ms. Laetner's pre-transcription memories, Dr. Predroyovich conducted extensive brain scans, comparing recollection of transcribed dreams to recollection of those that occurred pre-transcription. The neuronal activity was identical, showing no evidence of willful deception or creative embellishment on Bella's part. A number of other researchers replicated these findings.

Dr. Nathaniel Burff is a notable dissenter, suggesting that the hallmark of the delusional is how their brains can't differentiate between factual memories and those whose narrative has drifted over time. While his own database of patient data backs up his claims, there are some subtle variations in the Laetner case which introduce enough uncertainty that I believe Dr. Predroyovich to be the more reliable source on the subject. Other literature reviews conducted by independent observers throughout the field bear this out.

So then, keeping in mind that the account of the initial period comes not from the transcription phase, but post-coma interviews, let's begin. Even as a young child, Annabelle Laetner's perspective on life could be seen to foreshadow her unexpected coma. Her friends and family described her as occasionally aloof, but always wry of humor. From Bella's perspective, she describes it more as a perceptual disjunction.

"As a child, I wondered if perhaps I was from a different planet. Everyone around me seemed so satisfied, so self-assured, so content to follow the path set before them. Their lives seemed to be governed by a force I could not see—some singularity pulling them all in toward a rendezvous with the black unknown. Gravity always wins, doesn't it?

"I had no recourse for these feelings, but to withdraw into my dreams. Of course, imagination was not encouraged in a time when practicality and utility were prized above all. It caused some cognitive dissonance, you might say. My outward actions more or less in line with the masses, my mental journeys the height of idle exploration."

So this was the mindset of the child. As the saying goes, "Observe the young girl and therein shall you find the woman." Perhaps this duality, a tension between desire and reality, was the root of her coma. In interviews, she talks of having wanted to become an artist of some sort. A writer, or perhaps a documentary filmmaker.

As was the custom in those days, all children were given a battery of tests in the second grade to discern their aptitudes. These aptitudes were then mapped onto a course of study, which, in turn, led them to their eventual career. The tests indicated that Bella was slated to be a bus operator. Although autonomous vehicles have no need of human drivers, the government's "put people to work" plan ensured that fleshy redundancies proliferated. Even government officials themselves were superfluous. They acted as the human face for the mechanical gears and circuits that guided all of the decisions impacting our daily lives.

Thus, from third grade onward, Bella was enrolled in a rigorous training program whose ultimate result would be her bus operator's license. Manual dexterity, situational awareness, mechanics, maintenance, driving theory, and more were the subjects of her day. When she was tempted to complain over the family dinner table, her parents would "shush" her calmly and use her brother as exemplar. "Look at how practical he is. Please, Annabelle, don't rock the boat. Just follow your calling." There is a difference between what we feel called to and what science says we're destined for, of course, but such are the dictates of society—the illusion of productivity takes precedence over all else.

When she would try to air these concerns with her friends, they would quickly change the subject. "We always just thought she was a little crazy," said Janis Millhouse to one television interviewer who came seeking illuminating context. "Bella was one of the smartest people we knew, but sometimes, there can be too much of a good thing. It's not that it distracted her from the duty of her schoolwork, just that it sapped her passion for her true calling—a bus operator is a noble profession." As her friends indicate, despite her anti-practical predilections, Ms. Laetner was a model of productivity in the classroom, always earning the highest marks. She would come home promptly, do her homework, eat dinner with the family, spend her scant idle time reading or writing, then repeat her pre-bedtime mantra.

"Thank you for the day. Let the next day find my family and country safe, and my mind sound." And so it was on the fateful day. The same routine. Nothing out of the ordinary. She closed her eyes to sleep.

And suddenly, there in the garden was a bee in vibrant grayscale. Its stripes, black and white instead of the more typical honey-rust and black. It reminded her of a squirrel she had once seen, but as she got up to give it a closer inspection, the insect ascended toward the heavens, vanishing into the gray clouds high above. She felt as if she had just witnessed some secret process no one else had previously been allowed to see. These cloud-minder bees fly at high altitudes, scraping their legs as they go to salt the cumulostratus with pollen, thereby enabling the rain. They had an important job, and Bella would keep the secret.

Elsewhere, wasps gnawed on the wooden memorial bench. How long, she wondered, until they had chewed their way completely through?

"It's strange," said Bella, "though I can rarely remember my dreams upon waking in the morning—especially those that have numerous twists and turns—I clearly remember the very first image of what turned out to be my coma." She has openly admitted that her memory is hazy from this point on— our primary record being her unconscious writings—but adamantly adheres to this monochrome initial vision.

While young Bella was experiencing this and subsequent dreams, the outside world was fretting. It was her mother who first discovered her. Thinking Bella had forgotten to set the alarm, or willfully overslept, she eventually grew tired of yelling up the stairs for her daughter to get moving. The sun was starting to rise. Opening the door, things looked normal at first. The glow-in-the-dark stars affixed to the ceiling above Annabelle's bed were clinging to the faint memory of illumination. Her daughter's head was completely covered by the blankets. "You'll suffocate yourself if you sleep like that," was the constant cajoling refrain. Approaching the bed, she found Bella unresponsive, unable to be roused no matter how much she was jostled. At this, Priscilla Laetner began to grow increasingly concerned. A recording of her call to the emergency services is a heart-rending mix of panicked sobbing and hopeless wail.

"My daughter... she... sh... she won't wake up. I don't nuh... nuh... know what to do. Please help me. Come quick! Please help!"

By the time the medics arrived, the ceiling constellations had been overtaken by the ambient light of dawn, dissolving back into the off-white background from whence they came. Mrs. Laetner had exhausted herself from trying to shake her daughter awake. She just sat by the bed, stroking Bella's hair and holding her hand. The medics' efforts to wake Bella were equally futile, so they put her on a stretcher and rushed her to the hospital. All the while, Priscilla sat by her side, holding her hand. When she was forced to let go, the hand started flailing about. It was disquieting and only amplified the fear, so Priscilla chose to hang on as much as possible.

At the hospital, Dr. Alejandro Wunch, the attending physician, did not know what to make of the case. His words to the Laetner family indicated that it could be any number of things: stroke, aneurysm, seizure, breakdown. His patient notes indicate a different diagnosis. "Most likely an overdose on synthetic drugs, leading to complete sensory non-responsiveness." To be fair, there had at one time been an epidemic of drug use in the community, but it had not been an issue for decades. Dr. Wunch was decidedly old school in his opinions.

The initial flurry of activity in the hospital soon died down. The Laetners were given a private room and thus began their vigil. Priscilla and William alternated holding Bella's flailing hand. Her brother Jakob hung around the fringes, waiting until he could go back to his normal routine.

Throughout this entire period, we have no idea what Bella was experiencing. She reports a vague recollection of worms crawling through her hair and limbs mired in waves of

236

molasses, but no cogent narrative, no cohesive description of her dreams' imagery. In fact, if you ask her today to describe her dreams after the very first one, she can only point to her unconscious journals. "It's as if I'm reading someone else's words. I'm held in suspense like any other reader. Where were these episodes leading?"

At this point, enough references have been made to the "unconscious journal," that you, the reader, are probably fed up with the mystery. "Cut to the chase," you say. Very well then. On the third evening after losing consciousness, William and Priscilla took a break from their hand holding duties to eat dinner. While they sat there in the room, Mrs. Laetner anxiously watched her daughter's seemingly endless hand-twitch. "I remember saying 'our poor girl—even in her stupor, she has the precision of a painter.' But William said it was far too fine a motion for that. As if to prove him wrong—I grabbed a nearby pen and notepad and walked to Annabelle's side. The rest of her body was at peace, gently reclining on the hospital bed as if she was just sleeping. But there was her left hand, conducting a little symphony. I carefully worked the pen into her grip and slid the notepad under her hand. Honestly, I'm not sure what I was thinking—extended hospital stays will lead the mind to some strange places. But this was one of those times where the subconscious unleashed its strange logic and the next thing we knew, she was writing words across the page."

It's funny how the most momentous occasions often arrive without warning. This is the birth of the unconscious dream journal that has shaped careers and changed lives. And it all started on a whim in a hospital room. As the page filled, Priscilla stood in amazement, then did her best to hurriedly swap in a blank one so as to preserve the link. The hand stopped and started at random intervals over the course of the next three years. Not willing to lose any of Bella's scribblings, but accepting the reality that they could no longer sit by her bedside at all hours to manage the transcription, the Laetners went back to work, resumed their daily lives, and hired a "journal manager" to monitor Bella and ensure a steady supply of pens and paper.

Now, dear reader, lest you think I plan to present the complete musings of young Ms. Laetner in their entirety, let me assure you that it is not my goal. There are already several fine annotated volumes that collect her every word. The works of Tamra Smithfield and Dean Grosh are two prime examples of this. Moreover, all proceeds from the sale of those works goes toward repaying the medical bills incurred during her three-year unconsciousness. No, my friends, instead, my goal is to present something more of a contextual remixing of Bella's work and its stream of (un)consciousness. Disparate subjects, unconnected ideas—all of this merged to create something rather unique. However, as all authors must ultimately be subjected to the whims of the editor, I believe that with a little bit of trimming and rearranging, we can come to grips with some unexpected truths hidden in the dream journal. Most of all, I want to play the part of compassionate observer—even if Bella wasn't aware of it at the time, these are the thoughts of a real-live person, not some odd footnote in the annals of psychology. As such, I will try to contextualize more than analyze. The meaning-making, I entrust to you.

In what follows, I have kept with the chronological number system used in the Smithfield and Grosh works.

Other than indicating the real-world order in which they appeared, they have no direct bearing on the narrative. Likewise, I have chosen the controversial heading of "dream" to describe each of the visions. As "hallucination" has a derogatory meaning and "vision" has affiliations with mysticism, I believe that "dream" is the most appropriate choice. Moreover, it is something all of us have experienced, and so makes the work, on the whole, more relatable. Apologies if you take issue with that interpretation, but I assure you that no offence was intended.

Dream #5

Coming through the forest, we stumbled upon a clearing to find an entire section of violins sitting in the middle of a blank snowy field. The musicians took up their instruments, swaying in unison as they launched into a mournful drone.

Dream #12

We were laying siege to a walled fortress. A mass of people charged forward to batter down the gates. With their fists if they had to. As a deterrent to all would-be assailants, on the top of the fortress wall, the defenders had balanced a large, rectangular iron grid. At every intersection, a four-foot spike protruded ominously.

While the crowd fractured its fists on the front gate, the men above leaned-in to their contraption with a great heave-ho. Eventually, it passed through top-dead-center and gravity took charge.

The mass of metal swung down like a giant meat tenderizer, skewering people as it went. With thunderous report, it clanged against the stone walls, sending a shower of sparks and blood raining out over the crowd. It was a magisterial display underscoring the futility of the proletarian rabble.

We shrugged our shoulders and went home. After a while, the doorbell rang. A stranger dropped off a slew of new pets that became ours. One of us received a shorthaired puppy with no discernable eyes. Another a mournful-looking owlet. Someone else was given a rope, though I'm not sure what it was attached to. We had neither ordered these animals nor expected to become their protectors, but we did our duty.

Dream #17

Overhead, the brilliant deep blue of mid-October encased the world in its autumnal cocoon. We counted the leaves spiraling down. The first freeze had not yet come, so there was still life clinging to every twig and weedy shoot. Across the quad, at the picnic table whose top had been set askew by a fallen limb years before, we saw the writer, hunched up over his notebook, back to the sun. What was he writing? Would we ever get to read it? How many novels are written in this world, only to ultimately languish on an overlooked shelf?

So many questions, but we were late for class. Questions promptly forgotten when the chalk scraped its nail across the slate board. "SCREEEECccH." The accompaniment to every dying daydream.

Author's Commentary

What might stand out in this first set of dreams I've selected is Bella's authorial voice. You might be incredulous, unwilling to believe that these are the words of a bus operator-in-training. Part of this disparity can be explained by Ms. Laetner's innate interest in writing—she had long immersed herself in fine literature, so a certain amount of poetic mimicry is understandable. But is it the whole explanation? There is, after all, ample evidence that head injuries can lead to dramatic cognitive shifts, but we have no record of direct trauma here. Others might point to divine inspiration, but I prefer to view Bella's linguistics as evidence of the genius baked into every genome, just waiting for an opportunity to emerge.

Whatever the case, I also want to call attention to dream #20, where we will see the first reference to awakening or regaining consciousness. While by no means frequent at this stage of her coma, this type of dream ending appears with increasing regularity as the coma drags on. It is almost as if we readers are witness to the pitched internal battle taking place as her conscious mind struggles to resurface.

Dream #20

We were bicycling across the continent. Fans thronged along the route, screaming as the peloton whizzed by. There was no rest, only the open road and the unending rhythm of pedal, pedal, pedal, pedal. Our backs ached from crouching for so long, but we were determined. Everyone took their turn at the lead until we neared the final ascent. The road ahead looked vertical. Some in the pack simply pulled to the side and gave up. Others careened forward, their bikes wobbling wildly under the exertion. Our pace slowed to a crawl. The switchbacks were dizzying. The ribbon draped across the finish line came into view and we made our move. One by one, we overtook our competitors. There was a single rider left between us and the ultimate goal. Would we make it? I don't know. The dream ended in a pool of vomit as I came to at the gym.

Dream #22

We walked through the forest and down to the bay. Out on the jetty a gazebo was crumbling into the sound. The peepers in the pool behind us lodged their formal protest. The trail turned and we came upon the burned-out husk of a glass house. Even though it had only been abandoned for a few decades, substantial trees grew up through it. Vines completed the camouflage. Ashes to ashes, dust to dust.

Dream #25

Everything was under construction at my alma mater. It was familiar, yet different. The secret passage I used to sneak through was gone. In its place, stood a new-and-improved dining hall. Elsewhere, gaping holes had caution tape stretched across them. We lowered one boy in to explore a pit filled with water. He was taken. It seems the campus still held some mystery after all.

Dream #31

The moon was high overhead. It illuminated the mountains looming before us in blue-white monochrome. They looked imposing in their relief. Rugged, ragged, and jagged, covered in a billowing canopy that smoothed the sharper angles that lay beneath.

All at once, the mountains burst to life, lit from within, glowing gold and pink. The flashes were as brutal as they were instantaneous. Then the true contours could be seen. And the realization settled upon us that these cliffs were impassable, these canyons fatal.

We turned back, defeated, but newly content with our lot in life. The mountains dissolved as we recognized the lights of home. Steady blinking, beckoning. Each slow revolution of the control tower searchlight reeling us in.

Author's Commentary

Up to this point, the vast majority of Bella's dreams have at their root something of the quotidian life of a modern teenager. Orchestra rehearsals, sporting events, classroom work, the comforts of home, and the like are the prevailing kernels out of which the dreams sprout. However, after dream #31, there is evidence of a creeping paranoia. At this time, her vital signs—which had been steady thus far—exhibited a pronounced change. Her pulse quickened. Areas of the brain associated with fear and confusion began to become more active.

Dr. Jerome Cintas, a consulting neurologist who had been recruited by the Laetners, suggested that this was a good sign and perhaps indication that Annabelle's body was at last coming to grips with the coma. "Think of it like this. When you are first startled awake by a nightmare, your mind has not yet had a chance to differentiate dream from reality. It takes time for your surroundings to sink in and fully purge the fear you had been feeling. The same could be happening with Annabelle, only, in reverse—the surreal world of dream is giving way to panic as the mind realizes it has become trapped within itself." It is certainly a compelling theory.

In later interviews, Dr. Predroyovich attempted to determine whether there was some awareness of the change on the part of Bella, but to no avail. From Bella's perspective, the dreams were a continuous flow, building to a crescendo, not discrete units. It does beg the question, though, what was happening in the spaces between dreams? Perhaps, there is a clue in the fact that many of these dreams appear as dreams within a dream, with young Bella waking up at the end. Dr. Cintas pointed to this as further evidence that her mind was attempting to lift itself from its stupor, but expert opinion is divided on the matter. I promised you context over analysis, so I will stop here and let the dreams continue.

Dream #43

I opened my eyes and could not tell if I was awake or dreaming. My consciousness floated in that listless way one occasionally becomes aware of whilst in a dream. But being that everything seemed normal, I turned off my alarm clock, and stepped out of bed to start my usual morning routine.

I put on my clothes, brushed my teeth, and wandered downstairs to find my mother there in her usual place, getting ready to eat her oatmeal. We said our morning greetings, ate our breakfasts, and gathered up our things just as we did every day.

We got in the car and backed out of the driveway. Normally, my mother would ask what I had at school that day and if I had everything I needed. This time, silence. I was confused. We drove straight past our usual turn and into the parking lot of an innocuous strip-mall. She led me toward a psychiatrist's office.

Terror overtook me. I had always feared the clinical. In my numbness, my mother guided me into the waiting room. The doctor came out, took one look at me, and diagnosed me on the spot. My symptoms were prodromal and predictive of an impending psychotic break.

Suddenly, I realized that I was no longer (or maybe never had been) a girl. I woke up, clutching at my chest, happy to find my breasts still intact.

Dream #49

We watched the squirrel fall from the tree to the road below. A sickening squishing sound, improbably followed by the little fellow standing up and shaking himself off as if nothing had happened. While he stood there dazed, a passing car grazed the tip of his tail. He had used up two squirrel lives in the space of a few seconds, but thankfully, had a third and sprinted off. We wondered whether the tip of the tail would fall off, or simply atrophy and lose its color like people whose hair goes white after blunt-force head trauma.

Dream #52

We were sitting at home when a caravan of open-top vans came slowly pulling through the neighborhood. I felt anxious and remembered the last traveling salesman. He drank cleaning fluid to prove its worth, then smiled a big, toothless grin. One fellow stepped off the lead vehicle, came up to the door, knocked, waited, then walked back to the group. We just peered through small slits in the blinds, hoping they would go away.

After some discussion, a man who we could only assume was their leader emerged. He was outfitted with a bone necklace and leopard print sportcoat. Like a witch doctor, he blew through our door as if casting out a possessed soul.

Through our now open door, the group flooded in, pouring over our belongings.

When someone tried to walk out with our life savings in hand, I scolded them. At that point, they saw the error of their ways. We proceeded to have a lively discussion of mutual understanding. They told their tales and I gave them advice on the next house they should target. We left the encounter as great friends.

Dream #53

The Stasi were looking for us. I'm not sure why, given that we were neither in nor had ever been in East Germany. Nor was I sure of our transgression. But pursue us they did. We knew that they were hot on our trail, so we could not succumb to fear or exhaustion. We had to be clever.

If we just kept going, turning at random intervals, entering unexpected doorways, we could lose them. And so, we continued walking at a brisk pace. Our path led us through ancient cities, across unimaginable deserts, and into more opium dens than I can recall.

As we walked, we learned of our crime: remaining stagnant. It was then we realized that the people we encountered along the way had all been the same. They had the ability to inhabit different bodies, complete with new faces, but ultimately, their voices remained consistent. We lacked this shapeshifting ability. And accordingly, we were not trusted.

I woke up on the Post Office floor with the sweet taste of licked envelopes on my tongue.

Dream #55

I was a member of a smuggling ring. Whether it was antiquities or drugs, I wasn't certain, but there were large stacks of gold and briefcases of cash in a warehouse. I had a feeling that the cops were on to us. As the doorkickers came storming through the gates of the compound, we all scattered. I ran up a hill, a place I had visited the day before to read and picnic, and saw more government agents streaming in along the canyon floor.

I laid down and noticed an attack-wolf chained up not too far away. As I closed my eyes to sleep, I could feel a pack of guard dogs rush up to rip me to shreds. Their teeth closed on my limbs but did not pierce them. I stayed stock-still, completely relaxed. When I failed to react, I heard the wolf—now at the extent of its chain—whimper and lay down beside me. The other dogs of the pack followed suit.

Before long, I heard footsteps approaching in the grass. I opened my eyes and saw a grizzled old man there to offer me shelter. We walked back to his mountainside shack in the setting sun, puffs of dandelion suspended in the air, and that is where the dream ends.

Author's Commentary

Around the time of dream #56, two years into the ordeal, Ms. Laetner's situation took another turn. Her vitals fluctuated erratically. The hospital staff took to having frank conversations with Priscilla and William about their daughter's grim chances for recovery. Dr. Wunch predicted that Bella wouldn't last the year. Even the normally optimistic Dr. Cintas was not confident that the coma would come to a positive end. Hospice was called in at several points.

"We were terrified. As if it wasn't enough that we'd been living with Annabelle's condition for two years, the doctors began to broach the subject of when to best 'pull the plug.' That was my baby girl they were talking about." Perhaps then, it was these morbid conversations that colored the remaining dreams. From this point on, paranoia gives way to an outright contemplation of death. Time and again, Bella's dreams recount fear-inducing situations. A once wondrous dreamworld becomes a land of threats and imminent danger.

Dream #57

A peal of thunder found the resonant frequency of my chest cavity. A freight train grew increasingly closer. It was a tornado on an epic scale. I suggested that we take cover in the storm shelter. You objected because you didn't want to get wet in the rain. We sat on the kitchen floor until I awoke.

Dream #59

We sat in the car, watching the fine layer of snow inch up the windshield like sand in an hourglass. Soon, we would be entombed in silent white.

Only then did we realize it was not snow but ash. We looked out the side window and could see the central square below. The crowds danced around the burning city hall. Glowing bits of the town record flew high into the sky. We gathered them all and reassembled our collective history so it wouldn't be lost. What ash was too far gone to read, I gathered into a jar which I set on my shelf.

Dream #60

By then, the telltale flecks of blood had already appeared in the earwax. Soon, we knew what fate would befall us. Our memories would liquefy and spill out, dribbling down and collecting on our chins, before dripping to the floor. We had seen it happen to so many people. As the prions ate away at people's brains, they became incredibly gregarious and cheerful. We all had a good laugh about the end of the world.

Dream #64

The dream was vivid and intent on repeating. We were coming in for a landing. Everything was serene. The plane banked to the right. The bank became a barrel roll and we flew upside down, until smashing into the green dales of the upper Midwest. We were coming in for a landing. Everything was serene. The pilot looked ready to bank the plane to the right. Knowing what had happened previously, I suggested that we simply continue on our present course. Everyone saw the wisdom in the plan. We landed safely and I awoke.

Dream #72

We went into the office, but things were different. Our desks and chairs had been replaced by a series of glass display boxes on stands. Inside each was a lifelike diorama featuring some scene from the world. A cityscape here, a model of the planet there. Each box had a series of levers and buttons. We pulled the levers and watched in amazement as the city caught fire and was overrun by looters. Little bits of ash and debris billowed over the city model and drifted down. The planet didn't fare much better. An asteroid came hurtling-in, wreaking havoc. The dioramas were so detailed, we felt guilty—empathy even—in the modeled destruction. "Have no fear," the instructor said. We pushed a button on the back and everything was reset to the way it was in the beginning. Just another disturbing day at the office.

Walking home, we were talking about something-or-other when a passing natural gas tanker exploded. The sound split my eardrums and the shrapnel split my skull. As the flames incinerated what was left, the last thing I remember is a picture in my mind of someone walking over to the case and pressing the reset button. Someday, the scars on the sidewalk would fade, the leaves would resume their downward autumnal spiral, and it would be as if none of this had ever happened.

Closing Commentary

As Ms. Laetner scrawled these final words, her eyes opened and she coughed. The medical establishment was astounded and her family overjoyed. She had come back to the world of the living. Aside from the muscular atrophy that comes with extended periods of bedrest, she was apparently no worse for the wear. Bella's parents had decided to give her space and time to process her experience, but after a month, broached the subject of the dream journal. Bella had no recollection and was incredulous that it was something she could have written. "When I read it, it feels like someone else's narration, someone else's words added to the page." Despite her reservations, she consented to her journal's publication.

Millions around the world were enraptured by what appeared to be a real-world case of the extraordinary. The practical, regimented strictures of society began to fray as people more openly embraced the fantastic. Mysticism was resurgent. People began to follow their own paths, abandoning the career choices so carefully calculated by the state. But it was a gentle revolution, as you know. Despite some predicting that the sky would fall, the firmament remained intact.

Later interviewers asked Bella her thoughts about having sparked a cultural transformation. "It has never really felt like something I had anything to do with. Even now, I read my unconscious writings as a stranger. You all saw these bizarre vignettes as a sign that there was magic left in the world—possibilities beyond the expected. For me, all they are is record of the three-year void I've been left with. So what do I think about cultural transformation? Everything has a cost."

At the tender age of twenty-four, our dear young Annabelle reportedly stopped dreaming. To the best of anyone's knowledge, she has not had a dream since. Like many of her contemporaries, Bella abandoned her dictated path. Truth be told, during the three years she was in a coma, she had lost too much ground to become a bus operator anyway. And so, she took a job with a local florist. Though there are no doubt some among you who are appalled at such a scandalous turn of events, please remember that these are the events as they occurred. This is no tale being written by an unseen scoundrel, but the truth.

Occasionally, Annabelle lamented the fact that her dreams had deserted her and wished for their return, particularly the vivid daydreams that once served as her escape from everyday tedium. The poetry of her dreams proved to be fleeting, however. Now she stands at the counter, the bells on the door providing the meter, and the people passing through, the verse. A poetry of the mundane, but one that is well lived. Would that we all could find the escape Anabelle Laetner did with her seventy-two dreams. We can get close by reading, but to truly know it, we must be ready to embrace the opportunity when it presents itself. Let this be an instruction manual for doing so.

Part 7: Is There Something After a Coda?

❧

He went into the bathroom to take his afternoon piss and everything was going well until he noticed whispering coming from the adjacent stall. He craned his neck to get a look at the shoes, and judging by their patent leather appearance, whoever was in there must have been respectable.

When the whispering became a muttering monologue, he immediately recognized the voice of Bob Blumenthal, an accountant from the floor below. "Old Blumey" was well past retirement age, gout-riddled, and nearly blind. Why the man still worked there was beyond anybody's estimation. Maybe Blumenthal just liked the bathroom.

"This is a man I can respect," he thought. "Someday, I want to be paid to shit."

❧

"What has happened to me?" he wondered. "This is not creativity, it's garbage. My 'job' has sapped the lifeblood out of me. Either that or it is my having no time to read. Sigh."

He put away his notebook and walked back to his office to finish the glacially unimportant afternoon.

❧

It was his sister's birthday. He celebrated by crying like a little girl.

❧

His head was splitting, but he knew he must keep writing. Whether on account of the pain or the creative valley of death he had entered, his mind was entirely devoid of ideas. "If only I could remember it, I just had a good idea," he thought.

Well, if he couldn't remember today's thoughts, perhaps he could turn to yesterday's. These too were gone. In absence of all thought, he laid down his pen and took a nap.

✦

As he neared the homestretch of his novel, he began to become more and more self-conscious. Who would he show it to first? How would he choose the right cadre of readers? The poet at the local university? His college literature professor?

Perhaps even more vexing was the ending. He had so much momentum for a while, but his writing was hurtling toward no particular resolution. Other writers in the same situation had the good sense to leave their works unfinished. They either walked away from their manuscript mid-sentence or died before they could pen their last chapters. Either way, they were often heralded as tragic geniuses. He would take genius even without the tragedy, if it would be so kind as to visit itself upon him.

⌐

"Maybe I should just start over," he thought. Given that it had taken him ten years to get this far, he quickly realized rebooting was an impossibility. As they say, the only way out of a quagmire is forward. This is the type of wisdom that produces bog bodies. He took the thought as a good omen for his novel. Bog bodies last for millennia, after all.

✤

He lived with an unshakeable apprehension. An unrelenting sense of dread. He saw children and tensed up. He saw the workweek looming and tensed up. Yes, he was in an unenviable position.

"How will I ever finish my work amidst these demands?" he wondered.

He resolved to make an uncharacteristic effort at the end of the summer, just as his energy was waning. Into his diary went the words:

> When the last bats of summer have made their flights, the final thrushes have been flushed from their thicket homes, and the last vestiges of the day have disappeared beyond the horizon, I'll find an autumn field with windmill high above, and there, I'll take my rest. That is where you will find me completed.
>
> Until then, I'll be watching the setting sun paint brownish rainbows in the smog, gazing through the dusk at the grain elevators looming like the far-off peaks of which I dream. Damn this tractor and the fields I've yet to plow.

"Maybe people will believe I'm from the plains now," he thought.

He looked to the trees swaying on the mountainside and waited in vain for the first leaf to fall.

❀

The squirrel with the white tail had vanished in his absence, either to find a new home now that the trees had been felled or culled by the bitter winter cold. And yet, as he sat in his usual spot, here came the most peculiar insect—a wasp, completely black save for three white rings 'round its stinger. He decided that it was the spirit of the squirrel, come back to encourage him forward. Either that, or it was some sort of ghastly message from the garden architect, whose bones, he had recently learned, were interred in the wall against which he had long leaned. If it stung him, he would know for sure. But the sting never came.

∿

Would he ever find closure? At this rate, it was looking unlikely. To solve the dilemma, he planned to leave a blank lined page, with the instruction: "Write your own ending."

He imagined thousands of readers turning to the final page, confounded. Eventually, the more whimsical among them would fetch their pens and scrawl a fitting conclusion. Like a many-limbed exquisite corpse, it could go on forever. This would be how he cheated death and gained a linguistic immortality where everyone remembered him differently. And by that, he meant that everyone would remember him as themselves.

⊘

He decided that he would send copies of his finished work to authors whom he respected but had never met. Some were living, some were not. He imagined the bespectacled keeper of Kafka's estate wandering out into a graveyard and resting the book on his weathered headstone. There it would sit, swelling with each passing rain and slowly shrinking again as the rains stopped. But each drop of water would render the work irreparably changed, warping the pages and blending the words until it was nothing more than a solid mass of wood pulp and ink—physical evidence of the ideas that birthed it.

Dear _____,

I am not sure why I am sending this to you—you whom I have not met. Midway through writing

the book you have in your hands (in a volumet-
ric, not chronologic sense), I took a break to see
where I was and recharge my inspiration. Your
novel was one I read during that time. I found it
a moving experience and wellspring of inspira-
tion. It was the perfect novel for me at the
perfect time, encapsulating many of my small
struggles and triumphs along the way. Thank
you.

Yours Truly,

———————

7.

He had been writing this novel since the day he was born. He would not muster another unless he was born again. Upon hearing this sentiment, his editor began to take an interest in the science of cryogenics. Coincidence?

3

Previously, he had thought that six was his number. Upon re-view of his manuscript, he learned he was mistaken. Three stared him in the face.

"I'm only half the man I thought I was," he muttered.

9

Good writers don't write, they wrote. The verb tense being the defining characteristic. In other words—to make the tensical sensical—the best writers put the act of writing behind them. "I'm done," he thought. Followed immediately by the question "What have I done?"

❀

At last, he was finished writing. He closed his eyes and went to sleep.

( )

For a morning, he lived under the mistaken impression that he was done. He had not gone to writing school. Thus, he failed to realize that what comes after the writing is often more painful than the writing itself.

The editor brandished his pen like a scimitar, dripping red over the pristine pages. There was no escape from his terrible reign. "More. Different. Better." said the editor.

"Sigh," said the author.

Part 8: An Answer

The setting sun streams in through the window and into your eyes, signaling the end of another day at the office. Outside your seventh-floor window, birds flit cheerily about in the late spring air. You think they must be building a nest, as eager as they are. And so, before gathering up your things to go, you walk over to the glass for a closer inspection.

The birds, sensing your motion, disappear. Now that you're at the window, you notice a crowd of people massing in the street, trickling in from every direction. There has been talk for days of a general strike, and it looks as if it is finally coming to fruition.

Since you rode the bus to work, you will have to find an alternate way of getting home. Thankfully, with all of the recent unrest, you are experienced at navigating transit strikes. You hope that some industrious, picket-breaking cabbies are still operating. Sure, their rates will be extortionate, but it is better than walking up hill eight kilometers in your dress shoes.

The closest cab station is a couple of blocks west of your current location. The growing throng lies in between. While you have always sympathized with the plight of the proletariat, and even support their efforts in the silence of your heart, you aren't entirely sure you want to enter that fray. You've heard stories of these mobs doing awful things to outsiders. There was the banker they threw off the roof of the savings and loan a few months ago. And the local bureaucrat they beat and left naked on the steps of the parliament building. Clearly, it never pays to be an unwanted bystander.

And even if the crowd is relatively well behaved, there are always the riot police. Their affinity for tear gas, rubber bullets, and fire-hoses is well known. If you are unfortunate enough to fall within arm's length of the coppers, what awaits you may well be worse than a beating.

You survey the crowd, half-expecting to see the martial actions already being unleashed, but the police are nowhere to be seen. Your stomach rumbles almost imperceptibly. Since you did not eat lunch, you are looking forward to a nice, quiet dinner at home.

"Well," you think to yourself, "it's not getting any earlier. I'd better get going."

You look back out the window and the crowd seems to have doubled in size. The chants are beginning, the signs are being brandished. It is all looking a bit more agitated than just a few minutes ago. You want to leave, but the crowd gives you pause.

Do you choose to stay or go?

If you choose to wait in your office building until the crowd dissipates, turn to page 272. If you choose to take your chances on the street, turn to page 268.

There is a tense standoff for what feels like hours, which in reality lasts less than a minute. You slowly spin, looking into the eyes of the five men surrounding you. As the group circles, you sense an opening and take your chance to sprint toward the side street.

Though you have always fancied yourself a decathlete, it is surprising that you did not put more stock in your abilities as an orator. After all, you've had years of formal training as a mediator, negotiator, and speechwriter. When the Chief Minister of Finance needs to secure a deal, she turns to you to write the words. You have always had a gift for elegantly balanced rhetoric. If your father was here, he would wonder aloud if all those years (and the money spent on them) were a waste.

Oh well, it's too late to change your mind now. The belligerents follow in hot pursuit. You really are a gifted runner and quickly reach top speed. The doors and windows along the side street become nothing more than a blur. You glance backward and see your pursuers falling back only slightly. "Maybe I can lose them," you think.

You take a quick left, then a right, still in full-on sprint. I should tell you at this point that though you've worked in the same office for almost eight years now, you are still stubbornly unfamiliar with the local streets. You have your one route that you take every day like clockwork. You prefer to leave exploring for your weekend walks in your own neighborhood, wandering, lost in thought until you come to one of the numerous parks that dot the region. Then you sit and read or pull out your pen and notebook to work on the novel you've been writing on and off for several years.

But where were we? Right... Another quick glance back and you see that you have outpaced all but two of your assailants. You bring your head back around to scout your next turn and see only a dead end looming. "Curse these medieval streets!"

You look around frantically as you hear their footfalls drawing closer. A fire escape ladder dangles just out of reach on the wall. Since the men are closing in fast, you instinctively run toward the wall and scramble up it until your hands grip the first rung. The ladder slides down with your weight and you are able to climb it to the landing where the stairs begin. Though it was spring-loaded, it did not return to place once you removed your weight.

By now, the men are at the base and begin climbing up toward you. You've had better nightmares. You start sprinting up the stairs, taking two at a time until you reach the top. Here, you find a locked fire exit and another small ladder leading onto the roof. You ascend it and find yourself standing amidst a rooftop ecosystem of which you were previously unaware.

The two remaining men are still in pursuit, albeit they look winded. You've seen these kinds of rooftop chase scenes in movies before and know that they almost always involve reckless jumps between buildings. While your adrenaline has kept you ahead of the pack so far, you are concerned that even it would not be enough to propel such a leap should that choice arise. Long jump was always your weakest event. Nonetheless, you see few options left. There are plenty of vents, pipes, and HVAC units up here, so you could always hide. But, should that fail, encountering angry men on a roof does not seem like a recipe for continued health.

From the direction of the plaza, you hear muffled explosions and the screaming surge of a crowd. The first people to flee the commotion can be seen rushing through the street below. You see wisps of smoke, or perhaps tear gas, curling upward in the dusk. At least you are not part of that melee. Your pursuers will be appearing at any moment.

Do you choose to hide on the rooftop or jump to a neighboring building?

If you choose to hide behind a nearby air vent, turn to page 275. If you choose to make the jump to safety, turn to page 270.

I forgot to tell you that you work in the Government Ministry of Finance. Stupidly, in your hurry to leave, you forgot to put your ID badge in your pocket before heading out. Those on the edge of the crowd soon see the badge and begin hurling angry insults in your direction. They look to be inebriated and are already in an extreme frenzy.

You rip the nametag from your lapel and stuff it into your shirt pocket, hoping no one else sees it. You do your best to walk quickly and keep your eyes straight ahead. Your plan is to skirt the edge of the crowd, leaving a safe buffer. The side streets, while full of people streaming toward the plaza, seem to be quieter.

All at once, you see a glass bottle flying in your direction. It was not thrown well and crashes against the wall behind you. Nonetheless, it gets your attention. The bottle shatters on impact, sending bits of glass and droplets of whatever it once held toward you. You feel the light spray of liquid across your face and you pray that it was not piss.

As the characteristic smell of petrol hits your nostrils, you console yourself by thinking that your prayer came true—it was not, after all, a bottle of urine. Not that the alternative is much better in this case. "My god...they're throwing unlit Molotov cocktails," you think. It must have been a warning shot. Either that, or the thrower simply had bad aim. Whatever the case, you take it as a none-too-subtle hint that you shouldn't be here. Your only hope now is that they don't get the courage to toss another one before you make it across the plaza.

You feel the adrenaline swell but do your best to remain calm. You give a quick glance toward the crowd and notice that all of the eyes in your general vicinity are focused on you. "So much for hiding my badge," you mutter under your breath. Up ahead, you see your destination drawing near— just a few dozen meters and you'll be on the other side. You refocus your eyes on your feet and quicken your pace. The crowd grows ever-more riotous, hurling insults (and whatever else they can get their hands on) with reckless abandon.

Suddenly, you realize that one of the items they've managed to get their hands on is you. A small, especially unruly contingent detached from the main group and came up from behind. You feel someone's palm plant itself between your shoulder blades and heave forward.

You stumble into an empty table at a sidewalk cafe, sending it and its unattended place settings clattering to the ground. You try to right yourself but end up getting your legs tangled on a nearby chair. You collapse to the ground, landing hard on your knee. Instinctively, you reach down and find your pants ripped and knee lightly bloodied. "What a shame," you think, "I had just gotten these."

You stand up, dust yourself off and turn to look your assailants in the eye. Like a school of sharks, they sense blood in the water and begin circling. At your back is a relatively quiet side street. You think about making a break for it but are worried your sore knee might buckle. "Maybe I should just try to reason with them," you think.

Do you choose to run from, or reason with your attackers?
If you choose to sprint toward the side street, turn to page 265. If you choose to speak to the menacing group of people now circling you, turn to page 334.

I'm surprised that even you would try to jump a seven-meter span. When I said earlier that you were a poor long jumper, that was a bit of an understatement. In competition, there were several times you failed to even make the pit. You usually made up for this deficiency in the running and throwing events, but this is no track meet. A strange decision on your part indeed.

Nonetheless, you pick a favorable angle and sprint toward the edge of the roof. You plant your foot solidly on the edge and launch yourself across the void. Time stops. This is what flying feels like in your dreams. You are a true superhero. You have defeated gravity. Time unstops. You approach the neighboring building at what feels like ludicrous speed. You extend your arms, reaching madly for the upper lip of the wall. Your fingertips are filled with momentary hope as they catch, then dismay as they slide free.

Meanwhile, you absorb a full-on body blow from the wall. It literally feels like being hit by a ton of bricks. The wind knocked out of you, you tilt backward and gravity takes control. Before you black out, the last thing you remember is the peculiar sensation of falling.

Since you are temporarily unconscious, I will fill you in on the intervening details. Despite being a very bad jumper, you are, at the very least, lucky. Below you is an open and, thanks to the recent strikes, overflowing garbage bin. The refuse breaks your four-story fall without breaking your neck.

While you're out, your mind drifts in a dreamlike state. You picture yourself in a more peaceful time wearing a white smock. You're a consulting physician. Though you can't recall any training that would qualify you for this position, everyone, including the head surgeon turns to you for a diagnosis. Your opinion is respected, it seems. You are about to speak when you realize you've gone mute. A disheartening blend of fear and embarrassment courses through your veins. You instinctively open your mouth to speak, when...

The wind which had previously vacated your waking lungs floods back in a whoosh.

To regain consciousness in a garbage bin, turn to page 278.

You didn't get a job in the Ministry of Finance by accident—you've always known that discretion is the better part of valor. Despite sympathizing with the rabble, you decide to stay in your building until the police disperse the crowds. These things have a way of getting out of control quickly. What's more, walking through a crowd like that, there's a good chance that someone among them would peg you as a bureaucrat. At that point, all bets would be off.

Within a few minutes, the entire city square is full. The mob is looking angrier than usual. Wait, was that a... indeed it was. The first Molotov cocktails go cartwheeling through the sky toward the barricades ringing the bottom of your building. It's little wonder that frustrations have reached a breaking point. Not only is the nation in the midst of a stubborn recession with unemployment at an all-time high, but governmental corruption runs rampant. Just last week, there was an exposé run on the deputy minister of transportation. It seems that the recent fee, which had been instituted on all tire sales—to fund infrastructure maintenance and improvements—had instead been going to fund her shopping sprees in Paris. To be sure, your countrymen expect their leaders to be well heeled and a class above, but to spend a million on shoes and handbags goes a little too far.

You press your face up against the glass to get a better view of what's happening below. The security personnel behind the barricades are holding their ground, undeterred by the occasional projectiles. That's what body armor and flame-retardant suits are for. One security guard even has the gumption to pick up an unbroken bottle and hand it back to those on the edge of the crowd. You're pretty sure that's not standard protocol, but you appreciate any efforts, however unconventional, at keeping the peace.

Just now, on the fringes of the crowd, you are beginning to see the telltale signs of law enforcement. Navy blue uniforms, checkered hats, and large white vehicles blocking avenues of escape. Oh dear, they've brought in the water cannons and megaphones. Each warning elicits a wave of enraged chants from the crowd. Though the window between you and the action muffles the exact dialogue, you have a pretty good idea what is being said nonetheless. This may get ugly quickly. You are glad that you stayed inside where it is safe.

Without warning, the police mortars start launching tear gas into the middle of the group. At the same time, the water cannons pummel those on the edges. Chaos ensues. Those trying to escape the tear gas flee outward; those trying to flee the high-pressure hoses flee toward the center. The compressed agitants at the front of the group unleash an avalanche of projectiles toward your building.

Several years ago, in an effort to humanize the Ministry of Finance, the previous deputy minister had decided that the standard concrete and glass entrance wasn't welcoming enough. As such, it had been refurbished. Rough-hewn timbers replaced the concrete to create a mountain-lodge aesthetic out of character with the rest of the building. Nonetheless, the deputy minister looked upon what he had made and saw that it was very good. This entryway, as it just so happens, is now proving to be perfect tinder for the fire. Its notched roof cradles and nourishes the nascent blaze like a protective mother. That it seems to go unnoticed by the security guards is somewhat disturbing.

Their salvo relinquished, and the rest of the riot falling into disarray, the front line storms the barricades in order to escape. You watch in horror as the tsunami of humanity coming over the cordon scatters the security personnel. "What are they being paid for?" you say to the window. But upon seeing the fear reflected in your own eyes, you realize that you would have probably run, too.

You see various segments of the crowd being pursued down side streets by police detachments. As quickly as the protesters assembled, they dispersed. The square below your building is soon home to just a skeleton crew. A couple of law enforcement agents are handcuffing and loading injured protesters into paddy wagons. The fire at the base of your building has been growing all the while. By comparison, it now seems safer outside than in. That said, you never know when a contingent of protesters might double back and reignite the riot, so there is no guarantee of safety on the streets either.

Do you choose to leave the building on your own or call for help?

If you choose to carefully slink down the stairwell, turn to page 348. If you would rather place your life in the hands of others and call the fire department, turn to page 283.

For your sake, I really hope this was a good decision. After all, these air vents are not really that large. You hear your pursuers' footfalls nearing the top of the ladder. You choose the largest and most out of the way air vent, duck behind it, and curl yourself up into a ball. Confused footfalls on gravel. Heavy breathing.

"Where the hell?"

"One thing's for sure—there's nowhere to hide."

"Maybe jumped?"

"Yeah, look—I think I see someone over there!"

"You're not gettin' away from us!"

You are terrified that your cover has been blown, so you uncurl and look around the air vent to at least confront your assailants with some dignity. Instead, just as you poke your head around the side, you see the two men sprint toward the edge of the building and jump in unison in the direction of another roof. Wow. They look amazingly graceful. Until they smack into the side of the neighboring building and crash into a large garbage bin below. You are happy that you didn't try jumping that span, given your woeful history with the long jump.

The concussion from the tear gas mortars and abrupt change in pitch of the crowd noise means that police have begun their anti-riot efforts in earnest. Protesters begin streaming down the street between the two buildings. You are even more satisfied that you didn't attempt the jump when you see the roll-off your two pursuers are lying dazedly in set alight and pushed down the hill. Panicked, they attempt to dislodge any burning refuse, but it's all for naught as you see the garbage sled hit the curb and eject them and its contents through the window of a shop at the bottom of the street. That building is quickly engulfed in flames.

You begin counting your blessings until you notice that the Ministry of Finance is also on fire. Oh well, maybe that means you'll get next week off. After all, you remembered to bring your side bag, which has anything you might need in it. Wait. Are you telling me you forgot to bring your side bag?

I should apologize at this point for not reminding you to take your bag at the outset. There are several reasons to be upset. First, is the fact that your wallet may be inside of it—you have a habit of not putting it in your pocket where it belongs. You quickly pat yourself down, first your pants, then, finding nothing there, proceed to your jacket. Ah. There it is in your inside pocket. You like to put things in hidden places. It has always made you feel like a spy.

You are still upset at having forgotten the bag, as it contains the working draft of the novel you have been slowly writing for the past several years. You had recently been gaining momentum and were (by your estimation) only a page or two from wrapping the narrative up nicely. You had hoped you would be able to complete it over the weekend. Maybe even have had a chance to start reading back through and editing. Now, that draft is inside a burning building. The color drains from your face. There is a writhing sea of humanity between you and the flames slowly creeping up the side of your office. The office in which your life's work resides.

Do you run toward your burning building or wait to see if the riot dissipates before making your attempt?

If you choose to fight your way through the chaos and make a desperate attempt to recover the only extant draft of your novel, turn to page 331. If you choose to instead take a more civilized, less danger-filled approach, turn to page 280.

You find yourself in a large dumpster, cradled by bags of yesterday's kitchen scraps. At the other end of the container are broken-down cardboard boxes. Passersby see you and are incensed by your suspicious bureaucratic garb. A note to your future self: if you ever plan on spending time in a rubbish bin during a riot, make sure the materials in it are not flammable. Being that you had little choice in this instance, I will forgive you.

Since those you've angered are running from martial law, they favor streamlined acts of vandalism. One person, wishing to divest themselves of their protesterly evidence, smashes an unlit Molotov cocktail inside the garbage bin and continues running. Another person, also trying to dispose of anything incriminating, tosses in a lighter, which happens to snap open and set the now accelerant-soaked cardboard ablaze.

Seeing a fire, a wheeled container, and a hill with high street shops at the bottom, others in the fleeing group take advantage of the situation and give the flaming container a running shove. This all happens before you have time to process the chain of events. There is nothing like the efficiency of rioteers.

You ride the flaming roll-off down the hill, doing your best to expel the worst of the burning refuse. There is no steering such a contraption. The windows of the stores at the bottom of the hill rush forward to greet you. You duck as your vehicle hits the curb, goes airborne, and careens through a massive pane of glass. Mannequins, accessories, and the other detritus of haute couture scatter upon impact.

The trash bin comes to an abrupt stop when it meets a sizable jewelry display case. It flips on end, ejecting you and the flaming material into the middle of the room. Unfortunately for this proprietor, vintage 1970s apparel, while back in style, is still as flammable as ever. As piece after piece ignites with a whoosh of combustion, you realize that you need to vacate the premises.

Surprisingly no worse for the wear, you dust yourself off and hurry toward the rear exit. You make your way through the storage room and out into the alley behind the building. There, you find an idling car, empty of occupants. You look around for the driver, hoping that they will be willing to give you a ride to the safety of your home. But the alley is suspiciously devoid of all signs of life. For a moment, you debate walking out to find help. You hear the shouts of rioters on the other side of the building that is now engulfed in flames. You've never even dreamt of stealing a car before, but given your current predicament, the thought is tempting.

Do you choose to take the car or find help elsewhere?
You probably thought I was going to give you a choice in this matter, but you're wrong. Since you don't seem to learn much from previous mistakes, let me make this choice for you. As they say, you should never look a gift horse in the mouth. Please, take this stroke of good luck for what it is, get in the car, and get out of here. Turn to page 285.

You have a good head on your shoulders. Those, like you, who prioritize their personal safety, often live longer. Their lives are also more boring, but what the heck, some days, breathing is its own reward.

Hopefully, if you're reading ahead to try to see which is the correct choice, you stopped before you got to this sentence. Now that you have been hooked by the opening stanza and let your finger go from the previous page, it would be dishonorable to go back and make the other choice. There is only one way through life, and that is forward.

Just in the time you've been debating your choices, the crowd has already thinned by half. At the far end of the square, you see a group of people hurdle the anti-terror barricades ringing your building. Elsewhere, the police are continuing their enforcement tactics. Tear gas in the center gets the crowd moving. Water cannons on the edge help funnel them down predetermined escape routes toward choke points where the protesters can be scooped up and prosecuted as public nuisances. Like fish in a barrel. You are glad you didn't try to work your way through that rabble as your eyes would no doubt be burning by now.

Then come the dogs. Loosed from nearby police vans, the canines nip and bark, further herding the remaining protesters out of the central square. "Another thirty minutes or so," you think to yourself, "and the coast should be clear." You only hope that someone gets the fire under control by then. In the twilight, however, you begin to see orange, flickering glows elsewhere around the city skyline. The firefighters may have their hands full tonight.

For the next hour, you stand transfixed by the flames swirling up the side of your government building. They are really quite beautiful as they complete the dance of destruction. Like smoke from the congress of cardinals, you see the fruits of your decade-long labor wafting white into the sky. Does that mean a decision has been reached? Or is that for black smoke? You cannot remember and curse yourself for not having paid greater attention in your catechism classes. It suffices to say, your novel is probably long gone. You are unsure whether to feel relieved or suicidal.

You trudge the eight kilometers back to your home as darkness descends. Despair wells up in your heart. Maybe, if you hurry and spend all weekend, you can recreate your masterwork. Already, snippets of your choicest phrases are coming unmoored and begin drifting through your mind. There is a chance you could make this draft even better. It certainly can't take another ten years. You'll know what you're doing this time. If only that were true. Moments of inspiration are rare, and once exhausted, can never be reclaimed. New inspiration may come but trying to salvage what came before is futile. Maybe it's better to just be freed from the yoke of creativity—it did take up a lot of your time. Think of it as a gift from fate: take up a new hobby, meet some new people—viewing it as an opportunity is far more pleasant.

Meanwhile, your stomach, in an uncharacteristic act of solidarity with the rioters, lodges a formal protest and feels as if it is beginning to launch digestive pyrotechnics during the long walk home. You really regret not having eaten lunch today. But such is the choice you've made. Eventually, the hunger pangs subside. You suspect that your stomach has collapsed in on itself like a black hole. On the upside, if that is true, you may never have to eat again since your stomach, happy to have roles reversed, will now do the swallowing.

To complete your walk home and cry yourself to sleep, turn to page 333.

I should have told you that the fire climbing the front of your building began precariously close to the main phone system junction box. Hopefully, it hasn't rendered it inoperable. You pick up your desk phone and a dial tone chimes through.

"Hello. Fire department? The government building for the Ministry of Finance seems to be on fire. I'm up on the seventh-floor and don't know what to do. Can you please come rescue me?"

Of course, the dispatcher only heard up through the phrase "seems to be on fire." At that very moment, the fire severed your building's phone lines and your voice was interrupted on the dispatcher's side. You don't realize this and keep on giving details for a full minute, wanting to be sure they knew where to find you. Soon enough, you catch on and hang up the phone.

You go back over to the window and look down—the fire is continuing to creep up the buildingside. You're not one to be caught off guard, so you survey the area and retrieve all of the fire extinguishers you can find. When you count them, you're surprised that you've only collected two. It felt like a lot more work than that. Maybe you should exercise more regularly. It's not that you're fat by any stretch of the imagination, it's just that you've grown a slight paunch. Disappointing for someone who holds a collegiate record in javelin. The oxen-like shot putters would certainly scoff at your fitness as they let loose their primal growls.

It feels like it has been an awfully long time since you called for rescue. Walking back over to the window, you notice a discernible temperature gradient. A good deal of the building now seems to be bathed in flame. The fire will no doubt start snaking its way into the interior soon. Still no sign of the fire engines. Since the building will probably be suffering significant damage anyway, you decide you should break a window to make yourself more visible. You pick up your desk chair, wind up, and on the count of three, whip it at the floor-to-ceiling window by your desk with all of the force you can muster. The chair bounces back with equal vigor, knocking you flat on your back. Within a few minutes, the heat from the fire does the job for you and causes the window to pop.

All you have the wherewithal to do at this point is to wait for help. You have made your bed and you will lie in it. Turn to page 288 to do so.

You look around hesitantly and slowly sidle up to the car, trying to look as nonchalant as possible. If there was anyone here to see, your nervous glances would have drawn their attention long ago. You reach your shaking hand to the car door handle but pull it back instinctively. "I can't possibly steal a car," you think. "There must be another way." But the flames from the burning building are growing larger and the cries of the mob on the other side are growing louder. A sense of urgency descends. Still, you cannot help but hesitate.

Well, if you're not going to open the door, perhaps I can help. The latch on the car door, apparently sensing your indecision, gives way through no effort of your own and the door swings invitingly open. Unfortunately for you, this is just about the worst possible timing. Given your proximity to the car and your obviously guilty look, when the car's owner, who has just appeared at the far end of the alley, sees you, he flies into a rage.

You immediately take an instinctive step away from the car and wave your arms wildly in the universal gesture of "this is not what it looks like." The man sprinting toward you pays no heed to your entreaties.

I am concerned for your safety. If I could pick you up and deposit you in the driver's seat, I would. You really should get in the car and go. It will not end well if you stay here to greet the car owner. If it helps, you can think of what you have to do as "borrowing"—you'll just drive a few blocks down and park it somewhere safely out of the fray. You'll be doing the owner a favor.

Convinced, at last, that you are not actually stealing, you slide into the front seat, close the door, and start the car.

Surprisingly, the car owner seems to be running even faster than before, quickly closing the distance. For a moment, you pause to contemplate how, no matter how fast a person is running, it is always technically possible to push just a little harder and achieve a new personal best. The thwomp of your would-be assailant's screaming body on the windscreen jolts you back to the present.

The next series of events happens in rapid succession, as if you have no control. And really, since you can't see out the windscreen, it is all a matter of muscle memory and reaction. Your foot hits the accelerator. The man on the windshield's anger intensifies. He begins battering the car with his fists in an attempt to get your attention. You come to an intersection and jerk the wheel to the left because it's the only direction in which you have a clear view. The man on the windshield's weight shifts and he clutches at the edge of the hood so as not to fall off. You speed another few blocks and make another quick left, dislodging your unwanted passenger who somersaults out of harm's way.

Now that you can see where you're going again, you drive another five blocks at a more leisurely pace. This part of town seems relatively calm, so you decide to park the car on a quiet side street to try to find a taxi willing to take you home. You exit the borrowed vehicle, toss the keys onto the front seat, and look around to get your bearings. The street runs straight to the town center, like the spoke of a wheel, and you are now far away from the riot. In the other direction, the street heads up a hill. You really have no idea where you are. I'll leave you with an easy choice to reacclimate you to the idea of free will.

Do you choose to walk down the street toward the town center or up the hill and away from town?

If you choose to look for a taxi on the way into town, turn to page 295. If you choose to find a taxi on the outskirts, turn to page 297.

It is starting to get unpleasantly warm in your office. You catch occasional glimpses of fiery tendrils testing the edges of your drop ceiling. You brave the searing heat by the now shattered window and at last see the fire engines pull up outside. Luckily, they've brought a ladder company. Still, they may not see you. With the heat (and now smoke) verging on the intolerable, you decide that it is time to take action. You rush to a nearby closet where the ceremonial conference table coverings are stored. You grab all that you can get your arms around. Back at your desk, you carefully knot them together, one-by-one, testing each for strength. When you were a child, your grandfather, a former mariner, taught you all there was to know about knots. Bowlines, half-hitch, and catshank, you can tie them all. How fortunate. You loop the final cloth around the window frame, double knotting it for good measure.

Yes, it has come to this. You are planning to repel out the window on an improvised rope in the hopes a firefighter will see you and pluck you from the building's side. Did I mention you are afraid of heights? Well, this experience will serve to reinforce that healthy avoidance of high places.

You kick the "rope" out the window and carefully shimmy over the edge. To describe your clutch as anything other than a death grip is a disservice to your impressive finger strength. The worst of the fire has risen to the top of the building, which now wears a crown of flames. Hand by hand, you work your way downward until you make the mistake of looking at the ground. Fifteen meters might not sound like a lot, but it sends your body into vertiginous lock-down.

Thankfully, your antics have caught the attention of the ladder company, who immediately start moving to assist you. Before they can reach you (and honestly, you were out of range of their ladder anyway), you lose your grip and plummet earthward. You have time to wonder what impact will feel like and subsequently learn that it is bouncier than you had imagined. Quick-thinking firefighters know a lost cause when they see it—those involved here had rushed over and positioned themselves in the drop-zone with a large tarpaulin made for catching people in these very situations. Congratulations—you are not dead!

One last thing though... it seems in your mad rush for survival, you've forgotten your side bag. While that might not sound like a big deal given the ordeal you've just survived, it might make you sad to know that in it is the only existing draft of the novel you've been writing for the past seven years. You are old-fashioned and insisted on writing it by hand. You justified the inefficiency by telling yourself it: a) was how all great novels had been written in the past, and b) helped you write more fluidly since the speed of the pen was more in keeping with the speed of your mind. Or so you liked to think. You had been making good progress recently and hoped to possibly finish the draft this weekend. As you stare up at the burning building, all you can picture are the charred, curling edges of your life's work. Your heart fills with despair.

It has been said, however, that manuscripts refuse to burn, so maybe you'll get lucky this time. Tomorrow, as the disaster crews and insurance agents are poking through the ashy strata of destruction, a press conference will be called. The building, it seems, was a total loss, but one stack of papers improbably survived. They ask you to please step forward and reclaim your masterpiece. Tears of joy as you're reunited with what you thought was lost. The crowd erupts in applause. The city fire marshal announces a new initiative to insulate all buildings with the manuscripts of failed authors. You interrupt to say that "when you're saving lives, nothing can be considered a failure." It becomes the slogan for the new campaign. More applause from the crowd. Fade to black.

The End.

After years of hard work, you completed your novel. Even more surprisingly, you found a willing agent and a number of publishers willing to fight over it. Success, fame, fortune—all of these things are yours. You retire from civil service to an island you were able to purchase with some of the proceeds from your novel. Peace, quiet, and contentment are your daily lot.

Of course, to get here, you had to break the rules. Though I am a bit disappointed, who can blame you for your chutzpah? Government work taught you that there is always a loophole and you found it. I hope you're happy with your hollow victory.

The End.

Especially given the transit strike, you decide that you'd better not risk losing the only possible ride you might find tonight. You see the brake lights illuminate and hear the telltale sound of the ignition turning the engine over. Not wanting to be ignored, you sprint toward the taxi, shouting, whistling, and waving your arm. When you get to the back passenger door, the fare light on top goes out and you breathe a sigh of relief, knowing that you have gotten the driver's attention.

You open the door and climb in, the driver asks, "Where to?" Upon hearing your home address, the driver shakes his head, mutters, and makes a clicking sound with his tongue. "That'll cost extra with the police cordons." At this point, you don't care how much it will cost, you just want to go home. You agree to the terms and the driver begins circumnavigating the city center.

The taxi has seen better days. Its seats are stained, the protective Plexiglas between the back seat and driver is nearly opaque with scratches, and the whole cabin reeks of a combination of alcohol, cigarette-smoke, and body odor. You are not certain whether the smell is just part of the car or is emanating from the unkempt-looking driver. All that said, you've been in worse cabs. You are just thankful to be heading home at last.

Out the window, you see boroughs you have never been through before. Such is the arc of your route. The blending of architecture is really quite fascinating as you can see how, as the central city grew, it gobbled-up and incorporated surrounding districts of varying ages. "These are the strata of urbanization," you think to yourself. If it all burned down, you wonder if the ashes would be distinguishable from one another.

The taxi driver isn't particularly chatty, which is just as well with you—it has been a very long day and you don't have much energy for idle conversation.

Before you know it, you start recognizing your surroundings as the taxi makes its way through the neighborhoods adjoining your own. With home close at hand, you instinctively reach for your side bag only to realize that you left it back at the office. "Curse my stupidity!" you exclaim. This gets the attention of your driver. He raises an eyebrow in your direction. "It's nothing," you say with a nervous smile.

I should apologize at this point for not reminding you to take your bag at the outset. What has upset you is the fact that your wallet may be inside of it—you have a habit of not putting it in your pants pocket where it belongs. You quickly pat yourself down, first your pants pockets, then, finding nothing there, proceed to your jacket. Ah. There it is in your inside pocket. You like to put things in hidden places. It has always made you feel like a spy.

What is perhaps more upsetting is the fact that the bag contains the working draft of the novel you have been slowly writing for the past several years. You had recently been gaining momentum and were (by your estimation) only a page or two from wrapping the narrative up nicely. You had hoped you would be able to complete it over the weekend. Maybe even have had a chance to start reading back through and editing. "Oh well," you think, "what's one more week?"

At that very moment, you start smelling smoke. It seems to be wafting from a large fire in the city center. Those protesting hooligans have probably set another government office on fire. As the taxi turns onto the homestretch of your journey, you get a chance to glance out the back window. There is quite the conflagration in the central square. A tall building with its top swaddled in flames. The color drains from your face. That is your office building. And your life's work lies inside.

Do you tell the cab to make a beeline for the city center or go home in resigned defeat?

If you choose to speed toward the chaos and make a desperate attempt to recover the only extant draft of your novel, turn to page 331. If you choose to go home and cry yourself to sleep, turn to page 333.

You debate your options for a while and decide that you're likely to encounter a taxi in either direction, this being a main thoroughfare. Six of one, half a dozen of another, as they say. Still, to move forward, a direction must be picked, so you take your chances heading back toward the town center. After all, the worst of the protest mopping-up is probably over.

I suppose I should have told you that the protest is actually not over. In fact, it and its associated violence are spreading outward block by block. Oh well, too late to change anything now. For now, do your best to maintain blissful ignorance of the situation at the city center.

Your stomach gives an angry grumble, voicing its concern about the lunch you skipped and your overall decision-making skills. While you could probably wait until you get home, given the way the evening has gone so far, you should probably take advantage of any dining opportunity you encounter. Finding dinner has now taken temporary precedence over finding a ride home.

Lucky for you, you see what looks like cafe awnings lining a section of the street ahead. From here, you can see that they look a bit more upscale than your typical evening fare, but at this point, you're willing to eat (and pay) anything. Savory smells start to suffuse the air, tempting your taste buds and making your stomach rumble all the louder. Your mouth begins watering. "Maybe I'll have a nice, buttery quiche," you think.

Just as you are coming to the restaurant's front door, you notice a taxi stand on the street corner. What luck! What is less lucky is the fact that the only cab you have seen for the last thirty minutes seems to be preparing to leave to find paying customers.

With time ticking, do you choose to hurry over and hail the cab or go into the restaurant for dinner?
If you choose to run toward the cab, whistling and waving your arm, turn to page 292. If you choose to be slave to your digestive tract and trust fate to provide you with a taxi after dinner, turn to page 299.

You debate your options for a while and decide that you're likely to encounter a taxi in either direction, this being a main thoroughfare. Six of one, half a dozen of another, as they say. Still, to move forward, a direction must be picked, so you take your chances heading up the hill and away from the town center. After all, you don't want to get mired in the post-protest mopping-up.

I suppose I should have told you that the neighborhood you're heading into is probably the most dangerous in the entire city. Muggings, thievery, shootings—all are commonplace occurrences. Oh well, too late to change anything at this stage. For now, do your best to maintain blissful ignorance of the rapidly deteriorating streetscape.

Your stomach voices its concern with an angry grumble. While you could probably wait to eat until you get home, given the way the evening has gone so far, you should probably take advantage of any food opportunity you encounter. Finding dinner has now taken temporary precedence over finding a ride home.

Lucky for you, you see what looks like cafe awnings lining a section of the street ahead. Even from here, you can see that they are faded and a bit tattered, but food is food. The first waft of the kitchen exhaust is surprisingly palatable. Your mouth begins watering and your stomach rumblings kick into overdrive. "Maybe I'll have a nice, greasy piece of pizza," you think.

Just as you are coming to the restaurant's front door, you notice a taxi stand on the street corner. What luck! What is less lucky is the fact that the only cab you have seen for the last thirty minutes seems to be preparing to leave to find pay-ing customers.

With time ticking, do you choose to hurry over and hail the cab or go into the restaurant for dinner?
If you choose to run toward the cab, whistling and waving your arm, turn to page 303. If you choose to be slave to your digestive tract and trust fate to provide you with a taxi after dinner, turn to page 323.

Your hunger wins out with the rationalization that taxis, even during transit strikes, are not all that uncommon. With that, you watch the driver ease away from the curb and head off down the street. Your stomach is convinced you are doing it a grand favor. Let's allow it to live with that delusion for a while.

You turn your attention to the cafe. Its awnings are a classy goldenrod color and show no signs of sunfading. You squint to read the menu framed in a streetside pedestal and, as you suspected, everything is about fifty percent more than you'd like to pay for portions that will no doubt be smaller than what you'd like to consume. Nonetheless, you made this decision on account of your stomach. Finding its salvation at hand, biology will not be deterred.

You walk through the double front doors and are greeted by a skeptical-looking maître d'. Your entrance is drawing scowls from the assembled gourmands. It is for this very reason that you have always been negatively disposed toward haute cuisine. Fine dining halls are always thick with judgmentalism.

Trying to avoid eye contact with the assembled diners, you notice your reflection in the floor-to-ceiling mirror along the far wall. It seems that your adventures escaping the mob have left you looking a bit ragged. Your face is bruising, your pants are torn, and you are generally grimed-up from your time in the garbage bin. No wonder you are getting looks. If you could see my face, it would communicate disgust with subtle undercurrents of sympathy. After all, it is your choices that led you here.

Sensing that it would be better not to ask, and even worse to refuse you service, the maître d' whisks you toward the back of the establishment. There, in a secluded booth, out of view from the other patrons, you are seated and breathe a sigh of relief. You earnestly thank your host and he replies with a solemn nod. While you ponder the menu, you are brought the opening course of bread. It is crusty on the outside, light and fluffy on the inside. When it hits your stomach, it soaks up the waiting digestive juices like a sponge and you are grateful. The waiter comes back and takes your order. Just as you hoped, they have multiple quiches available. You indulge in a sausage, chard, and cheese variety and can already imagine its buttery crust dissolving in your mouth. It will only be a few minutes.

Some believe that there is more joy in the anticipation of pleasure than the pleasure itself. At this moment, you can understand the sentiment. Despite the rough series of events that led you here, everything has turned out alright. Soon, you will enjoy a fine quiche, then go home for a weekend's rest. As the waiter returns with your food, you instinctively reach for your side bag only to realize that you left it back at the office. "Curse my stupidity!" you exclaim. This gets the attention of your waiter. He raises an eyebrow as he sets the plate down. "It's nothing," you say with a nervous smile.

I should apologize at this point for not reminding you to take your bag at the outset. What has upset you is the fact that your wallet may be inside of it—you have a habit of not putting it in your pocket where it belongs. You quickly pat yourself down, first your pants, then, finding nothing there, proceed to your jacket. Ah. There it is in your inside pocket. You like to put things in hidden places. It has always made you feel like a spy.

What is perhaps more upsetting is the fact that the bag contains the working draft of the novel you have been slowly writing for the past several years. You had recently been gaining momentum and were (by your estimation) only a page or two from wrapping the narrative up nicely. You had hoped you would be able to complete it over the weekend. Maybe even have had a chance to start reading back through and editing. "Oh well," you think, "what's one more week?" Your hunger dictates your priorities at the moment, so it doesn't seem all that important.

Unfortunately, before you even get to enjoy your first bite of quiche, you hear some commotion burst out at the front of the restaurant. You crane your head to peer around your booth and see hordes of people running down the street. Some throw Molotov cocktails, others throw bricks. And they all seem to have taken an interest in the restaurant in which you are now seated. Great minds think alike, as they say. As if it wasn't incriminating enough to be a government employee, you are now eating with the upper-class muckety-mucks who frequent fine dining establishments. You have no desire to be mistaken for one of their ilk, and, having seen what this mob did in the city center, you know it would be best to leave quickly and surreptitiously. Your uneaten quiche stares back at you, grease pooling on the plate. In a frenzy, you wrap it in your napkin, shove the napkin in your pocket, and dart out of your booth to make an escape into the back hallway. You are confronted with the swinging door to the main kitchen and an access ladder that leads to the roof.

Do you head into the kitchen or take your chances on the roof?

If you choose to make a mad break through the kitchen, upsetting pots and pans as you go, turn to page 306. If you choose to shimmy up the ladder and wait out the hubbub on the roof, turn to page 310.

Given the realities of the transit strike, you decide that you'd better not risk losing the only possible ride home you might find tonight. Especially in this neighborhood. Of course, you could have chosen to ask the cab driver to wait, then ordered a takeaway meal, but you're not the quickest on your feet. You've chosen to get in the taxi straightaway, so that is what you'll do.

You see the brake lights illuminate and hear the telltale sound of the ignition straining to turn the engine over. Not wanting to be ignored, you sprint toward the taxi, shouting, whistling, and waving your arm. When you get to the back passenger door, the fare light on top goes out and you breathe a sigh of relief, knowing that you have gotten the driver's attention.

You open the door, climb in, and the driver says "Sorry, I am having bad luck today." You don't understand him and respond with your home address. The driver turns around shaking his head and muttering. "My car is broken, but don't worry, I've called my cousin." Cousins—even those with rough edges—are always there to help when we need them, aren't they? You, having been born to a third generation single-child family, don't know what to expect from a cousin, so are a bit concerned.

"Does your cousin also drive a taxi?" you ask nervously.

"No, but he can give us a ride."

You glance around to see if there are any other options, but this seems to be the only car, let alone only taxi, on this street. The rough character of the neighborhood really shines in the evening light. Boarded up storefronts, crumbling architectural details, broken bottles along the sidewalk—it's clear that this is not the best place to go wandering at night. The taxi you're sitting in has seen better days. Its seats are stained, the protective Plexiglas between the back seat and driver is broken and missing, and the whole cabin reeks of a combination of alcohol, cigarette-smoke, urine, and body odor. You are not certain whether the smell is just part of the car or is emanating from the unkempt-looking driver. There may even be bullet-holes in the front window. This may well be the worst cab you have ever sat in.

You're half tempted to tell the driver "never mind" and try your luck with the restaurant instead, when a battered car swerves into the parking space in front of you. The horrendous sound of metal grinding on concrete greets the car's arrival as its tires scrape along the curb. Your driver seems pleased by the development and says, "Ah good, he is here." He claps his hands, hops out of the car, and motions you to follow. Your driver attempts to open the rear passenger-side door on his cousin's car, but after a few straining tugs, gives up and walks over to the driver-side to give that a try. It opens like doors are supposed to and you are offered a seat inside. Wanting nothing but to go home, you oblige despite your misgivings. Your driver climbs in through the window of the front passenger-side and turns to his cousin who says, "Rough times with the car?" Both break into riotous laughter.

How best to describe the cousin? While I realize I didn't take the time to describe your driver, the cousin bears a close family resemblance. That said, his every attribute seems amplified. His arms more muscular, his facial scruff scruffier, his snarled lip more contorted, his odor more odoriferous. He has a large "Rx" tattooed on his arm, but you're fairly certain he's not a pharmacist. Let me remind you that one needn't be pleasant-seeming to be a good driver. Judging from the looks of the car though, driving is not one of this fellow's strong suits.

The cousin smashes the gas pedal, then shifts the car into gear. With a galloping lurch, the three of you go careening down the road. Thankfully, there are no other cars around, otherwise, you most likely would have hit something by now. As you swallow your heart back out of your throat, you attempt to remind the gentlemen of your desired destination, but they are so engrossed in conversation, that they don't seem to be interested in you. At this point, you don't care how much it will cost, you just want to go home. "I'll pay double if need be," you say loudly. You might as well be talking to yourself. The car speeds in the opposite direction from which you want to be heading. Rounding several corners, you feel it tip onto two wheels.

You feel hopeless and make peace with your creator, fully expecting to die at any moment. As you suspected it would, this wild ride comes to an abrupt end.

Turn to page 309 to learn your fate.

Recently, you have had some bad experiences with rooftop excursions, so an escape through the kitchen seems a safer bet. Besides, you have seen so many movies with kitchen chase scenes, you think it would be fun to recreate one. You steel yourself and make a mental note to send as much of the kitchenware and cutlery flying as you are able. This momentary lapse into a fantasy theme proves a painful mistake. The burly sous chef comes charging out to see what all the commotion is about in the front of house. She must not have seen you. Either that, or she didn't care. In any event, the end result is the same. The force of the swinging door transfers its energy to your skull and sends you tumbling backward. Somehow, you retain consciousness. Perhaps it is the mob of terrorized patrons now heading your way. You quickly get up and follow the panicked sous chef back into the kitchen.

The room that greets you is not at all what you expected given the genteel atmosphere out front. Instead of a spick and span expanse of chrome appliances and white walls, you're presented with a warren of wooden countertops and grimy tan tile. If you had the time, you could count the knife scoring, which like rings on a tree trunk, would tell you the age of the kitchen. There is no immediately discernible way out. You stand by the door, scanning the room in desperation, but all you see are nooks hiding sinks, and crannies cradling stacked cooking supplies.

By this point, the fleeing patrons have already found the kitchen entrance. You relive your immediate past, but in reverse. The door swings hard into the back of your skull and you tumble forward, sending a group of freshly plated meals clattering to the ground. You really should have learned your lesson about standing in its swing arc. Like a boxer who will not yield, you shake off your stupor, adrenaline coursing through your veins. You stagger up from the floor and take note of the direction the kitchen staff is now running. Along with the frightened patrons, some of the hooligans from the street are now coursing through the swinging door.

You had better get moving before this situation gets out of hand. Weaving through the various cooking stations (and scattering a generous amount of pots and pans as you do), you come to the rear exit. Freedom from this madness at last. Your plan, once you emerge in the alley, is to run a couple of blocks, find a quiet corner, then devour the crushed quiche whose grease is now soaking through to your undershirt. But you know what they say about the best-laid plans.

You step into the alley and find it awash in confusion. Patrons, chefs, and protesters running every which way. And police officers. The police have cordoned off the area, effectively trapping everyone in the dead-end alley. To get out, everyone must queue-up single file and proceed through the checkpoint. Those deemed suspicious are handcuffed and loaded into a van. The restaurant staff and patrons are consistently let through with no problem, however. Eventually, the chaos in the alley subsides and everyone—rioters and bystanders alike—joins the line and awaits judgement. At least it is moving quickly. You never imagined that government workers could be so efficient. Your waiter, it turns out, is in line in front of you. When he reaches the checkpoint, the police take one look at his attire and ingratiating smile and wave him through. He turns and gives you a wink as he walks away.

You enter the search zone and see the police officer grit his teeth. You nod a smile and take a step toward freedom. But there is a billy club blocking your path. The lieutenant it is connected to shakes his head disappointingly and gestures toward the van. "Surely, there must be some misunderstanding," you stammer. Reaching for your wallet to show your ID was the wrong choice in this case. Another officer slams you against the side of the van and gives you a full pat-down. They feel the quiche and disgustedly throw it to the ground. Your heart and stomach ache in unison as that beautiful potential meal comes to rest in a dirty, muck-filled gutter.

There seems to be no reasoning with these men. You are shackled to the floor next to some rough-looking characters. Luckily, they pay you no mind. When the van is full, its driver ferries you toward the local jail where you will all be put into processing. Out the front window, you catch a glimpse of a tall building bathed in flames. "What's that building?" you ask.

The driver, being more gregarious than enforcement-minded, is happy to respond: "That's the Ministry of Finance. Just heard a call over the radio—doesn't sound good." No, it doesn't. The flames are so bright they illuminate the city skyline. Your office is burning. And your life's work lies inside.

To spend the night in jail, turn to page 328.

"Am I dead?" you're thinking now. I'm so sorry. That was misleading language. Your ride comes to an abrupt end because the cousin has whipped into a garage and jammed on the brakes, flinging you forward against the front seats. You crumple into a whimpering pile while the car's other two occupants continue their boisterous antics. Your driver turns around, notices you on the floorboards and says, "Why are you laying down? We're here." He and the cousin get out and walk toward a man smoking in a dimly lit corner of the garage.

You carefully peek out the window so as to attract as little attention as possible and see your driver being handed a rope of some sort and the cousin, a tire-iron. At any second, they could be headed back to the car. Worried that there is some nefarious plot afoot, you sense that this might be your only chance to escape. The open garage door through which you entered seems to be the only way out. Nearby, in the opposite, dark corner of the garage, are stacks of old tires you might be able to hide behind.

Do you bolt for the exit or try to hide behind the tires?
If you choose to chance a footrace with people who might be violent felons, turn to page 312. If you choose to try to outwit your would-be assailants by hiding, turn to page 318.

Despite your recently developed fear of heights, you are more afraid of sharp objects, so decide to stay out of the kitchen. As you begin hoisting yourself up the ladder, a burly sous chef explodes out of the kitchen to see what all of the commotion is about. She sees you on the ladder and is about to shout you down when she sees the thundering mass of humanity bearing down on her. She turns heel and runs back into the kitchen.

Hoping no one disreputable decides to join you on your rooftop escapade, you scurry up the ladder until you reach the access hatch. You give it a mighty heave and it pops up momentarily, then slams back down. It seems the hydraulic pistons that once helped prop the door have long since failed. Nonetheless, you awkwardly squeeze yourself out the hatch without too much difficulty. Unfortunately, as you do so, the quiche in your pocket squirts out, falls to the floor, and is quickly trampled by the mob below. As you slither onto the roof, you breathe a sigh of relief at the rare moment of peace. You may have lost your dinner, but you escaped without injury. A fair trade in your mind.

You dust yourself off and look around to see the prototypical mix of gravel and tar, ducting and pipe-work. A few crushed beer cans and stamped-out cigarette butts tell you that this might occasionally be someone else's retreat as well. But for now, it appears as if you're all alone up here. The dusky city air is fragrant with the smells of protest. Diluted tear-gas, sweat, flowering trees, and alcohol, interlaced with the subtlest of smoky aromas.

For a moment, you are distracted from your olfactory bliss by the people lining up in the alley below. That looks awfully orderly for a bunch of people who just went screaming through a restaurant. The queue is single-file and in it, you see formal diners next to hooligans. At its far end, you see police lights and officers screening suspects into impound wagons. You are thankful you didn't emerge into that mess. Knowing your luck, you would be sitting in the back of one of those wagons as we speak.

But getting back to the smells. The smoky odor is getting stronger. It doesn't smell like kitchen exhaust. You scan the horizon and see several flickering orange glows quavering amongst the cityscape. On one particularly tall building, you can even see flames ascending the side, like a waterfall in reverse. The color drains from your face when you realize that the burning building is the Ministry of Finance. And your life's work lies inside. Why on earth did you choose to leave your bag behind?

Though you're tempted to rush back to see if you can rescue your manuscript, you wonder whether the protest itself is still raging. If so, there might not be any chance of making it through. But given the crowd that just rushed through the restaurant, it may be quieter in the town center now.

Do you rush back to your office or declare the whole endeavor a lost cause?

If you choose to speed toward the chaos and make a desperate attempt to recover the only extant draft of your novel, turn to page 331. If you choose to go home and cry yourself to sleep, turn to page 333.

You try in a frenzy to open the door, but it won't budge. Either the child-lock is engaged, or the latch is stuck. Whatever the case, there is no easy way out. The front passenger-side window is open, so you dive over the seats and scramble madly to squeeze yourself through the opening. Just as you are clearing the car, your driver and his cousin turn to see you and shout surprisedly.

You fall to the ground, but quickly pick yourself up and dart off before they even get a chance to react. For once, your legs do not fail you as you sprint down the block. You glance over your shoulder a few times but sense no pursuit. Victory and adrenaline course through your veins. The air rushes by your face, your clothes ruffle in the breeze, and you feel master of your own domain.

Confirming once again that you have lost your captors, you slow your pace and take in your surroundings. The street is bathed in dusky shadows. Abandoned buildings line it on both sides. You see huddled masses here and there and are unsure if they are garbage piles or people settling into their evening's accommodations. Two blocks down, on the neighborhood's far border, the streetlights begin again. Beyond that, you see more a more welcoming streetscape. You remember the unusually high murder-rate in this part of town and decide that you had better get out of here quickly.

While you've been catching your breath and surveying your surroundings, I should tell you that you've caught the attention of several locals. The buildings you think are abandoned actually are low-rent tenements. Some of the people watching you are technically squatters, but let's include them in this group for expediency's sake. You are oblivious to your observers until you hear footsteps approaching from behind.

You spin around, braced for a struggle, but the woman pays you no mind and continues walking. Further down the street, she walks up the front steps to one of the houses, fumbles for a key, and discretely opens the door and disappears inside. "This isn't so bad," you think to yourself.

Nonetheless, the man coming up the opposite side of the street could change that impression if you catch his attention, so you decide to keep walking toward the streetlights. Of course, you do look out of place, so you can't help but attract his attention. Out of the corner of your eye, you see him reach into his pocket, zero in on you and trot across the street. At five paces away, he pulls a gun and says, "I am going to shoot you." This is not how you pictured this encounter going. You focus on the barrel and see your life flash before your eyes. Up until that point, you had always assumed it was a figure of speech, but there, in rapid succession, are the defining moments of your life: your field trip to the factory where your father worked, the queue outside the observatory as Halley's Comet passed by, the vacation cruise your family took through the Strait of Gibraltar, your time in college, your first love, picking berries by the creekside, kicking through the fallen leaves every autumn, your swearing-in as a public servant, your favorite park bench, reading books on the weekend, Christmas morning at your parents'. You really wish it didn't have to end this way—there is so much more to be done.

You're so focused on the unfurling of your life's reel that you don't even notice the approaching car until it pulls up between you and the gunman. You hear a "You don't want to shoot this person!" followed by a "Hey, where do you think you're going?" that seems to be directed at you.

You turn and see your taxi driver and his cousin smiling and waving at you. There is something sick about people who can so cheerily engage in thuggery. No doubt, they have something horrible planned for you. So horrible, in fact, that they needed to chase off the man who was about to shoot you. But since you've been caught, you resign yourself to whatever torture might ensue. If they're just after your money, perhaps you can forestall their assault by forking over your wallet now. You instinctively reach for your side bag only to realize that you left it back at the office. "Curse my stupidity!" you exclaim.

I should apologize at this point for not reminding you to take your bag at the outset. What has upset you is the fact that your wallet may be inside of it—you have a habit of not putting it in your pocket where it belongs. You quickly pat yourself down, first your pants, then, finding nothing there, proceed to your jacket. Ah. There it is in your inside pocket. You like to put things in hidden places. It has always made you feel like a spy.

Wallet found, your disappointment lingers due to the fact that the bag contains the working draft of the novel you have been slowly writing for the past several years. You had recently been gaining momentum and were (by your estimation) only a page or two from wrapping the narrative up nicely. You had hoped you would be able to complete it over the weekend. Maybe even have had a chance to start reading back through and editing. "Oh well," you think, "what's one more week?"

During the entire length of this inner monologue, your driver and his cousin simply look at you quizzically. "Just get in," your driver snaps. The cousin shakes his head as if to say he cannot believe your stupidity. Remembering that the back passenger door does not open, you walk around to the driver-side, yank the door open and slide in to negotiate their demands. For a good minute, you all just look from one to another blankly, until the cousin has the good sense to speak up. "I'm sorry, but this will cost you."

At least he's a criminal with a conscience—it's a start. You pull out your wallet and relinquish it to your driver. "Take it all if you want, it's all I have with me." For a moment, there is more confusion. He rifles through your billfold, takes the three largest bills and hands the rest back to you. That was unexpected. "Where to?" they ask, while the cousin revs the engine eagerly. Slow to comprehend how badly you've misread this situation, you are hesitant at first to give them your home address. Sure, they were generous with your wallet, but maybe it's a ruse to get into your home. So they try again: "The address... where you want to go..." But your driver remembers that you told him when you first got in his malfunctioning taxi, so he chimes in excitedly. He and the cousin start their animated jabbering again and the car speeds off toward your home.

I'm really surprised at your behavior in these last few minutes. Did your mother never teach you to trust in the kindness of strangers? True, you have had some unfortunate events befall you recently, but these kinds of human interactions are the exception, not the norm. Fear of your fellow man drove you into exactly the kind of situation you had hoped to avoid. Oedipus would be proud. Take it from me—there is nothing to fear here. We both just want to get through this.

Out the window, the city passes by in a blur. You don't think you've ever been on some of these streets before, but the car is going so quickly, you can't be sure. The near-field buildings make you motion sick, but gazing into the distance, you start to recognize your surroundings. You have already made it to the neighborhoods adjoining your own. A wave of relief washes over you. Soon, this horrible adventure will all be over and you'll have a nice hot shower, then climb into bed. Maybe you will even indulge in a small fire. Curling up in front of it in your easy chair sounds awfully tempting. You have just a few chapters left in the novel you're currently reading, so with any luck, you'll learn how the author resolves the conundrum facing the protagonist. Or maybe you'll just sleep in front of the fire. It doesn't matter to you, since either way, you'll be home.

At that very moment, you start smelling smoke. It seems to be wafting from the city center. Those protesting hooligans have probably set another government office ablaze. As the taxi turns onto your home street, you get a chance to glance out the back window. There is quite the conflagration on the horizon. You can see a tall building with its top swaddled in flames. The color drains from your face. That is your office building. And your life's work lies inside.

Do you ask your driver to make a detour through the city center or go home in resigned defeat?

If you choose to speed toward the chaos and make a desperate attempt to recover the only extant draft of your novel, turn to page 331. If you choose to go home and cry yourself to sleep, turn to page 333.

You try in a frenzy to open the door, but it won't budge. Either the child-lock is engaged or the latch is stuck. Whatever the case, there is no way out. You could try scrambling over the front seat and out the passenger-side window, but the lack of stealth that would entail would make hiding behind the tires somewhat pointless. You are trapped. Out the window you see the three brutes chatting and gesturing toward you in the car.

In a flood of recognition, you realize that you have seen the cousin before. The large "Rx" tattoo on the man's forearm should have been a dead giveaway—he belongs to the notorious Rexwalder Gang. The self-same gang that your mother warned you about growing up. Rexwalders had long terrorized the area. They are known as a murderous band of ruffians and respected for their vicious disregard for human life. It's even said that the gang's matriarch once put a hit out on her own son, the snitch, who, failing to die despite absorbing fifteen shots to the torso, made amends by maiming her with an exploding teapot on Christmas morning. Once she healed, everyone had a good laugh.

When a family friend married into the Rexwalder clan, your parents lived in fear that you would all eventually end up in meat lockers scattered around the countryside. It was only later, when you found out that your father had been a willing participant in certain of the Rexwalder enterprises, that you had a change of heart. Your mother had wanted to give him a tongue-lashing but thought better of the idea being that he was protected by a gang of known teapot bombers. And she did like her afternoon teas. You had long wondered if your father killed in their employ, but never had the guts to ask before he died of carbon monoxide poisoning. Given the absurdity of your current predicament, you're half-tempted to ask the gentleman if he knows. Ultimately though, you give priority to your more immediate survival.

Your driver and his cousin eventually wrap up their conversation and walk back with the rope and tire-iron. I don't mean to frighten you, but they look fairly menacing. Maybe you can just pay them off. As they approach the car, you instinctively reach for your side bag only to realize that you left it back at the office. "Curse my stupidity!" you exclaim. This gets the attention of your driver. He raises an eyebrow and tap, tap, taps the tire-iron in his palm. "Never mind," you say with an air of defeat.

I should apologize at this point for not reminding you to take your bag at the outset. What has upset you is the fact that your wallet may be inside of the bag—you have a habit of not putting it in your pants pocket where it belongs. You quickly pat yourself down, first your pants pockets, then, finding nothing there, proceed to your jacket. Ah. There it is in your inside pocket. You like to put things in hidden places. It has always made you feel like a spy.

You breathe easier knowing your wallet is on hand. It still would be better to have the bag—especially since it contains the working draft of the novel you have been slowly writing for the past several years. You had recently been gaining momentum and were (by your estimation) only a page or two from wrapping the narrative up nicely. "Oh well," you think, "there is always next week." It's precisely these patterns of procrastination that have led to all of the unfinished projects in your life. But who am I to judge?

In the meantime, your driver and his cousin have re-taken their places in the front of the car. Each fleshy thwump of the tire-iron on palm fills you with a little more nausea. "Gentlemen," you say, "if you want my money, I'm afraid I'm not worth very much."

"In taxis, it is customary to pay for your ride."

Well that was an odd response. These guys are professionals, it seems.

"I'm sure I'll pay one way or another," you mutter. The passenger seat assailant clicks his tongue frustratedly. The cousin translates from the driver's seat: "He is upset." Great, now you've gone and made these men angry. If a tire-iron wasn't enough encouragement to hold your tongue, I'm not sure what will be.

"Where should we take you?" they ask, while the cousin revs the engine eagerly. Odd. You would have thought that thugs like this would know all of the best places in which to dispose of a body. Clearly, you've rattled them.

"You know, I've always imagined being buried at sea, so that's maybe a good option."

Silence and confused looks. It all feels ready to boil over. You close your eyes and expect to feel the iron impact your skull at any moment.

You know, I'm really disappointed in you. All of the times your mother talked to you about trusting in the kindness of strangers were for naught. True, since we've known each other, things have not necessarily gone your way, but negative human interactions are the exception, not the norm. Take it from me. I want nothing but the best for you. Suffices to say you've misread yet another situation.

You sheepishly open your eyes and see the front seat occupants staring over their shoulders at you. "You don't look well, friend. Hey, we won't even make you pay. Just tell us your address." Before you can respond, your driver remembers that you told him when you first got in his malfunctioning taxi, so he chimes in excitedly. He and the cousin resume their animated jabbering and the car speeds off toward your home.

Out the window, the city passes by in a blur. You think you see a mob of people running down the street at one point, but the car is going at a breakneck pace, so you don't know whether to trust your fleeting glances. To avert motion sickness, you fix your eyes on the horizon. Soon enough, you make it to the neighborhoods adjoining your own. A wave of relief washes over you. When this horrible adventure is over, you will have a nice hot shower, then climb into bed. Maybe you will even indulge in a small fire. Curling up in your hearthside easy chair sounds awfully tempting. Maybe you'll even have the energy to do some reading and will take notes on how the author navigates the protagonist through narrative conundrums. Or maybe you'll just doze, basking in the radiated heat. It doesn't matter to you, since either way, you'll be home.

At that very moment, you start smelling smoke. You either have a very potent imagination or the aerosolized fruits of the rioters' labor is wafting outward from the city center. As the car turns onto your home street, you get a chance to glance out the back window. There is quite the conflagration there alright. A tall building, crowned in flames. The color drains from your face. That is your office building. And your life's work lies inside.

Do you ask your driver to make a detour through the city center or go home in resigned defeat?

If you choose to speed toward the chaos and make a desperate attempt to recover the only extant draft of your novel, turn to page 331. If you choose to go home and cry yourself to sleep, turn to page 333.

Your hunger wins out with the rationalization that taxis, even during transit strikes, are not all that uncommon. Your stomach will thank you. Decision made, you watch the brake lights go off and hear the engine sputter and cough. The car shudders and the engine dies. The driver gets out and slams his door, cursing. Looks like you would have had to stay here anyway. Fate wanted you to have a meal, it seems.

You turn your attention to the greasy spoon diner. Its awnings are a tattered maroon. The neon sign in the front window flickers and hums behind a windowsill littered with dead and dying flies. You squint to read the menu plastered to the wall by the front door and it seems to offer the standard fare. It might not look that inviting, but as they say, hunger is the mother of bad decisions. Finding digestive salvation at hand, your stomach will not be deterred.

You walk through the squeaky screen door and are greeted by a pot-bellied cook behind the counter and a conspicuous lack of customers. Let me remind you that beggars can't be choosers. How bad could it really be? The cook looks you up and down, pulls a bottle of something off the shelf, fills up a glass, and slides it across the bar to you. "It's on me."

What a kind gesture. You thank him and take a seat at the bar. That is when you notice your reflection in the chrome behind the counter. It seems that your adventures escaping the mob have left you looking a bit ragged. Your face is bruising, your pants are torn, and you are generally grimed-up from your time in the garbage bin. No wonder you are getting a free drink. If you could see my face, it would communicate disgust with subtle undercurrents of sympathy. After all, it is your choices that led you here.

"Growl" says your stomach. "Food" says your brain. "I'll have some fried eggs and potatoes," says your mouth. "Comin' right up," says the cook. Soon, you'll have food in your belly and all will be right with the world. Of course, there's still the matter of finding your way home, but for the moment, that seems secondary.

There is a school of thought that there is more joy in the anticipation of pleasure than the pleasure itself. At this moment, you can understand the sentiment. The food arrives more quickly than you anticipated, so you don't get to enjoy that feeling for long. The eggs and potatoes are still sizzling as the plate is slid in front of you. You know it may burn your mouth, but you can't contain yourself and take the first bites. Greasy potatoes and eggs are hard to ruin. While these are maybe not the most flavorful example you have ever tried, they hit the spot.

As you near the end of your meal, bite after satisfied bite, you instinctively reach for your side bag only to realize that you left it back at the office. "Curse my stupidity!" you exclaim. This gets the attention of the cook who, though his back is turned, gives a sympathetic shrug. "It's nothing," you say with a nervous smile.

I should apologize at this point for not reminding you to take your bag at the outset. What has upset you is the fact that your wallet may be inside of the bag—you have a habit of not putting it in your pocket where it belongs. You quickly pat yourself down, first your pants, then, finding nothing there, proceed to your jacket. Ah. There it is in your inside pocket. You like to put things in hidden places. It has always made you feel like a spy.

Wallet found, you are still upset because the bag contains the working draft of the novel you have been slowly writing for the past decade. You had recently been gaining momentum and were (by your estimation) only a page or two from wrapping the narrative up nicely. You had hoped you would be able to complete it over the weekend. Maybe even have had a chance to start reading back through and editing. "Oh well," you think, "what's one more week?"

You pay for your meal, leaving a generous tip for the cook on the bar and head out into the dusk to find your ride home. The frustrated cabby is still there, only he has the help of a similarly proportioned fellow as they beat on the engine with a tire-iron. They're looking just about ready to give up and attach the towrope, when the driver sees you looking longingly at his broken-down taxi. "You need a ride?"

"Yeah, too bad," you say.

"No problem. My cousin here can give you a ride. I need to go into town to pick up some parts anyway. Half price."

You're pleased by the happy twist of fate, gladly accept, and tell them your address. After all, it doesn't look like there are any other rides to be found in this neighborhood. The cousin opens the rear driver-side door and invites you to have a seat. Once the three of you are situated in the car, the cousin starts the car and lets out a maniacal giggle, stomping on the accelerator before popping the car into gear. The tires squeal and the car careens wildly down the street. You are wondering if perhaps getting into this car was a mistake. But despite the wild first impression, and the rapid speed at which you are traveling, the cousin seems to be an expert behind the wheel.

Out the window, the city passes by in a blur. You don't think you've ever been on some of these streets before, but the car is going so quickly that you can't be sure. Your driver and his cousin are perfectly content chatting with each other, which is just as well with you—it has been a very long day and you don't have much energy for idle conversation.

The near-field buildings make you motion sick, so you focus on those more distant and soon start recognizing your surroundings. You have already made it to the neighborhoods adjoining your own. A wave of relief washes over you. Soon, this horrible adventure will all be over and you will have a nice hot shower, then climb into bed. Maybe you will even indulge in a small fire. Curling up in front of it in your easy chair sounds awfully tempting. You have just a few chapters left in the novel you're currently reading, so with any luck, you'll learn how the author resolves the conundrum facing the protagonist. Or maybe you'll just sleep in front of the fire. It doesn't matter to you, since either way, you'll be home.

At that very moment, you start smelling smoke. It seems to be wafting from the city center. Those protesting hooligans have probably set another government office on fire. As the taxi turns onto the homestretch of your journey, you get a chance to glance out the back window. There is quite the conflagration on the horizon. You see a tall building with its top swaddled in flames. The color drains from your face. That is your office building. And your life's work lies inside.

Do you ask your driver to make a detour through the city center or go home in resigned defeat?

If you choose to speed toward the chaos and make a desperate attempt to recover the only extant draft of your novel, turn to page 331. If you choose to go home and cry yourself to sleep, turn to page 333.

Try as you might, you have thus far been unable to convince anyone that you shouldn't have been arrested in the first place. It is a story that cops and criminals alike have become desensitized to. Even the friendly driver of the paddy wagon will have none of it.

The van stops at the city jail and you are all offloaded into a holding pen to await processing. Your compatriots in the cell have grown tired of your ninny-livered blathering and are contemplating shutting you up forcibly. Sensing that complaining may not be the best way to make new friends, you decide to calm yourself.

One particularly ornery fellow comes over to stare you down. His face is inches from your own. You can see every pore and grizzled, graying whisker. It didn't take being right next to him to notice, but he has a lazy eye intent on looking at your shoes throughout this exchange. In an act of dominance-asserting defiance, he jams his finger up his nose, digs around a while, extracts a large wad of mucous, and proceeds to wipe it on your lapel. You suddenly recognize him as one of the men you encountered earlier today in the square. Oh. This may not end well.

Always willing to see the best in people, you reach into your pocket and pull out a folded sheet of paper that you didn't realize you had until this very instant. You unfold it to reveal a complicated, hand-drawn maze you doodled in one of your meetings earlier today. At this stage in your misadventure, the boardroom seems like it existed in another time.

"What's that?" he barks.

"It's a maze," you say as you fish a pen (which you also didn't know you had) out of your pocket.

"Huh." He accepts your peace offering, begins tracing dead-end routes, and meanwhile, takes you into his protection.

Eventually, the paperwork official calls your name and you bid adieu to your new friend. You sit down at a desk in a small office and explain your situation, producing your ID from your jacket pocket. The officer apologizes for the mix-up, but acknowledges, "These things do happen." Despite your innocence, due to the nuances of the bureaucratic process, you are informed that you will still have to spend the night in jail. If it makes you feel any better, you get to pick your roommate. You choose the maze-lover and sleep the four hours until dawn.

When you are released, you are bussed back to the burnt-out remains of your office. Sheets of paper are scattered everywhere, floating on the breeze. Financial records, strategic plans, tax receipts and more all give you hope that your novel may still exist. The cleanup crews are carefully gathering the loose sheets one-by-one and assembling them into binders as the pages come. You wonder what use there could possibly be in such disorganized Franken-documents. Months later, in televised committee briefings, your words start appearing in the mix. The Ministry of Finance becomes known as an artistic haven and the broadcasts (which previously went unwatched as a public service) attract millions of viewers each week. Everyone can hardly wait to see how corporate taxation policy merges with the life stories of your fictional characters. Though you are never outed as the main contributor to this drama, you feel satisfied. After all, the resulting work is far more creative than anything you could have come up with on your own. You give up novelistic writing in favor of teleplays and are happy for the rest of your days.

The End.

Ah. A bold choice. You've earned my respect. You are a true artist, dedicated to your craft. Hemingway would be impressed by your gusto. I, on the other hand, question your sanity. If you want to reconsider, just this once, I'll let you go back and choose the other option. But if you do, know that your choice is final. I, like much of the electorate, cannot abide flip-flopping.

So you're still here. Good. Thankfully, the crowd in the central square has largely dissipated. There are still a few friendly rioters. Even larger numbers of friendly law enforcement officials. The setting sun peeks between the buildings and glints in your eyes. For some reason, the scene reminds you of the picture on a postcard you received from the only person you ever loved (outside of your parents): the tender folds of the Appalachians at sunset; the turquoise of the water filling abandoned quarries; it all fading into an early October haze at the edges. Somehow, you let that love slip away. And though you're content with your solitude, when the sun hits certain angles in the early autumn, you have your regrets. You are resolved that your forgotten draft will not become another one.

You take a moment to size up your options. There are bevies of uniformed personnel who have taken up position around the main entrance to your building. You do still have your ID badge with you, so they shouldn't give you too much of a hassle. Given all the goings-on elsewhere in the square, the sidestreet to the right of your building is surprisingly devoid of activity. You know there is a back entrance but aren't sure if it will be equally well-guarded. The building itself isn't completely engulfed in flame, but the fire is definitely having a heyday up top—as fires are wont to do. As it spreads, windows pop in the heat. The window by your desk follows suit. There is a fire engine with a large, retractable ladder on-scene, as well as a few other fire-related vehicles and personnel.

Do you choose the front entrance, the back entrance, or to impersonate a firefighter and go in through a window?

If you choose to show your credentials and march into the building in a forthright manner, turn to page 337. If you choose to wander around to the rear entrance, turn to page 343. If you choose to attempt the impossible and fool people with your play-acting skills as a firefighter, turn to page 345.

You get home, walk to your bedroom and collapse on your bed fully clothed and start sobbing. You didn't even wash your hands or face, which is surprising, given your obsessive dedication to pre-bed hygiene. You probably thought more would happen when you made the choice to come home, but I don't like to dwell on sadness. As you drift to sleep, you dream the perfect ending to your novel, while in the city center, its beginnings—years of your creative labor—turn to embers and drift silently to heaven amidst a symphony of sirens. Like the incense in the censer shaken back and forth by the priest, the smoke is your silent offering.

The End.

Though people have always told you that you were good at public speaking, it is funny that you did not place more stock in your abilities as a decathlete. After all, you competed all throughout college and even hold a record in javelin. Sure, that was some years ago, but you still run every day to keep yourself fit. By the looks of the five gentlemen surrounding you, you could easily take them in a foot race. They look more built for powerlifting than wind sprints. You're hoping your conversation doesn't come to blows.

You spin slowly, looking each of the men in the eye, trying to identify the ringleader. For all of the ruckus just a few paces away, a tense silence exists between you. Spotting one fellow who has the confident air of an experienced football hooligan, you decide to make your entreaties to him. You casually dust yourself off and your inner performer takes over. "Gentlemen," you begin, "I believe there must be some sort of misunderstanding." Your opening parry is met only with snickering. You open your arms wide, shrug your shoulders, and give a sheepish grin. "If I've upset you in some way, I apologize, because it was not my intent." A full-throated guffaw breaks loose behind you and the men seem nonplussed.

Perhaps this will be more difficult than you initially anticipated. Amidst the furor of the crowd, you hear knuckles cracking and clenched fists impatiently smacking into open palms. You sense that they are men of few words, so you try a different tack. "What do you say I buy you all a round down at the Brocket Arms? I have a feeling things are going to get ugly if we stay here much longer."

Surprisingly, this seems to have led to a breakthrough. One of the men steps forward and, chewing on his lip, looks you up and down. You missed him at first because he is smaller than the rest—a common, and occasionally fatal, oversight—but he clearly has the authority. It is always best to negotiate directly with the leadership. He looks you right in the eye and says, "A drink, eh?"

"It could even be a few if that suits you better."

He breaks into a broad grin and extends his large, sinewy hand. You reach out for it, happy to have solved another dispute with words. As your hands clasp, you feel his iron grip and sense just how formidable this man would be in a fistfight.

All of a sudden, he pulls you toward him. The next thing you know, his bicep and forearm are locked tightly around your neck. You reach up and tug on the arm, fully expecting to pass out at any moment. In fact, you are hoping to pass out, since you know there are inevitably sucker-punches coming from the hangers-on. But you, unfortunately, retain lucidity.

Your torso absorbs gut-punch after gut-punch. While it is excruciating at first, you soon become numb to the pain. Somehow, you are still able to look on the bright side. "At least I'm not in the crowd—it looks ready to stampede at any moment." No sooner does this thought race across your synapses than you hear the first telltale percussions of the tear-gas cannons. The crowd panics and begins to scatter. Your attackers, apparently satisfied with their evening's work, quickly let you go and flee ahead of the oncoming mob.

You're woozy with pain. You stagger toward the side-street your assailants just ran down. The first wave of the crowd is just behind you. In the state that you are in, you will not be able to stay ahead of the fray. Up ahead you see a doorway. You decide to make your way toward it. You arrive just as the leading edge of the crowd funnels into the street.

All around you people are screaming. You hear gun-shots, megaphones, and other commotion coming from the plaza. If the riot police are out in force, you are liable to be rounded up. That would be the end of your career—an undignified blemish for your CV. You consider your situation for a moment. "I can't run, but I can hide." You've always been clever. It is unclear where the doorway you're standing in leads. Looking around, the only other nearby option you see is a large garbage bin.

Do you choose to climb into the garbage bin or try the door?

If you choose to slink along the building and clamber into the trash receptacle, turn to page 278. If you choose to open the door, turn to page 339.

Slinking around to the rear is liable to raise suspicions. After all, who uses back doors but criminals or those with something to hide? Being a credentialed member of the Ministry of Finance, you have every right to enter that building. Thus, you decide to take the obvious approach.

You walk through the square, disappointed at the mess the protesters made. "Maybe if they weren't so slovenly," you think, "the government would be more receptive to their message." A good point. Organization and tidiness go a long way. The assembled police track your movements with watchful eyes. One gives you an especially incredulous stare as you approach.

"Halt. You cannot enter."

Fully prepared for the official bravado, you have already formulated a response.

"Thank you for your service, but I work here," you say as you reach into your jacket to retrieve your badge.

Unfortunately, your well-rehearsed plan to prove your right to enter looks an awful lot to the cops like you are trying to pull a gun. Dear, dear. You should be more cautious around people with itchy trigger fingers.

"A gun! A gun!" is the last thing you hear before being tackled to the ground.

"It's just my ID," you try to say, but with your teeth biting pavement, all the police officers hear is "Ish offa I yee." The recent retrenchment of nationalist ideology in your country belies an undercurrent of xenophobia pervading the government at all levels. The police are not exempt from this. To them, you sound foreign and that's all the more reason to

lock you up. They pat you down but find nothing worth con-
fiscating.

You try to explain your predicament and the importance of the bag you left on your desk, but your captors will
have none of it. "Tell it to the judge." You are herded onto a
police van that has just pulled up. It is already brimming with
recent round-ups. Some of them look rather rough, but you
can't muster the energy to be afraid. All you can think of is the
fire that will no doubt eradicate all proof of your creativity. It's
enough to make you seriously consider a life of crime. But who
are you kidding? You've never been one to go against the
grain. As the van makes its way toward the jail, an inverted
image of the towering inferno casts a bright reflection on the
tears welling in your eyes.

To take this van-ride to its inevitable end, turn to page 328.

Not wanting to take your chances hiding in other people's garbage, you opt for the doorway. You have always had a weak stomach after all. You try the handle and, finding it unlocked, open the door narrowly to slip inside. You find yourself in a long entryway. A "Welcome to Our Bed & Brakefast" sign hangs precariously above your head. At one time, it may have been suspended by two strings, but if so, it was long ago. Now it is just a cockeyed, Damoclean greeting, passing judgement on all souls brave enough to pass beneath it. It is little wonder you never knew this establishment was here.

Along with being poor spellers and sign maintainers, the proprietors must also be averse to standard customs of interior decoration. The entrance to the "bed and breakfast" looks like a mad scientist's lair. On shelves lining the entry hall, dozens of jars are stacked—jars containing a variety of pickled and preserved animal parts. You take a few hesitant steps forward and are greeted with a shrill alarm. The sound startles you. You wonder what kind of a mess you have gotten yourself into now. Is this really a bed and breakfast? Or is it something more sinister? Based upon your welcome, you have a horrible feeling that it may be the latter.

The alarm continues for another full minute before you hear someone coming to inspect. You are coiled and ready to sprint back the way you came. A large man without a shirt appears in the hallway to greet you. A cigarette stub is dangling from his lip. His potbelly glistens with sweat in the half-light. He seems delighted to have a visitor. "You have come for a room? Yes? Well, let me show you the options."

You haven't the heart to tell him you're only trying to escape the tumult outside, so you humor his salesman's pitch.

He shows you up the rickety stairs to the honeymoon suite. Everything in the room is bright pink. The walls. The linens. The toilet. Which happens to be conveniently located next to the bed. The floor has a concave slope such that you can imagine anything spilled would run to the center of the room and pool. When you think of all of the little lakes that may have formed over the years, a small shudder runs up your spine.

The B&B manager senses that this room might not be quite what you're looking for, so quickly hustles you into the adjoining offering. A stark contrast to the panoply of pink, this room is blue. Technically, it's more of a periwinkle, but your eyes are so pink-strained you cannot tell. Like the previous room, this one is floor to ceiling color. If you were a synesthete, you would be overpowered by the smell of ocean and sound of F#. Since you are not, you hear nothing and smell only the must of a room shut for too long. Instead of a proper toilet, this room features a trough along the wall, which, judging by the awkwardly affixed showerhead jutting out above it, also doubles as the shower stall. You would very much like to leave this place now, but the man seems intent on showing you each of the room's unique features. Apparently, there are only two rooms on offer, because the tour stops at this point. When he gets to the end of his sales pitch and looks at you expectantly, you equivocate about first needing to check with your nonexistent spouse. He gives you a knowing wink: "I know how this is."

By now, you're thinking that the worst of the protest clashes must have settled down outside. Your stomach gurgles audibly to remind you that your personal safety shouldn't be the only consideration—there is your stomach's comfort as well. Your makeshift host hears it and asks a leading question:

"Hungry?" As uncomfortable as the rooms made you, the thought of having to eat here causes you to vomit a small bit into your mouth. "Let me fix you a sample—free of charge."

How best to beg off the kind offer? You don't want to seem rude or hurt the gentleman's feelings, but watching the bare-chested man cook you one of his pickled specimens might just send you over the edge. How will you possibly hold it together? Serendipity saves you when you hear a shattering window downstairs. No doubt one of the last protesters trying to make a mark. As the man bounds down the stairs, you thank him for his hospitality and take this opportunity to hurry back out into the street.

From the shelter of the doorway, you see that the protest, while diminished, is still raging. The police who patiently let the masses assemble are now using the group's size against it. Such are modern enforcement tactics. You are thankful, for once, about being singled out for a beating. If those men hadn't chased you around the corner, you may well be one of those now facing charges. That would be hard to explain to your supervisors come Monday morning.

You continue counting your blessings until you notice that your office building is on fire. Oh well, maybe that means you'll get next week off. After all, you remembered to bring your side bag, which has all of your valuables. Wait. Are you telling me you didn't bring it?

I should apologize at this point for not reminding you to take your bag at the outset. It probably contains your wallet—you have a habit of not putting it in your pocket where it belongs. You quickly pat yourself down, first your pants, then, finding nothing there, proceed to your jacket. Ah. There it is in your inside pocket. You like to put things in hidden places. It has always made you feel like a spy.

I hate to be the bearer of bad news, but your bag also contains the working draft of the novel you have been slowly writing for the past fifteen years. You had recently been gaining momentum and were (by your estimation) only a page or two from wrapping the narrative up nicely. You had hoped you would be able to complete it over the weekend. Maybe even have had a chance to start reading back through and editing. Now, that draft is inside a burning building. I know you thought it would be more authentic to write your first draft by hand and that you carried it in your trusty bag because you never knew when inspiration might strike, but that's looking like it was a bad decision now. I've warned you before about prioritizing authenticity over practicality. Let this be a lesson in the importance of backup copies.

Your pulse quickens and your mountaineer heart scales your esophagus, planting its flag firmly in the top of your throat. There is a writhing sea of humanity between you and the flames slowly creeping up the buildingside. Behind those flames resides your life's work.

Do you run toward your burning building or wait to see if the riot dissipates before making your attempt?
If you choose to fight your way through the chaos and make a desperate attempt to recover the only extant draft of your novel, turn to page 331. If you choose to instead take a more civilized, less danger-filled approach, turn to page 280.

A frontal assault is liable to draw too much attention, so you wisely saunter around to the far side of the building. You are happy to find the back entrance deserted. Were it not for the flames beginning to peek out from the top floors, you could almost imagine this was a normal day. You swipe your ID along the card reader and hear the welcome sound of the door unlocking. Thank goodness the building still has power.

Out of habit, you walk straight to the elevator, climb in and press "7." The doors close and the elevator begins to rise. Only then does the "In case of fire, use stairs" pictogram posted prominently next to the keypad register on your synapses. Uh oh. This is a lesson we can all stand to learn at some point in our lives—stairs are healthier for many reasons. You are sure that the fire is consuming the lift machinery at this very moment. You steel yourself for the freefall that will come when the cable is melted through and the safety mechanisms fail. I should have told you (if it is not evident by this point) that common sense is not one of your strengths.

Ding. The doors open. You dive out onto the seventh floor, thankful to still be living. You didn't think I would let you fall with your goal so close at hand, did you? After all, I want to read your novel someday, so letting you meet an untimely end before you finish it would be a shame. Your office suite is filled with flames, but you feel a new courage coursing through your veins. If a soon-to-break elevator can't stop you, you will not let a little fire slow you down. You duck your head, shield your face with your arms and charge toward your desk. There it is, your side bag. You open it just to be sure your manuscript is inside. It is. Phew!

Just so you don't make the same mistake as the fool now turning to page 283, let me make this next choice easy for you. The phone lines have been destroyed in the fire. The power is out and the elevator is inoperable. There is only one possible way out—the stairwell. For the love of God, please turn to page 348 and get out of here.

How this even entered into your mind as an option, I have no idea. You often have trouble convincing the grocery clerk that you are there to purchase groceries, so how you will convincingly play the role of firefighter is beyond me. But you are feeling alive for the first time in a long while. In your mind, there is nothing you can't do.

You spot a truck full of firefighting gear and it looks to be untended. Waltzing by, you hoist a suit and helmet onto your shoulder. You find a secluded spot, out of sight from any who might object, and don your costume. I must say, you look rather convincing. You grab an axe off a different truck for good measure. Your ensemble complete, you confidently stride toward the ladder company barking orders. The incident commander has not yet arrived, but the truck operators are impressed by your gravitas and start extending the ladder, as per your directions. You begin climbing as it swivels into place below your seventh-story window. Everyone watching agrees that you must have been born on a ladder, so smooth is your ascent.

In all honesty, your father was a baker and your mother never allowed you to climb anything more than five feet off the ground. I could have told you that before you started in this direction, but it would have made no difference. You will not be deterred.

When fully extended, the ladder does not reach all the way to the seventh floor, but the windows of the sixth floor are within arm's length. You brandish your axe and tap the window which shatters easily. Thousands of tiny fragments rain down to the pavement far below and settle like sugar on a pastry. The heat from the fire is intense. Various bits of plastic are starting to deform. Ceiling tiles have come down to expose ducts and wiring that you never knew existed. The tiles are scattered and broken over the office furniture like crumb cake topping. Your penchant for delicious metaphors reinforces the fact that you should not have skipped lunch today.

But really, you ought to focus. Your novel manuscript is one floor directly above you. You could run to the stairs, but given the debris, that might take a while. Time is of the essence. Obligingly, a large metal beam crashes down through the ceiling and comes to rest at an angle perfect for climbing. You waste no time, hop through the broken window, and shimmy up the beam to see the fire beginning to encroach on your desk. Just like you've seen in countless movies, the world begins to move in slow motion. You sprint toward your side bag and dramatically hurdle through the flames. On this floor, there is a clear path to the fire escape—your officemates were thankfully more minimalist than the harried accountants one floor down.

Into the stairwell you fly, taking the stairs two-at-a-time and counting down the floors as they pass by. Six, five, four, three, two, one. At the bottom of the stairs, you shed your firefighter's garb, dust yourself off, and casually step out into the street.

The backside of your building is awash in the quiet splendor of civil twilight. Your adventure has left you bursting with energy and filled with the joys of life. You can feel inspiration welling in your chest. If the feeling holds, you may even be able to finish your draft tonight. With any luck, you'll have next week (or more) off as they decide where to temporarily relocate your office. It will be the perfect opportunity to polish up your writing. You can barely contain your excitement.

What a gorgeous evening. The eight kilometers home don't seem so intimidating now.

To learn what fruits your labor will bear, turn to page 350.

A prudent choice. Prudent choices are rewarded with prudent outcomes. You tuck your side bag tight under your arm to protect the only extant draft of your novel. If you make it out of here alive, there might be a few revisions you have to incorporate into the storyline. You've heard it said that the best fiction is written from personal experience. And your experience today has been a doozy.

The heat and smoke are increasing, so please, bustle off to the emergency stairwell. Until today, you've only ever used this exit to sneak out early, thus avoiding the watchful eye of the office overlords. You are excited to finally try using it during an actual emergency. Its unadorned concrete slab walls are comforting, given the visions of fire still dancing in your brain. You take the stairs one-at-a-time—no sense surviving a fire only to break your neck—and count down the floors as they pass by. Six, five, four, three, two, one. The rusty metal door at the bottom squeaks in approval as you open it up and step onto the street.

The backside of your building is awash in the quiet splendor of civil twilight. Your brush with death has left you bursting with energy and filled with the joys of life. You can feel inspiration welling in your chest. At least you think it's inspiration—you have been known to get the feeling confused with hunger now and then. I'm sure you'll work it out once you get home. I for one hope it is indeed inspiration. If so, you may even be able to finish your draft tonight. With any luck, you'll have next week (or more) off as they decide where to temporarily relocate your office. It will be the perfect opportunity to polish up your writing. You can barely contain your excitement. What a gorgeous evening. The eight kilometers home doesn't seem so intimidating now. You've been needing to exercise more anyway.

To complete your walk home, turn to page 350.

The whole walk home feels like a victory march. Your senses are alive to every input. You see tufts of grass you had never previously noticed, growing in rain gutters. Cracks in the foundation of a building you had previously thought faultless. Drips of water that seem to come from the sky above. Triangular-shaped paving stones that link all of the other stones together.

You arrive home after an hour and a half, feet aching, but mind full of energy. Even the hunger and regret that came with skipping lunch has abated. You sit down to write the final chapter of your novel. Your pen carries you far beyond that as you go back to add details you now realize were lacking. You also find ways to add enhancements based upon your recent experiences. It all fits together so nicely.

But I'm not going to put words into your mouth any longer. Here is what you wrote (please complete):

_____

_____

_____

_____

_____

_____

_____

_____

_____

_____

_____

_____

The End.

Part 9: A Double Coda

ℵ

"Maybe this is a manifesto proclaiming the independence of my voice—that I shall not be brought under the yoke of anyone else's dictates again. Or maybe this is all just a testament to the slow eroding of time."

He liked the sound of that last bit, so he went back and added it as an alternate title. A meaningless reveal saved for the very end. His readers would curse the plots he'd laid against them. (And those he'd left unresolved.) But such was the nature of his authorship.

It had been a decade of his life and now it was over.

Appendix A: Arthur Johnson Biography

Arthur Johnson was born February 18, 1923 in Schenectady, New York, to Archibald and Madeline Johnson. Archie was a sewing machine salesman at the time Arthur was born, but after a few fruitless years, took a job at General Electric and settled into a decades-long career in manufacturing. Madeline was a second grade teacher in the Schenectady City School District, though took some years off to raise Arthur and his five siblings.

Arthur Johnson's childhood was an uneventful and evidently studious one, as he graduated first in his class from Mont Pleasant High School and went on to St. Bonaventure on full scholarship. There, he studied journalism, with the intention of one day entering the professoriate. This did not come to pass, as he was drafted soon after America entered WWII. Johnson was first sent to England for training, then ended up helping to chase Rommel out of North Africa with the II Corps.

By the time Johnson returned home, the thought of academia had lost some of its appeal, but he still believed in the journalistic cause, so returned to St. Bonaventure to finish his degree. He later said that wartime taught him "the benefits of life on the frontlines" and figured that reporting was a more practical art than professorship. He graduated in 1948 and freelanced for several local newspapers in the Hudson Valley before finally getting on with the *New York Post* in 1953.

Shortly thereafter, Johnson met his wife, Doris, who was studying art at NYU. Upon her graduation in 1954, they married and settled in a walk-up apartment in Yorkville, Manhattan. Their first child, William was born in 1956, followed by Elizabeth in 1958. During this period, Johnson quickly worked his way up through the newsroom to become local news editor by 1961. He was the youngest to have ever held the position at that time. Despite the success, the increasing demands of newspaper life came into conflict with those of family life, so Johnson signed on with Smith Ralston Excelsior to produce a series of biographies for its non-fiction division.

Over the next 32 years, Johnson produced sixteen volumes in the American Visionaries series. Some of the most prominent of these include: *The Life and Times of Edward Hopper* (1963); *The Indomitable Elizabeth Cady Stanton* (1965); *Cayce and His Acolytes: The Occult in the Early 20th Century* (1968); *Bird Songs: The Tragedies and Triumphs of Charlie Parker* (1975); and *Winslow Homer: Wilderness and the American Subconscious* (1984). He was four-times a finalist for the James Tait Black Memorial Award in biography and once on the shortlist for the Pulitzer. He died in 1993, days after submitting his final biographical manuscript: *Nell Arthur and the Forgotten President: Marriage as the Model for Political Consensus*. His only novel, the posthumous work *The New Manifesto*, was first published by Smith Ralston Excelsior in 1994.

Appendix B: Letter from Arthur Johnson to Sam Ernst

Sam, Now that my last will and testament has been read, you've got to figure out what to do with the manuscript I left on my desk. It's a patchwork of notes and observations I've collected along the way—think of it as an experimental novel. Those are all the rage these days. I realize it lacks a real coherency, but for that fact, I am prouder of it than anything I've written recently. (My Arthur biography is utter garbage.)

As you can see, I've got the manuscript grouped into sections (I leave any editing in your capable hands). Publish the darn thing if you see fit, but please don't feel any obligation to do so. If it does see print, I think it would make for a handsome little volume decked in blue linen and gilt lettering. You can do whatever you want with the dust jacket—they always eventually get discarded anyway. And, God forbid, it ever hits paperback—all bets are off then. I'll leave those aesthetics to you. Your team has always had a nice eye.

Thanks for all of your help over the years. I think you know how much I valued your friendship, but in case I never made it clear, count this message from beyond the grave as proof. It's not often someone gets a letter from a dead person. Once the emotion of it all passes (and forgive me if I'm being presumptuous), I think it'll be a fun story you can tell at parties. I know how you've always needed fodder for small talk. Think of this as my parting gift to you.

A long and healthy life to you, my friend,
Artie

About the Author

Sam Ernst was born in Pennsylvania in 1981. He lives in Fort Collins, Colorado with his wife and son and works at Colorado State University as a grant writer. *The New Manifesto* is his first novel. Any other snippets of biographical information you may need are woven throughout the narrative.

CPSIA information can be obtained
at www.ICGtesting.com
Printed in the USA
FSHW011744050821
83648FS